Happy
90 th
Birthday
John

Lots of love
Sandy x

# FINDING MR ALFI

STEVE CARVER

# FOREWORD

There are a plethora of self-help books in the quest to find happiness. Often the West has looked to the East for answers, with meditation, yoga, mindfulness and Buddhism for example, elucidating a great deal of interest. This book is loosely based on these themes as our protagonist, Alfi, goes literally to the East in search for answers.

It's unusual in that the subjects we explore such as what is self, authenticity and the nature of one's reality, are told through an adventurous tale, rather than a dry academic account that purports to provide the answers. Indeed, the journey that readers are about to embark on will present them with more questions than answers, much like that of all philosophy, to make their own conclusions.

The book is unusual too, in that it provokes and entertains through a combination of genres and topics; adventure, comedy, philosophy, ethics and theology, set in Nepal's high Himalaya. A place where the author has lived for several years.

We begin with Alfi's earlier life in New York. Here he wrestles with journalistic work and the drudgery of routine. After a failed relationship, experiencing depression and even a conversation with Death, he begins his quest to find true happiness, leaving his city life behind.

In the story that follows, the audience is taken on a journey to enjoy the spectacle of it all; an adventure with surprising twists and turns, and the sometimes farcical situations that our character finds himself in, in this spectacular and mysterious part of the world.

Existentialism is a broad term that the book inevitably broaches; Kierkegaard's reflections to Nietzsche, for example, but the tale also pushes the subject towards a different direction, indeed, questioning does the individual exist at all, as well as traditional philosophical questions on the nature of our existence; and what it is meant to be human.

Ancient to modern philosophy and ethics are peppered subtly within the pages, as well as original thought, and teachings on meditation and Buddhism. Socrates' *The unexamined life is not worth living* for example, to Russell's pursuit of happiness, quotations from Shakespeare or Sartre's concept of freedom and 'mauvaise foi,' bad faith are considered within the context of the story, as we inquire inside the nature of the mind. The book is ambitious in that all the above is brought together in a dramatic and adventurous tale with light moments of comedy too.

In many ways, the novel is a debate, not prescribing any one theme or way of thinking, but instead taking a broader view, contradicting in parts, and asking the reader to examine, investigate and contemplate an overall perspective of their own. The book is as rich as the reader would like it to be.

There are some poignant and provocative reminders that the audience will take with them. Obstacles are constantly being thrown in our protagonist's way, as he meets interesting characters along his travels, many of whom teach him something.

In any novel you begin with an outline, a premise within which it shall be written, but then it takes on a life of its own, its individual performance, ultimately arriving at a different destination. The messages it shall possess change too. Simplicity, as one might find in this work, can be deceptive.

Despite its themes, the book is largely an optimistic one, not self-indulgent or dryly academic, but instead exploring the quest we all have for fulfilment, self-realisation and finding our way in the world and ultimately happiness - however even the need for the latter is also debated. All this, is told through actions, people and places with some humour too.

It is possible to write a novel that, like a song, transcends the meaning and even the words, yet not everyone will hear it.

'Tired of living. It's easy to do.
The things he wanted, never ended too.
Endless waiting, like sand in his hands.
The tighter he held it; it fell through his palms.
He thought of the future, and who that I am?
The mind that asked it, he did not understand.'

# PART ONE

# CHAPTER ONE

## Melancholia

It was the perfect Sunday morning and in all probability Alfi had become the wrong person. In the tale that will follow, he may no longer exist.

He leaned into his motorcycle as it rounded a turn, and like everyone else that morning, all his past, his hopes laying in their procession, had brought him here to this exact moment. But what for the present, and how would it dictate his future? He'd come to realise that to do nothing would have serious implications.

The frame of his silver mirror captured a man mowing a lawn in perfect straight lines outside a string of identical houses. He thought of the quiet, tidy lives behind the windows and what were they doing now? One task, then another, and what would they do if it all stopped? To cultivate oneself, *not* to want anything. Indeed, could this be possible? His eyes sank to the tarmac beneath his wheels. This dumfounded town.

Over the Brooklyn Bridge and it dawned on him that his life too, had been in cycles. Desire, achievement, failure, achievement; the desire for more things, both tangible or intangible, and the suffering it brings. The differences between necessitation to the folly of desire. Was there to be any end to it, or would the next twenty years be identical to the twenty before? And so, in this deleterious awakening, he had lost purpose and had become exhausted. Even the simple respite of pleasures eluded him. Youth had gone, and he had become more conscious, more serious, and now all the desires of the world were like strangers to him.

Along Fifth Avenue and the models looked down from their posters. Their eyes followed his. They teased at him as he rode by, telling him to want something. Entertainers laughed from their television screens within the shop windows, but all Alfi could see was madness.

Had he become too self-indulgent and should he just get on with it? Did he not realise how lucky he was, or was the game up? Could Alfi's humour and optimism save him and see him through? The past, no more than smoke in the wind, to learn rather than be shackled by it. Yet soon, everything was about to change for Alfi, and little did he know it.

The bells above the wooden door jingled playfully as he entered the bookshop which raised a disinterested eyebrow from a heavy looking woman at the till. He ran the backs of his fingers along a line of books in the 'Self Help and Spiritual' section, the tapping sound, as their images did their best to intrigue him. The only other customer in the store that day was a middle-aged, rather shapeless woman, in a long, tired looking grey cardigan. She silently purveyed some section or another, picking up publications before settling them back down again. He watched quietly, enraptured by her loneliness that had left her quite sad, and thought of the little girl she once was, running around playing. Where was the little girl now?

The titles on the covers called out. "The 7-day Detox. What

Colour is my Balloon? The Power of Now" as Alfi muttered to himself. 'Perhaps we just all need to be kinder to each other? Perhaps that's the simple answer?' His whisper raised an irritated *shush* from the woman in the cardigan as she set down another book.

By now, Alfi was struggling to carry the hard and paperbacks he'd been collecting and in all, appeared to be quite a lonely figure on a day that was becoming increasingly numb. His fingers felt the hard edges of the books again. Lifting up another he examined it briefly before adding it to his pile and approaching the till.

The heavy woman sat and peered over the rim of her bright red glasses that were halfway down her nose. There was an air of hostility about her and it occurred to Alfi, for some, how quickly the beauty of youth can give way, along with its enthusiasm. She ignored him and scanned his books - the only sound between them was the thud of their weight as she placed them from one side of the till to the other.

He became uncomfortable in the silence. 'You must enjoy your job,' he offered somewhat brightly, as she continued to flout his existence. 'I mean, what I mean to say is, that, meeting people. New people all the time, every day, is different. It's great to be working in something you like.' Alfi sighed but did not relent. 'It must give you...a buzz. A buzz to get out of bed in the morning.' He looked at his collection of books and turned one of them over. 'There's a really good one here,' he prompted. '*How to Win Friends and Influence People.*'

She pushed her glasses up along her nose with a rigid forefinger. 'That'll be $43.95.'

Alfi exited into the street and into the rain, where a man stood to the side of a car arguing with a police officer as he waved a parking ticket. Another fellow, dressed in dismal grey, was calling out and trying to sell newspapers to no one who was listening. Some lovers passed by, in a world separated and of their own, giggling as they struggled with an umbrella. A busy woman, serious on her phone, clicked along loudly in her heels, as a mother pushed her pram against the angled rain. Then a gleaming car sped past, accelerating angrily and sending up splashes from the gutters, as a fragile old man shoved along the sidewalk with a stick, the young man he had once been, had died years ago.

And it seemed, in that exact moment to Alfi, that all the world and its sinews were against him. People were a summary of what they've done, and what they've not done before - along with their fortunes and misfortunes. And in the silence, a wave of solitude drowned and consumed him. Everything, all and sundry, had no purpose. He had lost his fascination with the world and nothing was worth it. His eyes had become dead and nothing could enchant him. There was little point for the fight. This creeping wisdom had begun to encircle his feet. Was it an awakening or a curse? It was desperate, so desperate, and its heaviness would not leave him. Even the wind along the high street blew brutally against him.

It wasn't always like this.

## SIX MONTHS EARLIER
*Life is meaningless for a reason*

It was night time as Alfi and Claudia entered Alfi's apartment. He opened the door, reached in awkwardly and put on the light. Dropping down their suitcases, they were in a flutter of conversation.

'How was I to know we'd be over a nightclub?' Alfi pleaded. 'The brochure did say "lively area" they just forgot one word: *"underneath."* What the hell has happened to copywriters these days? Just add the word! "Underneath." They had space!'

Claudia brushed some fingers over her forehead. 'One of the reasons you go on vacation is to sleep! And from the very beginning.

The *very* beginning of this...holiday...why didn't *you* book extra luggage?'

Alfi shrugged. 'Not that again.'

'It's not nice Alfi. Starting your vacation with a $89 fine. For just five more pounds!'

Alfi pleaded. 'I told you before, not to pack so many shoes! How many shoes do you need for fourteen days anyway? Um? In the great words of any world explorer...adventurers, people who put their lives on the line in dangerous places to better understand the world. Bring footwear that's interchangeable.'

She shook her head. 'And that airline rep!'

'Who gave *me* the fine remember?' Alfi interrupted. 'And who trains these people anyway? The Gestapo? It's like *"meet and greet"* at a gas chamber. All they could do...was point and grunt.'

'And the hotel Alfi. That bathroom!' cried Claudia.

'Trying to get the shower temperature right, I'll give you that. Was like trying to crack a safe.' Alfi muttered.

'And the beach. Oh, now the beach!' said Claudia.

'It had sand, water,' responded Alfi half optimistically.

'It was too packed! We were like sardines! Beach towels, parasols, sunbeds. The music, the noise! And that couple, the one who said she'd put on weight to allow a bigger canvas for her tattoos!' And with that, Claudia continued with a tirade of grievances, something that Alfi had been accustomed to.

His thoughts drew inward. 'This is my ex, Claudia. One of the reasons two people come together, well I believe, is so that they can complain together. Let off gas against the world. Someone once said that lovers shouldn't stare into each other's eyes, but look outwards in the same direction...I bet he was single! Claudia and I had different views.'

He looked at Claudia's lips as they sent out words like bullets. She, the type who never questioned her own mind. What she liked was good, and what she didn't like was not so. It was as simple and as ignorant as that. Her face, with all the years of dissatisfaction from the repeating patterns of her mind, was beginning to look tired - the world could never be perfect but she preferred to bask in its imperfections.

Alfi's thoughts moved inwards again. 'Life, they say...love even, should imitate art. You should create a good painting together. But the truth was, that she was more renaissance - as popularised by Di Vinci in the mid sixteenth century, with his use of colours to create body, shape and form - whilst I, I suppose, was just too abstract.' He walked to the window, oblivious now to Claudia who was unpacking ferociously. Touching a curtain, he drew it back and peered into a grey city sky. 'I used to call Claudia, *Cloudy*,' he pondered. 'It's the kind of weather I like. It's not too cold - or too hot either. It never gets too *close*.' This last admission shook Alfi and brought him to look to his feet, then up again to the slate-coloured sky. 'And you never know? Just never know if the cloud's going to break and let the sunshine in, or if there's going to be a downpour. I always expected rain.' He hesitated, and with a thoughtful smile shook his head. 'She called me Bunny, I don't know why, just *Bunny*. Funny how things change. Now it's bastard...Relationships? Why do we do it hey? Why do we do it! It's instinct I suppose? The call of the wild! Marriage - it's the *great call of nature.*'

Claudia blurted some words, shunting him from his daydream. 'I gave you the best years of my life Alfi! The best years! And what have I got for it?'

'The best years?' Alfi was perplexed. 'When were your best years?'

'2006 to 09,' she replied.

'Really? 06 to 09? Those years weren't so kind to me.'

Claudia paused as he read her thoughts. 'Don't you feel?' she said.

'Not again,' he interrupted.

'Do you feel, that this life, this relationship, is not going anywhere?'

'We've just been to Mexico.' Alfi sighed.

'You know what I mean.'

'Ok, ok. I know where this is going.' Alfi replied, 'Children. I told you. I don't think it's fair to give someone else my genes.'

'What about my genes Alfi? Don't they have a say in this?'

'And you know my theory of genetics!' Alfi continued. 'We've tried. Sperm carries a lot more than the way you look you know. It carries who you are, as a person. Your character. Personality traits. In my case, mine swim half way up, it gets dark, cold, so they turn back. What can I do about it?'

'You can try harder.'

'Harder?' asked Alfi. 'What do you want me to do? Sit down and talk to them? Kids. All that noise. Missing out on life...on freedom, just to be near good schools. Besides, I'd only be having offspring as a reaction to my own mortality. Living vicariously through others to conceal my own underachievement.' Claudia gave off a long, tired sigh as he continued. 'And marriage? For life? It's a long time! We're living longer these days. And marriage, you know it's one step closer to divorce.'

'The trouble with you is that you think too much,' snapped Claudia.

Alfi was surprised. 'I think too much?'

'Yes.' she replied more assuredly. 'Why don't you just do! *Do things*, and stop just thinking about them!'

'What do you mean?'

'Have children. A family. What else is there to do? You keep trying to find some...' she hesitated trying to find the words. 'Higher meaning Alfi! Analysing things. You analyse too much. You're procrastinating when there is no bigger picture! You're looking for something that's not there! You just gotta get on with life. Before it's too late.'

Alfi was stopped in his tracks. 'Maybe she's right?' he thought. 'Maybe there is no meaning to life? And if so, is this...is this not a release?' He scratched his head and turned. 'Or maybe life is meaningless for a reason? That's a distinct possibility?'

And so, amongst the noise; the petty battles and vexations with Claudia, he began to abandon himself once more from the present and asked himself, as he watched her, as he watched those lips, was he paying too much to avoid his loneliness?

'It wasn't always like this,' he thought. 'Where have I, where have *we*, gone wrong? What changed?'

## A YEAR BEFORE

Alfi's bedroom was softly lit. He sat on the edge of the bed and was shirtless. Claudia had positioned herself behind his back and held both his shoulders as she squared his body and giggled playfully. There was love in her voice - and he knew something sweet was coming.

'Ok, now sit straight. Sit still,' she said. 'Now look forward. No turning round.'

The room, safe, and they, private together, and all their days so far had brought them to this. 'I can't see anything anyway,' he playfully protested.

'Ok,' she said. 'I'm writing on your back. Ok? Here's another one. Guess the letters.' She started to trace her finger down his skin.

He felt the straight line and called out. 'I?' he said.

'Yes,' said Claudia as she continued to trace her finger.

'That's an L,' said Alfi.

'Yes,' she said again and so it continued as Alfi called out the letters she etched onto him. She, she was the calligrapher, painting out and brushing beautiful words.

Alfi spoke softly. 'O. V. E.'

'You!' chirped Claudia with a light surrender.

Alfi paused and asked. 'Really?'

'Yes, really. Really, I do. Forever. I do.'

And yet, even then, within this moment of togetherness, and the need for their togetherness, there was a suggestion to Alfi. "Was he running away, rather than to something?"

## THE HIMALAYA

The long undulating road was so remote, it was as if the whole world had forgotten it had existed. Alfi lightly gripped the handle bars and eased into a gentle acceleration. Despite the beauty of the place, the quiet of his surroundings, he held a sadness in his eyes. His bike had been packed heavily that day. An old orange holdall, scuffed and tired looking, was strapped tightly onto the empty pillion seat behind him. Side boxes carried spares. He thought he'd planned for everything.

To his right, the green hills of the lower Himalaya climbed steeply. These were peppered with wild flowers; quivering lilacs, crimsons, whites and yellows in a dancing breeze. And to his left the land disappeared downwards into deep forests and jungle. He glanced up once more to the slanting hills, where later behind them, the pure white peaks of the Himalaya appeared against a sapphire sky.

It was then, just then, that his mind's eye noticed. Noticed as he caught sight, the sight of her lips. That gave him a conciliatory smile. And he watched. Watched, as his hand limply left hers and fell loosely away. They both turning. Turning in opposite directions to begin their absence from one another. His whole life seemed full, unjustifiably so, of farewells.

His boots rested on the bike. 'The earth turns at a thousand miles an hour yet no one seems to notice,' he thought. 'But on a motorbike, you can see it spinning, just a foot pedal away. This concentrates matters, one clear moment after another. I guess what a Buddhist monk would call mindfulness. And if you wait long enough within the mindfulness, you can leave everything behind and find peace. But then something comes and tries to disturb you.'

A stream of whistles entered like ghosts into his helmet as a vicious wind encircled him. It buffeted the bike - first one side, then the other - pounding at him, until he quickly turned off the road and drove down into a little ravine. He got off the bike and shielded himself behind its curved fuel tank as a haze of stones and dust pelted at him. 'You just have to wait,' his mind said. 'Wait long enough.'

And so, in time, as if by magic, the storm began to recede until it finally vanished itself, leaving Alfi huddled alone in the quietness. The sand had fallen back to earth and in the stillness everything, all the sky, had become clear. He lifted himself up and rode again, up into the hills, leaning easily into one long rising bend after another. Until, in the chilled air, he was along the crest of the highest mountain where all the world was below him. Alfi was flying!

His eyelids blinked briefly. Just closed for a moment.

※ ※ ※

His eyes opened and he looked carefully at the monk's hand. To the bony angular wrist with a mala necklace of sandalwood beads wrapped repeatedly around it. The fingers moved precisely, touching a percussion stick to the edge of an old brass singing bowl which gave off the gentlest of chimes. It was tapped a second time, but this time more deeply, sending a long ethereal sound into the room as the class, along with Alfi, consumed it. Brother Iblan put down the stick and sat still in his saffron robe. His round concentrated face, under a neatly shaved head, broke into a satisfied smile.

The room was simple, yet intimate. There were small pictures scattered here and there, of religious figures; gurus staring out benevolently from old gold frames. In fact, everything, amongst the rows of flickering buttermilk candles, the saffron, orange and yellow walls, had a golden, glowing, hue to it. There was a cluster of incense sticks, like those found everywhere in Nepal. These were tightly arranged and fanned out from a small brass vase below a window. They smoldered; their smoke snaking upwards and rising through white shafts of morning sunlight, until they seeped through a half-open shuttered window, escaping to the outside.

There was a slow intake of breath before Brother Iblan spoke with a liveliness in his voice that elevated the room. 'Try *not* to follow the flow of your mind,' he said. 'And see how hard it is - to do this? *Not* to follow the mind? Concentrate on the inbreath, the outbreath. And when we sit, here and try to focus *just* on our breath, you may realise you cannot even do that! You cannot even control your own mind to concentrate on the breath for one single moment!'

Brother Iblan became both excited and perplexed at his own observation. His head circled the class to see if they understood. 'It moves from one thought, one subject, one feeling to another. You cannot stop it. And this is serious! As you have to live with your mind twenty-four hours a day! All day long. We're thinking, planning, experiencing, perceiving. Our mind gives us feelings, memories, perceptions, and some of these can bring us down or create a lot of problems for ourselves or for those around us. So, we need to go beyond our mind, to our stillness and then calm our mind: and make it our friend.'

Brother Iblan's voice became more serious as he lent forward as if telling a secret. 'When you train your mind. You can reduce or end suffering. Suffering from frustrated desires. With a controlled mind you can now just watch your desires pass by, without reacting or grasping for them. Just observe as they come - and eventually they will go again. Like watching a train come towards you and then disappearing again. You can educate your mind to let desire go. To let all negative thoughts disappear too! Rather than being driven by them. Everything: desire, happiness, even unhappiness is impermanent.'

Alfi thought back to his life in New York.

# CHAPTER TWO

*Samsara*

Alfi sat on the slow-moving, juddering underground train where a fluorescent light shone back at him from the black windows. He was smartly, casually dressed, with a brown weathered looking briefcase beside his feet - like a loyal old dog. Other commuters sat with unfortunate, sullen looking faces, as he turned the pages on one of his newly acquired books. It was a publication of short stories about how people had changed direction in their lives.

It prompted him to think. "When would he ever reach the point where he would be truly happy? Next year? In five years? When I get this, or achieve that, maybe? Would he always *not* be there yet? Was it passing him by? Was happiness potentially within his grasp already? But was he too blind to notice?"

A story '*My Spiritual Journey to Nepal*' caught his eye as the carriage reached a station and jolted, telling him to leave the page and examine the other passengers. He defined them playfully according to their outfits. The suits and ties, the dark blue formal wear of the ladies, or their long, whimsical dresses that were in fashion recently, that would have taken them a while to decide over, in some far-off store somewhere. The heavy overcoats, the younger boys in their sneakers and badges. He wondered, how had the world shaped them? Was it their fate? Or had they shaped themselves?

In fact, being on the underground and seeing their quiet faces without expression, pointed him to something. He pondered on what they would be like above ground when their mouths were to become animated? What would they sound like? It was true of course, that any public transport creates such a show of quiet solemnity; buses, trains and so on, for the single traveler. And then he remembered the underground where his father first took him as a child. His Dad had lent down to take his hand, explaining that they were to go on a train that would take them 'deep under the ground.' He recalled the sheer wonder of it that he'd had that day as a child, amongst the fear of it too. Indeed, it *was* wonderful, and now, as he caught his sombre reflection in the black curved windows, all that wonder had gone. Was then, fascination always needing something anew? And would the joy of it, the joy of life, if you let it, diminish with age? Could intellect, at least in some instances, be the misfortune of man? For the shine of most things becomes speckled with age.

Nearby, some parents fussed over a spoilt little girl. She tugged at her mother's arm as her little legs skittered. Alfi thought. "Were they chasing immortality unconsciously, obstructing a fear of death through their children?" Opposite was a man not dissimilar to Alfi, but older. The suit, even with the characterful briefcase by his side. "Do we leave too much of ourselves to chance?" Alfi thought again as he surveyed him. "A family, and did he ever step back to see who he really needs to be, before he made the commitment, and began to become diluted? Did he make real choices or was he pulled about by circumstances?" Was there a hierarchy about it? Granted, there were a few men who made themselves great, but how could you do wonderful things if you were born without advantage or opportunity? There were human slaves too, he considered, who despite their freedom, lacked the intellectual capacity or gifts to direct their own fate? They thought they did but their lives were trivial. Alas he thought, perhaps we should just treat our lives as if they were a holiday, knowing it will end, but enjoying each day?

How much then, was it down to chance and good or bad luck? He looked at the man opposite again - and were they both the same? A wandering cycle in various guises. Life felt then, like an endless knot from which there is no escape, Samsara - as one of his books had labelled it, a constant churning between karma: actions and consequences, and desire.

Had Alfi too, chosen instinctively, to become part of the herd? Was he being led by something called '*bad faith*? Something he'd learn about soon enough in this tale. Consumed by a culture that had possessed him with all the wrong values and prejudices, with no exit from its deceit? Oh, *what a fool he'd been*! The man and Alfi exchanged glances.

You would assume that, as Alfi worked for a philosophy magazine and in studying the great thinkers, he would know better - or at least take a more educated view. But the absorption of the philosophers had made them look dull, and there was no laughter in them. Were they educated fools who felt themselves too wise to be happy, wrapped in an intellect and superciliousness? Was it that, the vanity of their propositions had carried them to such a height, that none of them could have an interest in the other, apart from how the other could serve them? They had become too ridiculous, too vain to be happy, and there would be no satisfaction of love.

He looked at his distorted reflection in the window again, where now his figure seemed to be on the outside of the train and mused on something he'd found in his philosophical work. 'You know there's the story of the *"Paradox of the Ass."* Sometimes wrongly attributed to Buridan. *"A hungry donkey comes up to two identical hay stacks, but can't decide which one to eat, so he starves to death."* Alfi looked at himself. "What we could have here, is a dead ass."

The rhythmic sound of the train picked up. It swayed the carriage along the tracks. It neared Chambers Street station, Alfi's station, where he mumbled to himself amongst the noise. 'Routine.'

❀ ❀ ❀

Inside the consulting room the doctor considered Alfi, giving him a half-smile. 'So how long have you been having the headaches?'

Alfi shuffled nervously. 'I don't know. I mean, I'm unsure,' he sat up a little in the slippery, reclined leather couch. 'Maybe it's been a couple of months. Maybe I'm also suffering with a little memory loss? It's hard to tell. The pain, it comes hard, right on the front...the frontal lobe, then it can move round a bit, to the back. Sometimes, the pain. It can last for days. Whatever it is, I want you to tell me straight doctor! Tell me what it is. Just be absolutely honest. Maybe it's...I hate to say the word. A tumour. I'd like to know what I'm dealing with. Or maybe it's something psychological, and the onslaught of *severe debilitating manic depression,* so I get off lucky.'

'Open up,' the doctor commanded.

'You mean, talk about myself? My life history? Feelings?' asked Alfi.

'Open your mouth Mr Singer. I'd like to see your tonsils.'

The doctor looked carefully into Alfi's mouth and began making inaudible noises as if he'd just discovered something quite intriguing, then familiar. 'Mm. Ah. Oh,' he confirmed in several successions, a little to Alfi's annoyance. He eventually pulled back and spoke just one word, an elongated, 'Ok!' Followed by an indifferent stare to the window.

'Ok?' Alfi asked. 'Did you find anything?'

The doctor ignored this remark, retreated to his desk, sat down and pondered. 'I think,' he said, before pausing again on his elbows. 'I think, I need to do some tests.'

'Tests?' cried Alfi. 'You'd like to do some tests? At a time like this! You gotta do *tests?* I thought you were fully qualified?'

'Tests on *you* Mr Singer!'

Alfi's expression was not dissimilar to someone on the tracks and facing an oncoming 10:22 from Boston. 'Tests?' he repeated, his mouth half open. 'What kind of tests?'

'Well, there's blood pressure, any hypertension of course, but...'

Alfi was still mesmerised. 'Tests?'

'Perhaps a computerised axial tomography,' the doctor continued matter-of-factly. 'What you call a CAT scan.'

'A scan?'

Within half an hour Alfi was lying face upwards towards a polystyrene clinic ceiling on a slow-moving conveyer - looking as if he was about to be minced. The CAT machine focused him somewhat.

Later, the doctor stood in the consulting room examining some images on an illuminated white screen. He pointed at various shadows. 'Bloods good, the rest here, nothing, nothing. It seems, Mr Singer,' he said turning to face him squarely. 'There is nothing wrong with you. I can't see any abnormalities, there is nothing serious to worry about. All pretty normal.'

'Are you sure?' Alfi asked. 'I mean, really sure? I'm *normal?* Do we need a second opinion?'

The doctor cautiously lowered his voice. 'These could be, well simply, they could be tension headaches. Are you having any difficulties at the moment? Do you sleep well? Perhaps stress, anxiety in your personal or work life? Sometimes we just need to calm things down. Approach things differently.'

'Maybe I *could* change my approach to things?' replied Alfi half addressing himself.

The doctor began scribbling a prescription. 'Look,' he said

holding out a piece of paper. 'I can prescribe these "serotonin reup-take inhibitors." They will help you just calm things down. Take these, two times a day for a couple of weeks and see how things go. You can always come back if the symptoms persist.'

Alfi walked down the high street with a palpable joy in his steps. He was alive, he was healthy, and how often did he not celebrate this? Is not the absence of pain the greatest of all pleasures? And there would be no need for pleasure seeking. This was his thought at least at the time - for however fleeting it lasted. Then, the entrance to the metro station loomed and it beckoned him. His footsteps slowed. There was the job.

❀ ❀ ❀

Ted, the manager of the magazine, leant backwards in his chair. He was opposite Alfi in a large, mostly unoccupied meeting room with bare white walls, apart from a collection of framed posters illustrating covers from previous magazines. Each of these carried philosophical, slightly amusing, nonsensical headlines designed to lure the reader in, such as "The Quest to be Normal" or "Why now...Why Me?"

Ted's sycophantic young assistant, Daniel, sat aside him with beginnings of a smirk along his narrow Irish lips. They both looked at Alfi from across a long table that might as well had been from another universe.

'Your writing.' Ted continued. 'Has...changed. Recently it lacks anything...compelling. Do you know what I mean? Do you know what I mean? It doesn't draw the reader in. I can't put my finger on it.'

Ted was the right man for the job. It was only his intelligence that had been lacking. Alfi stared back at him, at his behavior, and remembered the olden days and how sweet the work had been. When the ego worked so obviously. How difficult it was to criticize those who complemented you. It was a game easily played, but lacked any merit or fortitude. Yet Ted was committed, despite books, magazines and their words, even their education, being the mere frivolousness of entertainment. Their significance nothing, apart from what their perpetrators pretended it to be.

Ted continued. 'What I mean to say is, it needs to grab me. And, it doesn't grab me.'

'Thank you for pointing out some of my perceived failings,' replied Alfi. 'Would you like me to point out a few of yours?'

Ted picked up a pile of papers and turned to Daniel. 'Those last articles he submitted?'

Daniel folded his arms and lent back to survey Alfi. 'There were three,' he said coldly, before announcing. "In Praise of Alcohol."

Ted interrupted. 'You see.'

Daniel sensed the beginning of a roll. "Ageing Equals Ugliness."

Ted sniffed, looked baffled and turned to Daniel. 'And what was the last one?'

Daniel glanced to the ceiling light and back down again before shuffling with some papers. "Happiness - and How to Avoid It."

Ted punched the table. 'You see! They're not big sellers are they Alfi! We need something more...aspirational!'

Alfi cut in. 'I was making an exploration into something new. Perhaps we're all going down the wrong path here! Philosophy, it just...it just seems like some dry academic luxury for the upper classes. Don't you think? It needs to offer something original for the common people. Something practical. Even Socrates, he was a man of the people. He used to wander around Athenian markets asking questions to peasants.'

'Never mind Socrates for a minute,' Ted countered.

'We need to offer questions and answers for the common man. The modern, twenty first century...peasant.' remarked Alfi.

'We need to offer something. Agreed,' said Ted. 'We need to grip readers in. Something that will give them some benefit. Who's going to buy these magazines anyway? Hey? We buy magazines to inform, to entertain - to illuminate, that's what people want. To gain insights. Know what I mean? Articles. They must hit you on a gut level...I'd like to be hit, on a gut level.'

Alfi glanced at Ted's potted stomach behind the starched blue and white striped shirt, and imagined the satisfaction.

'Compelling,' Ted added dramatically as if the word in itself was a wondrous thing, so wondrous in fact, that he repeated it again. 'Compelling! I just need you to focus more. We need to offer...*positivity*. That's where it's all going these days. Positivity. Get me kid? Do you get me?'

'Yes focus,' Daniel added wryly.

'Can you do that kid? Ted asked expectantly. 'Can you do that? Give me more positivity?'

'Positivity?' Alfi looked puzzled. 'I don't think that's my field.'

He stared at the two of them. Their keen, anxious, motivated, and desperate faces.

❀ ❀ ❀

It was night time as Alfi lay alone in bed. It was true that these past few weeks he'd not been sleeping well. It had made the nights long, the days tired, where he would do his best not to take out his exhaustion on others. He stared, motionless, at the patterns on the textured ceiling, making images. Lights out, and waiting for the shroud of sleep to take him - where, at last in the darkness, he could remove himself from a reality given to him by the day, and enter a new actuality - one not limited by words. Which one, he thought, is more true? How abstract feelings had the ability to take him. His eyes, finally, heavily, fell shut. Time passed, there was no measure to it, and then there was a jolt. Something shook him a little. Was he in a dream? He looked down to the length of his bed in the darkness where there seemed to be the unnerving sight of a dark figure sitting. It became real when he felt the weight of it shift on his mattress. He called out timidly. 'Who? Who is it?'

'It's me,' came a whisper. The figure moved again slightly.

'Me? Me who?' Alfi asked.

'Death,' was the reply.

'What?' asked Alfi.

'Death,' came the thudding reply again. 'You heard me!'

'Death?' Alfi asked.

'Yes Death! Are you hard of hearing or something? You know. Kaput. As opposed to life.'

'What are you doing here?' Alfi asked.

'What do you think I'm doing here?' came the reply.

'Me? Me? You've come for me? But I'm not ready yet. I've just been to the Doctor's. I had tests? I've got the all clear!'

'That's what they all say. No one's ready *yet*,' remarked Death, as he looked to his watch. 'Look I haven't got much time. I'm on a schedule.'

Alfi became anxious. 'Is that all I'm going to get from you? Just short answers? Give me some time here, to take this all in! And it's just...Just so much of a shock. I mean, I didn't think things were that bad, I'm at a younger age. I could get hit by a bus, yes. But in bed?' Death shrugged his shoulders as Alfi continued. 'And I didn't think there was anything wrong. I mean, I eat well. I exercise...sometimes. I often eat organic. And the tests! There must be some kind of mix up? A mistake. Have you checked? You've the right paperwork? You're at the wrong address? Do you go by zip-codes?'

'No, no.' Death replied. 'It's definitely you. I rarely make mistakes. Well rarely.'

'And you, you look so...typical,' Alfi interrupted. 'Is this a dream?'

'What do you mean? Typical?'

'Well. You know. Dressed in black, the cloak and all that. Is this fancy dress or something?'

'Fancy dress?' Death was insulted.

'The shadowy face,' continued Alfi unabated. 'Perhaps this *is* a dream?'

'Dream?' Death was agitated. 'And don't knock black either! It makes me look slimmer. And what do you expect anyway? Something floral? Shorts? I'm death.'

'I suppose.' Alfi said. 'I suppose we all dress for occasions.'

Death fumbled inside his cloak. 'Look I tried Lycra once. It didn't work.' He drew out a cigarette and lit it. The dark silhouette of his face blew out a perfect line of grey smoke. 'Truth be said, now that we're in a conversation. I get lonely.'

'Lonely? Lonely? Are you surprised!'

'The job. It's the pressure of a one-man band you see,' replied Death.

Alfi tiptoed out of his bed, crept down and rested a hand, hesitantly, on Death's shoulder. 'I'm sorry. Sorry to hear that. Do you? Do you need to talk?'

'I feel ignored,' Death confessed before taking another draw on his cigarette. 'And I'm always around you know, but no one seems to notice. And who likes being ignored these days? Tell me? Umm? Nobody - that's who! Yet most people like to forget me. And it gets busy sometimes. You try working with a plague! To tell the truth, after all these years I think I'm more of a team player.'

'I'm sorry to hear that. I didn't...I just didn't realise, responded Alfi. 'It makes sense.'

Death continued. 'If people could just think of me every once in a while, not all the time of course, I get that. But it might just give them a little more momentum, spur them on to do something with their lives. Perhaps take more chances, as they know it's all going to end, to come to nothing anyway. What have they got to lose? Instead of keeping putting things off, or playing safe. As they say, *it's later than you think.'*

'It's a point I suppose.' Alfi sighed. 'Well, maybe you're right? That's it, and I should have thought about you sooner. I might have done more.'

Death looked at him squarely. 'And now it's too late.'

'Yes, too late,' Alfi repeated, and hearing the words out loud, the tangibility of them, it hurt him a little. He stared with eyes wide-open, into the blackness. 'Maybe, in all my years I just didn't do anything. Beyond the normal really. And what was expected of me. I just played safe.'

'In fact, there are many deaths,' Death added more brightly. 'The death of childhood, adolescence, young adulthood. And for some, old age. Your previous incarnations all pass away at some point, don't they? But you don't seem to notice exactly when. You can't pinpoint it. But they all go. It's just a matter of time. You know, it's also true that time speeds up through the ages. A month to a playing child seems infinite, yet in the later years, as time is measured in the mind not the clock, it speedeth so. This is a little trick of mine that people have a suspicion about, but is ignored by the sciences for it has no reason. Old age, despite its frailty, runs quicker to you than an infant's feet! And then I come along. To end the whole show. Tough, isn't it?'

'You're right, and we're not, most of us, making the most of it.'

'Yep.' Death said. 'I've heard it all before.'

'The end then?' Alfi mused glumly. 'But you know, at least I'll get to see my ancestors, right? My parents, Uncle Graham, my gold-fish. Elvis?'

'Uh. No.'

'What do you mean...*no?*'

Death took a deeper drag on his cigarette. 'There's no afterlife,' he said.

'No afterlife? What do you mean?'

'When it's over, it's over,' said Death.

'But,' Alfi protested. 'Look, we've been depending on it! Depending on something. It can't be the end? This can't just be it - can it? Are you sure? I mean...well I did, I must confess, worry that in some notion of heaven you might get a little bored. What would you do with your time all day? All that lying around? Looking at things. It's like a student's gap year. Maybe God didn't think it through. Heavenly pleasures...they have their limitations you know, and eternity's a pretty long time! But are you sure? There is no heaven? I mean, it's the shock.'

'How can I *not* be sure? I'm Death. I know these things.'

'But what about you?'

'What? What do you mean *me*?' Death asked.

'If there's no such thing as an afterlife. Then who employs you?'

'I'm self-employed.'

'You're self-employed?'

'Look, don't knock it. Ok, the work can be hard - it can be unpredictable, but you get to choose your own hours.'

'Self-employed?' Alfi repeated. 'Now you're sending me into a panic. Do you know that! You're sending me, you're sending everyone, into a panic!' Alfi calmed himself a little and asked. 'Ok, now look. Listen to me. Is there any way. I mean anyway, I could ask for a little longer?'

'Longer?'

'Well, you know. Think of it as a reprieve. Some kind of pardon or something? Give me a few more years.'

'Well. What for?' Death asked.

'What for?' retorted Alfi.

'Yes? What for? Just more of the same?' asked Death blankly.

'What for?' Alfi repeated rhetorically and scratched his head. 'Well, yes, maybe...more of the same! Life with all its pain, the let downs, striving for something, not really even knowing why you're really doing it...the heartache, people leaving you, people cheating on you...all the disappointments, the bad weather, old age and disease. It's all over far too quickly.'

Taking another deep draw on his cigarette, Death circled his lips and expelled three perfect hoops of smoke, watching each one carefully as they dissipated a few jaw lengths away. He was both a patient and impetuous sort and enjoyed smoking as it helped calm the nerves, despite the health risks. 'You want more time?' he eventually asked.

'Yes.'

'Ok then, I'll give you more time.'

'You will?' asked Alfi.

'Why not?' Death said. 'You seem like a nice chap. And it would be a shame to see you disintegrate to nothingness, to oblivion, and to begin to be forgotten by the universe so early. Think of it as an experiment. For you, I'll make the exception. But do something with it this time! And stop ignoring me.'

Alfi's head turned on his pillow. And whether this was a dream or not, he heard the words repeating themselves deep into his ear. 'Stop ignoring me.'

✵ ✵ ✵

Alfi sat on the rolling underground train as it slowed and entered the station. The familiar letters aligned themselves outside his window 'Chambers Street.' It was his station, back to work, yet his face - amongst the noise of the wheels on the track and the shuffling, disinterested passengers - was ambiguous. The carriage doors slid open but time hung suspended. It was as if the occasion was telling him something - and he couldn't move.

Had he given up? Had he lost the power to imagine future good anticipations? Could he not keep up the sensible routine, behaving like this - and wasting his life; wasting away *the Self* and what it possibly could be? It was true, like most of us, that hardly anyone knew him beyond his close circles, so what did it matter anyway, if he did not exist at all?

The doors closed awkwardly again as he just sat. Sat. His lack of significance whispered to him like spiteful words in a dream. The train shuddered as it began to move, lulling him forward and disappearing with his figure into the darkness.

❀ ❀ ❀

That night, he sat in a bath of warm soapy water as Claudia knelt on the bathroom floor beside him. She washed his back in slow thoughtful circles; the same skin upon which she'd etched those loving words, so long ago. Her eyes watched, as the suds fell back into the water in slow motion. And the silence held them together. She eventually moved her lips. 'I'm seeing somebody else,' she said, and Alfi's head dropped. An emptiness consumed, and it drained him. He had become a lonely figure as she continued to bathe him.

# CHAPTER THREE

*Butterflies*

Brother Iblan delicately struck the singing bowl and Alfi's eyes opened. The class rubbed their palms together, and placing the heel of their hands over their eyes, they felt the heat for a moment. They then stood up, still half within a dream, and without saying a word began putting things away.

Brother Iblan walked to the garden and sat with Alfi to drink tea. There was some incense burning in a flower pot. Alfi glanced at it uncomfortably and gave out a light sneeze before turning apologetically. 'Sorry' he said. 'Of all the places, I've come to Nepal and find I have an allergy to incense.'

The monk raised an eyebrow ruefully. 'Meditation is like learning to play the piano Mr Alfi. You have to keep practicing; first the musical scales over and over. You keep making mistakes, it will be very boring, but you keep at it. Practice, practice, practice. Some people just come here, close their eyes for a little bit and say there is nothing in meditation and never return to it again. They expect to play the piano in just one day! But I feel you're committed to it. So, when you go, you must continue practicing.'

'I will. I promise,' answered Alfi.

Brother Iblan shifted in his seat. 'So, tell me? About your trip.'

'It's a small village for a story,' Alfi said. 'Called Madrakani.'

'Oh Madrakani, I know it. It's a long way, a very long way. And might I know why you're going there? What is the story?'

'Yetis,' said Alfi. 'I am investigating the existence of Yetis. New York Times.'

'Yetis?' Brother Iblan quizzed with a smile. 'I wonder why people want to know if they exist or not? What is the reason? They are always seeking *wonder* I suppose. People like stories don't they? Religions are told all over the world, through stories.' The monk considered Alfi more carefully, lowered his voice and added. 'Do you think...you would like to make your own story one day Mr Alfi? Instead of just telling those of others?'

'What do you mean?' Alfi asked.

'Don't be afraid of making mistakes Mr Alfi, otherwise you'll do nothing. You must give yourself, give your life, some direction. Give your life a map and some purpose. Otherwise, there is no reason to it. You'll just go about doing things. Why go on a journey without a map? Eventually...you'll become lost. And if you're not careful, it will be too late. With no time left. Remember this, Alfi. The *unexamined life* is not worth living!'

'Unexamined life?'

'You need to think about your own values,' the monk continued. 'Not the values of those around you, of others,' he laughed by way of a pause. 'You know, before man was domesticated, he was free and wild and perhaps in a more sophisticated way, you'll become that way too! Most importantly, you must decide what sort of person you want to be. How to live your life must be decided by you and you should not - as much as possible - be driven around by things that happen around you. If you do, then you've lost your autonomy and you're not the governor of yourself.'

'Mm,' Alfi reflected.

'You must be a thoughtful human being, who makes choices that you've reflected upon carefully. Are they good choices? And your choices must take into account being compassionate to others,' the monk laughed gently. 'What is a life without virtue Mr Alfi? And you can direct your own fate - if you're clever about it. The past is gone. And it has brought you here. But what you do in the present will dictate your future.'

Brother Iblan stood up, walked to the end of the garden and peered thoughtfully over a high wall. On the other side the poor were going about their daily chores in a busy marketplace. Men were bent, carrying heavy loads. A woman struggled to heave a trolley of vegetables: people, cars, traffic and cattle all convened in sublime, almost poetic, Nepalese chaos. He considered the view.

'So many people out there Mr Alfi,' he said shaking his head. 'And they struggle just to survive. They do not have freedom you see. Many will never get the chance to realise their potential. *Eudaimonia*, the ancient Greeks used to call it - *to flourish*. To flourish is a route to happiness and almost the same word for it. Some of them out there, over that wall, might had been great scholars, scientists, made a difference to the world and to those around them, but they will never have the opportunity. Instead, we're led by fools. All their time you see, is taken up with their survival. Life is so unfair, don't you think? Maybe that is why many of us become monks!' He laughed mockingly but with a sense of guilt. 'However, you're lucky Mr Alfi. In this life you were born a Westerner. You have education, freedom and choice. And in Nepal you're between cultures. You're outside your own culture and outside ours. You have autonomy. Freedom! You're in an interesting position. So why waste it? You have come a long way here for a reason. You just have to find it.'

Brother Iblan stopped as he noticed a butterfly flying over the brickwork and into the garden. He sat back down next to Alfi who asked him. 'But happiness, Brother Iblan? That's the Buddhist philosophy isn't it? To be happy. To find happiness. To be content? Although, sometimes it does sound a bit selfish.'

'Ah. Happiness!' Brother Iblan quipped. 'Easy thing to say isn't it. *Happiness.* Maybe happiness is the wrong word and they cannot find an alternative for it. And what does happiness mean? And us Buddhists teach that we must seek happiness!' He glanced at the butterfly as it floated clumsily above the garden, hovering from one leaf, one flower, to another. 'Happiness is like that butterfly. It might come to you. It might not. And even when it does it only stays fleetingly. You must enjoy it while it's here but not become attached to it.'

With that, the butterfly landed perfectly on the back of Brother Iblan's hand - much to his delight. His eyes marveled at it. 'Try not to hold on to it,' he said, studying the insect carefully. 'The moment you try to hold on to it, to keep the happiness, it will disappear again.' And with that, the butterfly opened its wings and lifted away as quickly as it had come. Brother Iblan leant towards Alfi. 'Do you think that we must spend our lives chasing butterflies?'

Alfi spoke. 'You know someone once said to me that happiness is like holding sand between your two hands: the tighter you try to hold it, the faster it disappears.'

'Very good,' exclaimed Brother Iblan. 'Perhaps that person is right. But Mr Alfi. You know, there is a place, far from here, up in the mountains, that teaches an alternative to Buddhism - an alternative to happiness.'

'Oh? Really...' asked Alfi.

'I've never been there,' Brother Iblan continued. 'But I know it's run by a former Buddhist monk - a Lama, his name is *Thay*. He left Buddhism a long time ago. He used to be a great teacher, he was my elder and also my friend.' Brother Iblan smiled in recollection. 'But he began to question Buddhism, particularly that the life goal should be "to be happy" or content. After all, a cow in a field with all its banality is content!' The monk broke into laughter. 'Instead, his teachings were that life should have *meaning* - and that only a life with meaning had importance - and that happiness in itself was irrelevant! A man without purpose, may attempt to fill the void with pleasure or quiet routine, but it will never do. It will never be adequate. He also taught that we must be *authentic.*

Do you know what this is Mr Alfi? But most of us are not authentic at all! This was quite a revelation at the time to a community of monks who all lived in the same way and who all appeared to be the same. And by being authentic, Thay argued, our lives would have meaning. So in the end, he just left and created a new place, far away from here and on the other side of the Himalaya - where people could go to start anew. They would go there to be reborn, to live authentic lives, rather than the lives that had been given to them accidentally, or through causation from the circumstances around them. They were even granted new names so that their old selves would completely disappear, be rubbed out...their former selves would simply vanish! They say some of those who've "gone missing" you know, from the West, are living quite happily up there.'

Brother Iblan looked warmly into Alfi's eager eyes. 'How would that appeal to you Mr Alfi? To recreate yourself? *"To thine self be true."* Wasn't that, one of your clever writer's words?' He then reached into his pocket and removed a small tattered envelope, handing it to Alfi. 'Go on,' he said nodding. 'Open it. I have this for you.'

Alfi carefully unsealed the envelope and took out a hand drawn map on some old parchment paper. 'It was given to me many years ago,' said Brother Iblan. 'It's a map of how to get there, to that special place. I never did go. And now? I am too old! Ah, maybe in another life Alfi,' he sighed.

Alfi studied it carefully, where below the map were just a few

33

words written in brushed painted strokes, quite beautifully. He read them aloud. *"Mindgarten at the End of the Universe."*

Brother Iblan's face shone. 'Nice name isn't it! And perhaps, after you find those yetis of yours, you should go there - to the Mindgarten at the end of the Universe! Who knows? You might find many butterflies there?'

# CHAPTER FOUR

## The Non-Imperative of Freewill

It was three days before his thirty-ninth birthday as Alfi set out in search for yetis, and like the dust spinning out from behind his wheels, he'd left his old New York city life behind. He gripped the throttle and his head tilted back to enjoy a flurry of acceleration. Getting stories in Nepal this first month had proved interesting, and within the soothing breeze from the hills he was sent into another daydream of past adventures.

❀ ❀ ❀

With the back of a hand, Alfi wiped the smoky little round window to the side of him. He looked out. The rutted airstrip, not long enough he thought, ended abruptly with a vertical drop over the hills. The propellers span noisily and invisibly in the terrific wind, as the little aircraft turned to face the runway along the top of the black mountain. Dark clouds were descending, they moved like veils over the peaks. He turned to the other five passengers who sat wearing thick jackets to keep out the cold.

The plane's small front wheel rasped some more over loose stones as it finally aligned itself, and waited. Alfi looked behind himself again, this time at the heavy cloth sacks and luggage stacked haphazardly, then at the two heftiest of passengers - he wondered did they feel any guilt?

Over the pilot's leather shoulder was the narrow windscreen. His arm pulled back the lever with such a fierceness, that with a shunt, they were off. They bounced along the ridge in a rage of noise, struggling to find speed. And then they were over it like lead, over the edge and dropping, until miraculously, the winds got under their wings and took them up again, where they rose in a gliding curve, up over the oncoming peaks.

❀ ❀ ❀

Alfi came back to the present, eased his hand on the throttle and turned off the road. 'This should be it,' he thought as he dropped down a narrow track that led into the base of a steep, secluded valley. He rode for a while alongside a little stream until the trail he was following petered out almost to nothing. He stopped to take in the view and began to wonder where he was going? The track ahead rose uninvitingly behind an ugly stone hillock. A wind shuddered some nearby trees. Yet apart from the crackling of their branches there was nothing, nor even a bird in the sky. He clicked the bike into action, continued around the hillock, and up the hill.

Hours passed, along what was little more than a mule trail and then came the rain. It was a fierce, unforgiving rain, the water coming in sideways which made the route he was following barely visible. He was now mid-way up, and along the angled edge of a mountain. The stones to his front wheel turned and rolled down the slope - the narrow track he was riding was disappearing behind him - could he ever go back?

At last, he reached the top of the hill. The trail widened and he rode more quickly, until rounding a bend it slowed again into a wide muddy slush. He was beneath a broken escarpment, its jagged edge, and riding into the remains of landslides. Large rocks and the ugly black upturned roots of trees were being surrounded and turned over by the slurry. Like lava it took them across the road in front of him, and down again into a slanted black forest below.

He drove through it, knowing it was dangerous to stand still. The mud spilt up to his knees and into the lips of his boots, then eventually he came to higher ground. Hour after hour he climbed, the hills never ending, and in concentrating on his wheels, he'd failed to notice that the sky above him had changed remarkably - and was now a clear indigo blue. Rounding another bend and now he was near the very top of a last mountain. Further, and finally he reached the plateau where, beyond all his imaginations, the vista became wide and epic, unlike anything he'd seen before. He stopped in awe of the view. Could a place like this, so empty, so bright, exist?

In any direction the land gave no marks. It was desolate, flat, endless. The elements had spilled the floor in places with white, silvery shingles, sometimes in large heaps and gushes, that shone like precious stones under the blinding light. He clicked into gear and drove as fast as he could. Across the land, he was directionless now - alone and free, with only the far-off mountains to guide him. Then the colossal winds came. They surrounded his bike in all directions at once, shrieking and howling, pushing and pulling, rising in tempo then falling again - were they playing with him?

Further, and as the day was fading, he rode across a giant orange horizon. As far as he could see was a string of wild-looking clay-coloured boulders, the size of small hills changing colour in the shadowy light - that had been carved into ethereal sculptures by the gusts. He rode along their bases, into the noise of the wind, yet even here and sounding within the gusts was a sign of human habitation.

A torn weather-beaten Tibetan flag, vibrant looking in glittering red, blue, white and gold, shook noisily from a yielding wooden stake. He stopped and reached out momentarily to touch it.

Time later and with the sun at its lowest, the bike's engine began to run weak. It was telling him something. The terrain had changed, and now his wheels struggled over sharp slippery stones and skidded sideways over dust. The meagre direction the mountains had once given him, now began to err Alfi. Was there to be any end to it? Then up ahead, his eyes caught first sight of a black tumbling river, that ran like a scar across the moonscape. If he was to go further, he would have to cross it.

He stopped exhausted, just short of it. Flipping down his side-stand he walked to the water that was flowing wildly, carrying sheets of bobbing ice. Yet it seemed shallow enough. He remounted the bike and accelerated into it, but immediately the river turned malicious. Riving and splashing madly at him - as if he were an intruder - it was already half way up his wheels, pushing and turning, and as he fought against it, the gushing white and black, he felt his arms grow weak. And then with a clout, the bike was hit sideways, into the vicious surf and the engine died, and he was being dragged downstream. With the bike leaning, he tried to pull it upright again and pushed forward against the torrent that was now near his chest - and then, all of a sudden, he became engulfed, his wheel trapped between rocks. The sky changed again; from deep violet, to grey, to black, as the river tried to sink him, to take him in. And yet even then - at that exact moment - there was a delectability to it. For within the solitude, a fight with the wilderness to survive and the fear of death, in each scintillating second, he was truly alive.

❀ ❀ ❀

By nightfall, Alfi's bike was parked on dry land. He sat beside his small tent and watched, as the little fire he'd made crackled and popped. Scooping food from a tin, he stared at the flames for a while, when a thought occurred to him that seemed to come like a whisper from the mountains. That in the drama of his new life - both good and bad - there was a kind of *'dialectic click'* about it. The more you cling on to life, he considered, and the safety of it, the more you would lose it. But to let go, you would truly be free.

He played with the last smoldering branches. And, under a multitude of stars that looked down on him on that blackest of nights, he felt he was the only man on earth. A luscious adventure had taken him, and within its seduction he fell asleep. It was a delicious deep sleep.

The next day he awoke to find the sky a brilliant blue that warmed his shoulders, filling him with optimism. He rode on for hours; he and the bike had a new appetite for the world and everything within it. This was living! The ground ahead was a shimmering white; sparkling beneath his wheels - and all under an enormous rising sun - that seemed close enough, like a ball, that he could touch it. Was this the feeling of hope? Could every day be like this?

❀ ❀ ❀

Alfi stood next to his motorbike and stared at his flat back tyre. Opening a saddle bag, he shrugged in easy resignation and took out an innertube; he was amusing himself now. Nothing could upset him, because his mind thought differently. Differently about the outside world, and how its mild troubles could or could not, affect him - for today at least. He rested the innertube on the saddle and mumbled. 'An innertube. But no pump.' But he was being watched.

She looked inquisitively at him at first, from a small hillock where she was hunched amongst the bushes. She wore a thick, multi-layered dress that stretched all the way down to her ankles, and over one shoulder was a crooked wooden stick with a cloth bag dangling from one of its ends. Around her was a flock of goats, some of the smaller ones clambering to her feet. She watched Alfi for a while, making her mind up about what to do. He seemed harmless enough. No danger, she thought, and called out. 'You need sky inside.'

Alfi's head searched for the voice. 'Hallo?' Eventually his eyes met hers. He was relieved to see someone. 'Yes. I need air and you speak English! I haven't seen anyone for a while.' He gave a sincere smile. 'Do you know where I can get some help? To fix this?' Then holding up the innertube. 'And I'm trying to find the town of Madrakani. Madrakani? Do you know it? It shouldn't be far from here.'

'It's not far,' she said. 'Maybe a days' walk from here.' She looked at Alfi's legs carefully. 'Maybe longer. Why are you going there?'

'I've come to write a story.'

'Story?' she asked. 'There are many stories. Which story?'

'I want to find out about Yetis.'

'Yetis? 'What is that? Yetis?'

'It's difficult to explain. Look it doesn't matter.'

'Oh, difficult to explain?' she said. 'You know, I see many pictures of foreigner. They are difficult to explain, but I've studied their languages and it makes it easier for me to understand how they think. They are always searching for something - aren't they? And upset the nature of things. They get angry when they cannot get the things they want. And when they get it, they want more. One thing after the next. One thing after the other. And then they die. And they want nice coffin.' She laughed to herself and was becoming more comfortable with Alfi.

'That's a pretty good account,' Alfi said. 'But not everyone's like that. Right now, all I want is some air.'

'You're the first one, the first foreigner, I see for real.'

'Disappointed?' he asked.

'Somewhat. To some extent,' came the reply.

Alfi ruffled his own hair. 'Thanks. Look, I've had better days. I was much fresher when I started out. These roads, the weather, sleeping outside...it takes you out of your hair care routine.' He sensed the girl found him silly and was trying to make her mind up about him. 'And don't worry,' he hastily added. 'I haven't come here to take anything. I've just come to find out about the *Yeti*. It's like man-monster. It's a big animal. Like a bear. Like a human.'

She looked at him with a degree of examination. 'Maybe you are a Yeti?' and broke into laughter. 'What you mean is...Gumbran. Men with fur. Yes, sometimes we have them here. Not often you see them. But they come here.'

'So, you've seen one?'

'You ask many questions.'

'Sorry,' he dropped his head a little.

'What is your name?' she asked.

'Alfi. Your name too?'

She studied him again before answering. 'Rita. But why did you decide to come here Mr Alfi? Was it a voice in your head, that told you to come here?'

'Voice? I don't understand? What do you mean?'

She continued. 'If you just followed your mind then maybe *you* didn't decide to come here? Maybe, it was already determined you would come. You have to understand the difference between your mind and *you* Mr Alfi. How it leads you.' She tapped one of her goats with a stick. 'Maybe that voice in your head, sending you here, is your ancestor voice. From a previous life? Maybe they lived here before and they want to come back.' She paused and added limply. 'Ok, you don't understand. You don't understand the difference between what your mind tells you and who you are. I think on this journey you will learn about that. But for your information, about the Gumbran. For me, yes one day, the Gumbran came to me, a long time ago. And I was with my goats. Minding my own business,' she paused in recollection and added sorrowfully. 'He threw me into lake.'

'He threw you in a lake?'

'They're not friendly,' said Rita. 'Why would they be? They are angry because they are not humans and they're driven about by nature. They do not have the power to control themselves, to reason. The Gumbran, he then walked away. My father always told me never mix with wild species. It's not good, is it? They are like ghosts and won't play our games. Their mind is different you see. They won't like you. No wild animals like humans do they? Even the birds fly away. They're frightened of us.'

'It's a point,' said Alfi.

'Come to think of it. Even my own goats may not like me. But these are different. They are not wild. They just put up with me. My goats. They give me trust which will one day be broken.' She looked down to them forlornly. 'They have been brainwashed you see. I have replaced their instinct with mine. They think they make their own decisions but they are too foolish to realise that I am making their decisions for them. They are lucky too, as they don't have any memories - they don't carry any resentment or upset with them. Each day they start afresh. I have become their instinct. I have become their mind. I can control them, how they think, and they do not even know it.' One of the goats looked back innocently. 'They follow each other. Even though they are not chained, and if one of them runs away he will always come back. He must always come back, because he thinks he is a goat. Because he feels it safer, to be like the others.'

'You seem to know a lot about goat psychology? It's an expanding field.'

'Is a human a goat?' she said.

'You speak like you're not a human?' replied Alfi.

'I live in the mountains,' she replied randomly. 'Away from people. My name Rita means *child of light*. I am not part of a tribe -

and never can be. And I will make my goats go up that hill, just like that voice in your head makes *you* go up that hill.' She looked away from Alfi and toward the mountains, then spoke more gently. 'Who would you be Mr Alfi? If you were born in these mountains, away from the West and away from your country? And who would be your shepherd? What kind of person would you be?' She gently prodded one of her goats again. 'That's enough,' she said abruptly, and walked towards him and sat comfortably cross-legged on the ground. She untied her cloth bag, drew out a selection of colourful purses and displayed them along some stones. 'I make and sell these purses. You can have one.'

'They're nice. But.'

Rita interrupted. 'You *must* have one.'

'I'll buy one.' he said. 'How much?'

'No, for you, one is free.'

'I don't mind buying one really.'

Rita looked in disagreement as he fingered one of the purses.

'This one is nice,' he said.

'Then you must have it.' She handed him the purse with an outstretched hand.

'Really? You're sure?'

She nodded.

'Thanks,' Alfi said and looked admiringly at it. 'So. So, what happened? What happened with the Yeti? The Gumbran.'

'When he threw me into lake?'

'Yes.'

'I just swim to other side and I watched him walk away. He didn't even attack my goats.'

'And what? What did it look like? The Gumbran.'

'Well. It was about your height. Covered in fur. Big feet. But he had a limp. One leg, not same as other.'

'A yeti with a limp?'

'Many around here have sprained ankles if they're two legged. It's all the stones and the ground. Everybody slips.' She pointed to a hill and changed the subject. 'And up there. That is where you can walk to get to Madrakani.'

Alfi's eyes followed the direction of her pointing. 'Up there? Ok.'

'And after this, in the distance, you will see a steep hill. You go up there,' she added.

'Right,' said Alfi. 'A steep hill.'

'And from there, you will see a mountain with long track. In the distance, with flags around. It is up there.'

'Anymore?' Alfi asked. 'Can you throw in another hill or two?'

'No,' said Rita, not understanding his humour.

'Thanks.'

Rita watched as he began to chain his bike, removed his luggage, and slung it over his shoulder. She then announced. 'Maybe you will go to the *end of the universe* Mr Alfi?' The words affected him, but she did not allow him to speak. 'Have you ever thought about responsibility Mr Alfi?' she asked. He stopped, surprised again by the question. 'Being responsible for others,' she continued. 'Outside of yourself? Like me with my goats? You are on your own. And have nothing else to think about, to worry about. It's dangerous to have a mind that is selfish in this way. Looking inwards - it can turn against you.' Something stirred inside Alfi but he couldn't quite fathom what it was. Rita rolled up the rest of her purses into her bag. 'There is also the bus,' she said.

# CHAPTER FIVE

## The Dialectic Click

The old ramshackle bus heaved its way up the hill. Alfi sat on the roof which was overcrowded. A tethered goat trembled - hunched down on its front knees as it tried awkwardly to balance itself and gormlessly faced the track. A meshed metal box glinted in the sunlight, it held a clutter of live chickens who were lying motionless and sideways, their feet tied with cheap yellow string, and pink eyes fluttering in the dust. A young girl sat silently with her parents, her mother leaning into a tired husband's shoulder. Whilst young boys dangled their legs over the sides of the bus, and down the windows - thinking they were brave and making yelps.

'You're lucky!' Ruben, the young, happy looking monk called out from amongst all the noise. 'To be here on the roof. No space below. And we get free air conditioning.'

A much older holy man sat on the edge of a useless spare tyre clutching prayer beads. He moved these vigorously, counting them through his dry chapped fingers as his scorched lips chanted, the words lost in the blustering wind. Ruben followed Alfi's eyes. 'Oh, that's Brother Tikum,' he added. 'It's a mala, a garland, he's holding.

He pray' with this. As he is worrying about journey. Sometimes the buses roll down from here. Over and over and over. They roll over so badly, so we have many ghosts of dead people. We've ghosts in Madrakani too.'

The bus shunted forward some more, sometimes leaning so far that it raised louder playful shouts from the boys and terrified groans from the women. Beneath them, and sticking out of the open windows, was a countless muddle of arms and elbows, the corners of sacks and bruised suitcases.

Ruben smiled again. 'Madrakani is only four hours. You will find good hotel there. And air for your motorbike.'

The bus continued over the hill and leant badly again, creating a new shrill from the passengers.

❀ ❀ ❀

Ruben skipped briskly with Alfi along a main ragged road that was lined with the shabby looking wooden houses of Madrakani. Their entrances had lean-tos, that opened out onto the street, these were half covered porchways where people sat, the older ones rocking mindfully in slow creaking chairs - in and out of the shade. They looked inquisitively at Alfi, the man from somewhere else, but there was a kindness about their round, rosy weather-beaten faces, smiling to him as he went.

The occasional yak or buffalo cart rolled by. Each slow turn of the wheels crushing dry stones to dust. Alfi stared at one for a while and wondered if this old town had ever seen rain, perhaps it lived reliably from the streams from the upper glaciers. Some dogs laid sideways, utterly still and under the angled shade of the porches, whilst up above cats yawned from the tin roofs, and reclined into another dream.

Further along, and a middle-aged woman sat quietly on a high chair. There was an air of superiority about her as she was having her boots polished by a thorough looking boy. Alfi was struck by the clothes she was wearing, the tall top-hat, her thick long black dress and a dark cloak that hung heavily, almost to her ankles. And most of all, she was smoking a pungent looking, thick short cigar. Its smoke concealed her face for an instant as the boy glanced up to Alfi, before nervously settling back down to the boots.

Ahead of them, the end of the road disappeared again. Down a steep, sad looking slope, with a row of similar looking houses, their chimneys falling out of view. Beyond the street, the jagged peaks of the white Himalaya rose up and into a brilliant blue sky. Ruben followed Alfi's gaze.

'Oh those,' he said, finally breaking the silence of their walking. 'Those mountains over there. We don't give them names. They are on the other side. In Tibet.' They continued into a side street as Ruben eagerly continued. 'Here! Here you will find this best hotel. Well, it's the only hotel. It has been here a very long time - but good place. They don't get much guests. It'll be comfortable for you.'

And so, that night, on a new, old feathered pillow that felt cold to the cheek, Alfi rested and dreamt about the comedy of his new life so far. He thought of Rita too, out there somewhere, the child of light, and her blissfulness. As free and without direction, as any of the mountain winds that blew about her. Not even nature could dictate to her. Was such an existence possible?

❀ ❀ ❀

The sun rose like an orange spotlight over the hills, as Ruben and Alfi stood below a large pair of green iron gates that towered above them. The gates had been elaborately sculpted into the shapes of trees and lotus blossoms and standing with them was an elderly man, who had a pronounced limp, who Ruben had previously announced, quite officially, as *"Mr J P Joshi* or Mr Joshi for short." Looped around the old man's wrist was a large iron keyring with three equally large keys. His hands were shaking but he looked at Alfi with an assured smile.

'It's a pleasure. A pleasure to see you here sir,' Mr Joshi said. 'Marvelous.'

'Mr Joshi was educated in very good English school you know,' added Ruben. 'In the city.'

'Yes, I was sir. Very fine memories too,' Mr Joshi interrupted, his eyes now warm in recollection. 'Marvelous. A marvelous time indeed. Education can shape one somewhat.'

'And Mr Joshi is very excited to meet you!' supplemented Ruben. 'You are the first foreigner here. Mr Joshi has the keys to monastery and he will show you. He is caretaker.'

With that, Ruben ceremoniously lent both arms against the gates and pushed forward. They fanned open to reveal a long, richly planted and untamed garden. Wild poppies, clusters of thick green bushes of all shapes and sizes, and most of all, a sea of purple lilacs flooded the floor everywhere and clambered for light below Cedar, tall Birch and Pine trees that moved sideways a little in the breeze.

Ruben admired the scene. 'The purple flower,' he said with obvious joy in his voice. 'Is the colour of the spirit. That is why we have many of them here.'

They walked through a pathway that cut its way between the shrubs where, at the far end, a small domed monastery merged into view. A few elderly monks, serious looking and wearing large crescent shaped yellow headdresses, were sitting below the shadows of some trees. They saw Alfi and there was a kerfuffle between them. They picked up long ceremonial horns that had been resting on the grass beside them and blew fiercely. It was a thunderous sound that filled the air and shook Alfi.

Ruben giggled. 'These are great Dungchen horns! It's part of the ceremony here.' The horns stopped abruptly. The holy men rested them on the grass and then, as if on cue, a small boy monk appeared who was little more than five years old. He stepped forward timidly at first, his little saffron robe touching the ground, and clutching a small conch shell to his lips, his head titled back and he puffed into it. Another older teenage monk appeared from behind, and thumped a colourful pigskin drum unrhythmically with a crooked looking percussion stick.

'Who's the boy?' Alfi asked, enjoying the entertainment.

'Oh, this is Dundram,' replied Ruben.

'A very good boy sir,' Mr Joshi added. 'He often lives here.'

'Boy novice monk,' said Ruben. 'He cannot speak you see, so he communicates his feeling through the shell. He wards off evil spirits, we have ghosts, I told you, and he make them go away quickly. He's lucky.'

Ahead near the monastery, an older monk was planing a door on a simple bench. He looked up from his work and smiled with Ruben continuing. 'They're making improvements here,' he said with a glow. 'Great improvements! We think many foreigners will want to come here, to see this place. It will make the village prosperous and very famous. Many people will come to see what we have. You coming, Mr Alfi, you first foreigner! Make everybody happy.'

They treaded to the monastery door as Mr Joshi carefully selected a key. His hand trembled as he grappled to find the keyhole. 'He is very nervous,' Ruben observed.

'Would you be so kind as to give me a moment sir,' Mr Joshi said, quite poshly, as he continued with some difficulty over the keys. Finally, entering another into the keyhole, the door clicked and drew itself open - like a warm hand inviting them in. They stepped inside, into a pillared, richly coloured room painted in saffron, yellow and gold where, at the far end, was a long wooden altar which was festooned with fresh garlands and flickering butter-milk candles.

Along the altar's beautiful decoration were seven equally spaced offerings - pure vessels of water - and at one end, a tilted portraiture on a stand of an elder monk who looked out with a quiet indifference to the world.

It dawned then, on Alfi, how Buddhism like all religions, was rich in symbolism and nuanced in detail. The strict order of the objects he observed, once designed by those now unknown, invisible and dead - a ritual well beyond the generations and unquestioned. It had made these creators mystical, as if the ideas themselves had come down from the heavens. He examined the precision of the elements again. Their arrangement, the chalices of water in strict alignment along one side of the altar to the other. Was this too a symbolism of the discipline of the mind? Had such a discipline been missing for Alfi?

A gold shining image of the Buddha looked telepathically at him from where it sat, deep in the middle of the garlands. The Buddha's right hand was held outwards, in a gesture of learning and reassurance. Yet in front of the Buddha, and in front of the altar, was a small, simple looking green cast iron safe. And next to this, was what looked like, a tall upright carved sarcophagus painted in greens, yellows and golds. It gave the scene a curious and rather odd significance. Even the Buddha now appeared to be watching over the little iron safe rather than toward Alfi, and the burning incense below it.

Ruben waited a while before pronouncing. 'Here,' he said grandly, tapping the top of the little safe. 'Inside here, is something very special. That you'll want to see.'

He nodded, and Mr Joshi stepped forward and fumbled with his keys again. 'These keys can be awfully fiddly sometimes,' he observed, glancing to Alfi apologetically. 'I believe in the West keys are much smaller. But up here we take a more dramatic view.' Eventually, he inserted a key and the lock clicked. He reached forward and drew the door open along a creaking hinge that added drama to the occasion - as if one was needed.

Alfi peered inside. The object facing him sat alone on a single shelf, protected within a tall glass dome. It looked to be a skull - or at least a fair proportion of it. It was larger than any human's, conical in shape and covered, in part at least, with patches of white and tan pelt. The eye sockets were close together; too close Alfi thought, as they stared back to him from their shadows. And it entranced him. A flat nasal bone dropped down to what was left of a mouth and a wide protruding jaw, with only two remaining long discoloured canines.

Ruben eventually spoke. 'It is the skull of a Gumbran! What you call a Yeti. And it is very lucky.'

'Yes.' Mr Joshi nodded. 'It is that. Very lucky indeed. One can only marvel at it.'

'The skull of a yeti? repeated Alfi. 'Really? Are you sure? How old is it?'

'It must be three hundred years old.' Ruben said, sensing Alfi's delight.

'He's quite right sir. Give or take,' added Mr Joshi - as Dundram, the boy monk, entered. He skipped forward, danced with a twirl and whistled as loud as he could into his shell.

'And it's been here for three hundred years?' asked Alfi.

Mr Joshi smiled. 'I look after it sir. My father before me, and before him, you can guess. You might get the picture.'

'So it's special,' continued Ruben. 'And every year it will come out on the Yeti festival.'

'Festival?' enquired Alfi as Dundrum eventually stopped whistling.

'Yes,' Ruben said. 'Isn't that why you are here?'

'I didn't know about a festival?'

'Then you're indeed very lucky,' said Ruben. 'You have come at the right time! The festival is soon. This is why the monks are outside. They are getting ready and making music.'

Alfi studied the object more closely. 'Well, I am lucky! Has it been looked at? You know. Checked, by any scientists. Verified by a laboratory or anything?'

'Not that I know of,' replied Ruben as Mr Joshi nodded in agreement. 'It has always been here.'

Alfi shuffled into his bag. 'Is it possible to take a photograph? I mean, take it out of the dome?'

Ruben looked to Mr Joshi who immediately began lifting the glass cover. 'Our pleasure sir,' Mr Joshi smiled. 'Our pleasure indeed.'

Alfi fiddled with his camera. 'And when's the festival?'

'The Abbot will decide the actual day, but it will be soon,' replied Ruben. 'And each time we have the festival we take it out and put it here.'

'Where?'

Ruben proudly stepped to the upright casket alongside the safe and began to unfasten it. Inside, and balancing precariously on bamboo dowels, he revealed a headless skeleton, complete with long arms dangling loosely, and well beyond the hips. It was indeed - a curiosity.

'This,' he said in a bold announcement. 'Is the body! The body of what you call a Yeti. Very fragile, but beautiful isn't it! Tall too! The skeleton of Gumbran. Also, many years old. We're not sure if the skull, the skull in the safe here, is the actual head from this same body. But it doesn't matter really. It is the coming together of the head over the body you see, which symbolises the coming together of mind with body. It has great spiritual significance for the festival. As when the mind is in harmony with the body, we will have a healthy, good life. This is what we believe in Madrakani. But when the mind is not in harmony with the body, when it wants too much - and goes against it: like too much drink or food or other pleasures, this makes the body unhealthy and unhappy, this in turn, makes the mind unhappy. This is why harmony; a mind that cares about the body, and a body that cares about the mind, is very important. Earthly pleasures, they are only moving things, and temporary you know. They cannot bring about anything lasting.' Ruben pointed at the top of the skeleton. 'We put the skull on top. Here. Very carefully in a special ceremony, just one time in a year. Everyone...everyone comes to see it and pray to it. And one day, people from all over the world will come to see it too. Like you! Just to see it and pray. The town will also make money!' And then, as quickly as Ruben had opened the casket, he refastened it again.

'Here you go sir!' called Mr Joshi. Alfi turned to see he was holding out the skull with both hands. 'It will do wonders for that magazine of yours. Make a wonderful, photograph, don't you think?'

'Why don't you put it on your head?' asked Ruben flatly. 'It's very good luck you know - and big enough too, the chief of the holy men sometimes does it. We have elastic to hold it on.' Ruben pointed at two limp looking rubber bands attached to the sides of the skull that Alfi hadn't noticed earlier.

'Oh no,' he protested. 'Just rest it down somewhere. I just want a photograph.'

'Go on!' urged Ruben. 'Put it on,' and in an instant before Alfi could resist, his shoulders were being steadied and he was being coronated by Mr Joshi who was busy adjusting the straps.

'Here you are sir,' he said, as he straightened it a little more with a glare of approval. 'If I might say so, it's a wonderful fit. Wonderful fit isn't it!' Dundram blew his conch shell, circling the room.

Ruben clapped. 'You're wearing the skull. The skull of a Yeti!'

It was then, amongst the sound of the clapping, that Alfi glanced sideways to the burning incense. Its vapour curled upwards and for some unfortunate reason, decided to turn into his direction. First, his nose twitched, and that was it. Out came a sneeze with such a vehemence, that it sent him backwards and into Dundram, who was busy twirling around the casket. The boy fell back into it, it wobbled and, as if in slow motion, the casket lent forwards again until it finally passed forty-five degrees, and collapsed like someone fainting. The resounding sound as it crashed to the floor, left all four of them in a steely silence.

Dundram stumbled up to his feet as Alfi rushed over and knelt beside the casket. He paused, lifting it slightly, as one would a fallen soldier in the field, and shook it softly as the others looked on. The sound of the broken pieces, sliding about in the receptacle made Mr Joshi's bottom lip quiver somewhat, as if he was about to say something without full use of a tongue. Alfi jiggled it mildly some more - the bones moving this way then that, and then rested the casket, respectfully, on the floor again, as if the soldier had nobly deceased. He turned to the other three.

Mr Joshi was the first to speak. 'Is it broken sir?'

Alfi looked up. 'Is it broke? Is it broken! What do *you* think?'

'Oh,' said Ruben. As Dundram made a pathetic, rather piteous blast that descended two octaves.

The four stared at the casket. 'Oh dear,' added Mr Joshi inadequately. 'That's terribly unfortunate. Awfully terrible indeed.'

Ruben hurried over, unclasped the casket and gazed in eagerly. His head dropped, and without saying a word, he re-fastened it again, ever-so-carefully and scratched his right ear. He had the expression one has, when staring at a veterinary surgeon after your favourite pet's heart has stopped beating.

'When's the festival again?' asked Alfi.

'Soon,' replied Ruben limply.

'Oh, I must say, we were looking forward to it,' said Mr Joshi. 'Damn shame, awfully regrettable really, and all that. Quite a blow. Quite a blow indeed. Hits you in the back of the throat. Do you...do you think we can fix it?'

'Fix it!' called Alfi. He then added with a delivery which could had won an award theatrically. 'Do you think we can fix it?'

'So, what are we going to do now?' Ruben asked. Suddenly there was a knocking at the door. One aggressive thump followed by an unattractive staccato of others.

'I believe there is someone at the door?' observed Mr Joshi.

'We've had it!' called Alfi. 'We've had it. We've ruined the festival. Come on! Put it back! Put it back upright!'

A voice, that might had been untrained baritone, called from the outside. 'Open up! Who's closed this door? Open up! What's going on?'

'We need to make this place look like nothing happened,' said Alfi.

The three hurriedly lifted and straightened the casket. 'We can say it was a ghost.' Ruben said.

'Ghost?' asked Alfi.

'We can say it was a ghost that did it.'

'I'd better attend to who it is sir,' Mr Joshi announced, as he trotted towards the door as if attending to a party guest. The others stood and waited.

Opening the door, he revealed several, rather stern looking male characters. The nearest one, who looked to be some kind of uniformed town Sheriff, was a short rotund man - with what would've been a kindly face - if it wasn't for the circumstances. Alongside him was the tall languid figure of his Deputy, and behind them, and struggling to gain a view, were the elderly monks seen earlier, still in their elaborate headwear and clutching their horns. They peered over the Sheriff's and the Deputy's shoulders with a bitter religiousness. Most of all, they were captivated, quite agitated of course, by the sight of Alfi who was wearing the skull of a yeti.

# CHAPTER SIX

## *Power over mind, powerless over events*

The Sheriff looked thoughtfully from across his desk, scratched one of his chins and began to speak. 'I think what we've got here,' he said. 'With you being from out of town and all that, is an *inability to assimilate.*' He turned his eyes in Ruben's direction who was sitting alongside Alfi. 'So, let me get this straight. What you say is. What you claim is. You say a ghost. A *ghost* did it?'

Being a monk, and not so akin with the enormous benefits of telling untruths, Ruben occupied the middle ground quite uncomfortably, and only half nodded.

There was a long pause, which gave Alfi the chance to survey the room; the bare wooden floor boards, the patchy timber walls and a couple of lassos wound over large iron wall hooks. A hat stand was cluttered with spare sombreros and ponchos - the whole place looked like it could have come from an American Western. On the wall was a shining, recently polished, glass framed certificate, signed by some authority or another, with the Sheriff's name on it, no doubt asserting his significance in the field. The Sheriff folded his arms beneath it and stared at the four of them sitting; Alfi, Ruben, Mr

Joshi and a blank looking Dundram whose legs were swinging, as they weren't long enough to touch the ground. His Deputy - a tall chap called Ronson - stood to the side and was poised eagerly with a writing pad and pen.

Indeed, it dawned on Alfi then, looking of the two of them, that the Sheriff and Ronson had very much modelled themselves on their mid-western counterparts. The large Stetsons, beige uniform and big, shining silver stars; a large one on the hat, and a smaller effort on the left chest. They even had spurs on their boots, which was unusual in a town that didn't have any horses. Most eye catching of all, was the thick black belts that they wore. These held, instead of a gun and holster, a dangling small crossbow and assortment of colourful feathered little arrows as ammunition dotted along their waists.

Deputy Ronson began scribbling feverishly, the way busy waiters do when taking complicated orders, as the Sheriff continued. 'So, let me get this straight. We get one foreigner in this town.'

Ronson wrote hurriedly, repeating. 'One foreigner in this town.'

The Sheriff added. 'The first foreigner in town.'

Ronson scribbled and muttered. 'The first foreigner in town.'

The Sheriff looked to Ronson with a fair degree of annoyance but continued. 'To come here, and now the Gundrum…is in pieces.'

'In pieces.' Ronson jotted down and flamboyantly added a full-stop from a height of ten inches.

'And you say it was a ghost?' said the Sheriff, flabbergasted.

Ronson continued jotting. 'Ghost,' he said.

The Sheriff, heavily irritated by Ronson's paraphrasing grimaced. 'Ronson please!'

Ronson muttered. 'Please.'

The Sheriff stamped a heavy cowboy boot. 'Please Ronson!' He then calmed a little and looked to Alfi. 'Now, just to let you know, I'm almost as new to this town as you are. And like you Mr Alfi. I, the two of us, myself and my deputy here Ronson, have been sent up from 'Du' down South.'

'Du?' enquired Alfi.

'Kathmandu' finished the Sheriff. 'And I realise, and do *you* realise, how important this skeleton is to this little town? It was supposed to be the main reason, well it's the *only* reason, for anyone wanting to come all the way up here. To this...place. They were trying to build a pilgrimage town you see. Bring in a bit of money. Why else would anyone visit? They've got nothing. And now, since you coming here, in these few short hours Mr Alfi, they've got even less. We get one *pilgrim*! One pilgrim! Our first pilgrim to this town - *you Mr Alfi* - something that they were very excited about. And now that Gumbran in the box over there, the only important thing in this town, is in bits. Not a good start, is it? What we've got here, with you that is, is an inability to assimilate.'

Ronson interrupted with the word, 'bits,' again which upset the Sheriff, as Dundram played a short tune on his shell, a sound which for some odd reason, seemed to make the Sheriff a little more conciliatory.

'Look. Mr Alfi,' he said leaning on his elbows. 'It's small town.'

'Small town,' repeated Ronson.

The Sheriff tutted again before continuing. 'A small poor, frontier town. Next to Tibet. There's not much going on here...so it seems. But I've been sent up here. We're right on the border you see. And while this place doesn't have much; we don't want much trouble either. Being a border town, we get a lot of people coming and going. Coming through. All kinds of people from China and Tibet. And that's why, for a few months anyway, I'm here. I'm making...let's say...a few investigations to bring in some discipline - there is no need to say more about it than that. And you say you're one of those journalist fellas?'

'Yes. Yes, I am. Of sorts.' Alfi replied sheepishly.

'Of sorts?' repeated the Sheriff who turned to Ruben. 'And you say, you can fix it? Fix the Gumbran? Glue it together?'

'We have glue,' the monk nodded readily. 'I can do my best. I can work on it.'

'I'll help him too sir.' Mr Joshi added brightly as Dundram made another blast on his conch-shell.

'So why don't we just let Ruben here do the fixing?' The Sheriff said. 'And you don't do any writing about this town, no sniffing around. And in return, we'll just let this whole thing go. Just let it pass by. Hey? Just this one time.'

'That sounds sensible officer,' replied Alfi. 'I can live with that.'

The Sheriff added. 'And you say you're having some trouble with a motorbike of yours, down on the hill? Well, Ronson here, he can help.'

'We can get a pump for his bike soon,' Ronson said smartly. 'Maybe tomorrow or the next.'

'Ok then,' announced the Sheriff pleased. 'So that's it. Meeting adjourned fellas! In a day or so, we can get that wheel on that bike of yours some sky. And then you'll be on your way. But in the meantime, you just lie low here. You hear? Just relax. Don't go snooping around, you got that? No writing.'

'That's perfectly clear,' said Alfi. 'No snooping, guaranteed.'

'Just enjoy the simple hospitality we have, and soon you'll be on your merry way. Now tonight. You'll need to eat. We've only one restaurant in this town, and it's near your hotel, called Bleaches. Enjoy it.'

Dundram blew into his shell again. It seemed, at the time at least, to be a satisfactory conclusion.

❁ ❁ ❁

Alfi sat alone at a small round table, where a tired looking waiter stood over him holding a pad and wearing an apron that showed evidence of meals over the years. 'Have you seen my specials?' he asked, scratching his testicles and looking to a blackboard.

'Can't say I have,' replied Alfi, as he perused the menu with a forefinger that stopped. 'Um. I'll have this,' he pointed. 'Just a sandwich. Sandwich of the day.'

'We've got ham and cheese. Or if you prefer, you could have ham. Wait,' the waiter added, thinking carefully. 'I'll check with the kitchen but I think we can also do cheese.'

By now the restaurant had started to fill and there were a good number of single women sitting in the wings wearing dark multi-layered frocks. Some sat alone in quiet, stoic anticipation whilst others were huddled together in faintly menacing little groups. All were wearing tall top hats and virtually all, were smoking cigars and sending out puffs of smoke like miniature nuclear explosions. There was a distinct air of superiority about them which was making the waiters nervous, especially visible when they had to sidle past them balancing their trays.

Ahead of Alfi, a clearing of chairs had been made into a makeshift dancefloor that nobody was using. Three musicians played from a small platform above; an old drummer who was having trouble with his sticks, a short male double bassist who wasn't tall enough for certain chords, and another grey bearded lost looking soul, vacantly strumming a beat-up guitar as if he'd just lost something but couldn't quite remember what it was. The whole ensemble was pushing the envelope in terms of the repertoire you could achieve with three chords - whilst ahead of them was a lone female vocalist, also wearing a top hat and long frock, who was singing some lament about lost loves and the open road, the way people do when they want to appear noble and poetic. She was waving a cigar with its thick ash threatening to drop to the stage at the salient moments.

The dance area began to fill as a small scattering of men walked on, mostly in ones and twos. Alfi watched the men dancing in a way he'd never seen before. They shuffled about in slow circles as if in a team. Stretching their arms straight upwards into the air as if reaching for something quite strange and invisible, and then out again in front of them as if about to sleepwalk.

Alfi bit into his rigid cheese sandwich that was curling in one corner towards him. He looked at the men dancing again. They seemed drunk. Drunk enough to be revelous with their thoughts lined with beer, and those who were revelous earlier so, now with their energy depleting. He was not sure if the dancing was lifting them up, or invisibly bringing them down again. They were away from their tables, and away from their drink that was waiting for them in half-empty green bottles and also becoming sour.

A man called out from a table. 'Most of the women around here have two or three husbands,' he declared in dramatic disappointment. 'Some more. They can have as many husbands as they want. Depends on how much money they have. She can have the body, face, and attitude of a mule, and get anybody in town. Most of them do. They're not too good at conversation either.' He took a glug of his drink and half fell from his chair before stumbling up again on an elbow. 'There's a shortage of women you see. That's the problem. I blame global warming. They've got the upper hand, especially if she's got money or goats. We look after them. We cook for them, we do the housework, put them in clean clothes. Meanwhile, all they do is come home late. Drunk. You can't get a decent woman. Then they go out and cheat on you! After all the work you do to keep the house going. Women! You can't live *with them*, and you can't...' he hesitated trying to gather the words, '...*live with them*. We're dropping like flies. We're doomed!'

There was a thud as he passed out onto the floor. Two young

waiters, as if they'd been waiting for the moment, took him by both arms and slid him to the skirting boards.

The evening went on and the music grew louder. Alfi struck up another conversation with another local called Rishi. 'So, it is your birthday tomorrow?' Rishi announced, holding out a glass ceremoniously. 'Drink!' They touched glasses as Rishi asked. 'Do you want to dance?'

'Dance?' asked Alfi, surprised.

'Come on!' he smiled. 'This is how we get noticed. Women like it if you can move well. It's important to show off what you've got.'

The two of them joined the others on the dancefloor where in the middle, was a huddle of saddle bags which they all jigged around. Their dancing soon developed into a kind of exaggerated walk in slow motion, with waist high steps and arms stretched up to the ceiling, twisting and turning their hips, meanwhile their heads moved ever-so-slowly in the opposite direction - it was as if they were trying out new necks. Alfi tried to follow, looking one way then the other, until he caught sight of a woman watching him carefully from under the brim of her hat. She took a thoughtful drag of a cigar and broke into a half smile, that could had been wind, where behind the drifting smoke, she revealed two large gold front teeth. She made her approach.

'You wanna dance?' she said, which had a hint of a command about it - and so Alfi began dancing. Her moves seemed to mirror his, one way or another. Yet she said nothing, and although she was a bit low on the small talk, he guessed she might had had been Sagittarius and had a liking for him. There was the occasional glint of gold behind her bulbous purple lips. This went on for a while, without even the mention of names or what they did for a living.

❀ ❀ ❀

Alfi half-saw the punch coming. The thick forearm that it was attached to, came through the crowd and over their shoulders. He was quick enough to lean away from it, but heard the hiss of it as it passed his cheek, and landed on someone else - a happy go lucky, quite large sort, who was doing a good virtuoso and grasping towards the ceiling lights. It knocked the man sideways and tripping over the saddle bags, but he was up quickly with both fists flinching. Soon, amongst the hollers, the vigorous eyes - a bar brawl developed. Chairs and tables were thrown, yet the band continued to play, albeit in a more energetic bossa nova that matched the scene before their eyes.

❀ ❀ ❀

It was late at night and, as he often did at that time of day, the Sheriff sat in a relaxed, untroubled poise, with his legs resting on his table. It was his time, quiet time in the office, when he would muster up thoughts and enjoy pondering on the day's activities. Yet this time he was rudely interrupted at the door. Deputy Ronson led in Alfi who was wearing handcuffs. The Sheriff looked up. 'Holy cow!'

Ronson replied matter-of-factly. 'Drunk and disorderly Sheriff. Caused a fight over at Bleaches.'

Alfi interrupted. 'I told you! I didn't do a thing. I just go for a meal, a dance...everything, the whole thing was out of my control!'

The Sheriff butted in. 'Well, what the hell is it? What is it with you Mr Alfi? Who the hell are you?'

'I did nothing wrong Sheriff,' continued Alfi. 'I just go for a drink, it's the night before my birthday.'

'Happy birthday,' conceded Ronson.

'And then this fight breaks out. Maybe this man, the man who saw me dancing, was jealous of my dancing partner.'

'Dancing partner?' asked the Sheriff.

'He was dancing with one of the Millighani girls,' added Ronson. 'The big ones. Six footers with big feet, from the big family.'

'What kind of town is this?' interrupted Alfi, switching tact.

The Sheriff sat up squarely. 'Dancing? Drunk, disorderly?' He thought for a moment and looked to Ronson. 'Ok, put him inside.'

'What!' exclaimed Alfi.

'Inside Ronson! You heard.' the Sheriff commanded with obvious disappointment in his voice. He shook his head.

Ronson guided Alfi down a short corridor and to a large caged cell that stood as an adjunct to the office. He opened the barred gate, released the handcuffs and guided Alfi in. 'Sorry Mr Alfi,' he whispered.

In the darkened light Alfi was surrounded by other prisoners. 'I thought this was supposed to be a small town,' he remarked, loud enough for the Sheriff to hear. 'How come you have so many prisoners?' They all looked at him.

'Never mind that,' called the Sheriff from behind his desk. 'We're busy. I told you! I am cleaning up this town. Zero tolerance, I like to call it. I'm just disappointed in you Mr Alfi. Why can't you just assimilate! We get just one foreigner! One foreigner, and look what happens.'

The Sheriff got up and was obviously frustrated. He reached for his Stetson from a coat stand, plonked it on his head and adjusted it before turning to Ronson. 'Make sure you get them bedded down for the night,' he called out. 'We'll see you in the morning...Mr Alfi. When you'll have some explaining to do, after you've done a lot of thinking, in there with your new friends tonight.' The Sheriff opened the door and began to stomp out. 'You've let me, you've let yourself, you're letting everybody down! Why can't you just assimilate?' The door slammed and the Sheriff was gone. Ronson shrugged his shoulders and seemed pretty pleased to be left in charge.

Alfi turned to see a prisoner in a torn shirt who looked like a depressed car mechanic. 'So uh, what? What are you in for?'

'Murder,' came the reply.

Alfi nodded as if this was half expected. 'Murder,' he repeated.

Another prisoner called out. 'Theft.'

'And um, what did you steal?' Alfi asked.

'As much as I could.'

Other prisoners got into the swing of it and began to call out.

'Assault.'

'Arson. Accidental. Dropped a match.'

'Attempted murder, two counts. Shame really.'

'Just kidnap,' came a timid call. 'But it didn't work out. Wasn't really cut out for it.'

'I burnt down a school, there were no kids in it.'

A silence followed where Alfi glanced at a large man, well over six foot, who was sitting on the cell floor without saying a word. A smaller, older prisoner called Gildesh followed Alfi's gaze and whispered into his ear. 'Oh, that's Horse,' he said. 'He hasn't done anything. Don't worry about him. He just lives on the streets but as he's so tall, they bring him in at night as he frightens the bullocks. They let him go in the morning. He like' it here.'

Alfi looked through the metal bars and back along the short corridor into the jailhouse office. By now Ronson had picked up a guitar with two strings missing. He watched as the deputy stretched his dusty spurred boots to make a clearing over the Sheriff's desk, and began to strum the remaining four strings and sing something quite sad, about one lost love or another. There must had been many lost loves in Madrakani, Alfi thought. Meanwhile, the prisoners stared, stone faced, some sitting or others standing and gripping the bars a little more tightly to the music. Alfi called out. 'Is there any chance of solitary?' But Ronson continued to lament.

# CHAPTER SEVEN

*The problem is how you deal with the problem*

A cockerel shrilled in the distance. Its first call was an energetic one, so much so, that it jolted at least some of the rising and falling stomachs of the snoring prisoners. There was a stale smell about them, that would have taken several sorrowful months for the body to ferment, as the bird took its breath and gave out two more cries; each one more listless, more descending than the other. It was pathetic. As if the bird, like everyone else in the jailhouse that morning, had given up. Alfi scratched his eyes to find himself propped up against the bars next to Gildesh. Two other jailmates opposite were already awake and huddled together, looking at him with no expression.

Gildesh lent into Alfi's ear. 'Those two, over there,' he whispered. 'I know them. They bring in gold. Smugglers. Regularly. From China, over Tibet. They'll get out. Believe me. Mr Teshi will get them out.'

'Mr Teshi? Who's Teshi?' asked Alfi as he wiped his eyes some more.

'Oh Mr Teshi! Why he's is the most powerful man in this town!

He's like a Major. He owns everything, he owns land. He runs every-thing. No one can touch him. Not even the new Sheriff.'

Just then Gildesh looked to both sides to see if anyone was watching, and began to unravel a small cloth hidden inside his tattered shirt. 'Look at this,' he said, revealing a miniature Swiss file. 'This is my key. My key to freedom,' he held it aloft to demonstrate. 'I'm going to get out with this. You'll see! I am. They can't lock me in forever. They can't! Each day, each day I file a little on the bars by the window...I just file a little bit more. Just take a little more at a time. So each day I get closer. Closer to my freedom. It gives me hope.'

Alfi looked at the trivial file and back again to the thick steel bars at the window. 'What are you in for?' he asked.

'I'm not quite sure,' he said, scratching his head. It was then that a thought occurred to Alfi, and he began to feel inside his own pockets.

The Sheriff entered with a bang at the door. 'Well, looky' here' he called out. 'Wakey, Wakey.' He ran a truncheon that bounced along the bars as the other prisoners were jolted from their sleep. 'Nice and early start! Hope you got your beauty sleep. We've got a busy day today fellas. It's court day! Sentence time. All of you will find out - if you're found guilty - how I'm not going to tolerate any more bad behavior in this town. And Mr Alfi, did you sleep well? I hope you're enjoying your visit?'

'I got a couple of hours in,' said Alfi still checking his pockets. 'Can't grumble.'

The Sheriff looked to him oddly. 'Now what's wrong?'

'I think I've lost my wallet.'

'Your wallet?'

Alfi looked to the collection of ragged jailbirds who vacantly returned his stare. He checked his pockets once more, lowered his voice and whispered to the Sheriff through the bars. 'My wallet. It appears to have gone missing.'

The Sheriff scratched an ear vigorously. 'I think, I'm getting tired of this.'

'But...' Alfi tried to interrupt.

'We've all got our tether, and sadly, I'm at the end of it,' said the Sheriff.

Alfi turned to his cellmates. 'Look boys,' he said coolly. 'I am not saying anything. I'm not pointing fingers. We all have a cross to bear. We all need to survive in this difficult world. Some of us were not given the best start in life. We were not dealt the best of hands. Perhaps a pair of jokers. And I know I'm surrounded by thieves. But my wallet...it's gone missing. What did I expect hey?' he added agreeably. 'Stealing? Well, it comes naturally, like second nature. But now, I just want to say, that someone might have 'borrowed' my wallet.'

The prisoners shuffled about in the limited space they had, and were beginning to look unsettled. The Sheriff stepped forward. 'I don't think you should be making any accusations.'

'It could have been by accident, easily done,' Alfi conceded. The Sheriff attempted to speak but Alfi raised a finger. 'If I may say Sheriff. Just two minutes. On my own terms.' The Sheriff clenched his lips grudgingly as Alfi took center stage. 'Look. I'm going to turn around,' he said. 'No questions asked. And I'd just like to hear...to hear the sound of my wallet, as it's dropped, delicately, onto the cell floor. And we won't say anything else. No repercussions. No accusations. No pressing of charges. That'll be the end of it. The end of it all. Ok? I am now turning my back.'

Alfi turned away from his cellmates, and gestured for the Sheriff and Ronson to do the same - who reluctantly followed suit. They waited. There was silence. A kind of difficult, uncomfortable one, like listening out for a gas leak when your kids are playing with matches. Alfi briefly turned to face them and looked away again. 'Okay, on the count of three. One. Two. Three.'

More stillness followed, where you could have heard the proverbial drop as the Sheriff shrugged his shoulders and took a step closer to the bars. 'Now what Mr Alfi?'

'Ok, ok good!' Alfi readdressed the cell again. 'Look, maybe we got off to a bad start fellas. The wrong foot. Maybe you're a little worried about being found out here. If we could *all* just close our eyes. Yes, close our eyes for a minute, just *one more minute.* And if the person, the person, who took my wallet could just drop it on the floor anywhere in this cell. Far away from their feet...that should make the difference. And we'll say no more about it. Go on. Close your eyes. No one will see. Everybody.'

Alfi nodded again to the Sheriff and Ronson who were becoming uncomfortably impatient. 'Go on, all of us,' Alfi reiterated. 'It will give that person a chance to redeem himself, and from this moment on, they might even turn the corner, turn their life around. Believe me. It will show all of us, from wherever we've come. That we can become better individuals. We can become fair, honest; upstanding and with, most of all - *morals.* Perhaps my visit here would not have been wasted after all. It could give someone a new life. Turn their life around. A second chance.'

Everyone closed their eyes and waited. More silence followed. 'Okay, we can give it a few more seconds,' Alfi persisted. 'And then we'll have not one, not *one* more word about it!'

Still, there was no movement. Everyone gradually opened their eyes and the Sheriff spoke, this time more assuredly. 'We're well aware of your games Mr Alfi,' he said looking at the ceiling as if it was telling him something. 'Look, to you, and your fancy ways, these people might not amount to much, but we have a respectable collection of prisoners here. They're seasoned, yes. And they are, and I am very much aware of your complicated English literature, *'down on their uppers'* but I also think it's fair to say that, despite the ramshackle nature of the situation, we do have a sense of pride here too. Dignity.' Alfi scanned the dirty faces and torn clothes as the

Sheriff continued. 'And your way of doing things doesn't come to much, does it?'

Alfi was about to speak when there was a sound at the door. A well-dressed, demure looking man entered. He had a slight limp, that was propped up with an expensive looking walking cane. Alongside him was a large, completely bald fellow, menacing in a way but softened by a gormless look about him - he was the bulky muscular type who, when wearing a dinner suit, would look more doorman than gentleman. The Sheriff turned to the man with the cane. 'Ah! Mr Teshi.'

'Good morning Sheriff. I believe you have two of my...' he pointed up slightly with his stick.

'Of course,' the Sheriff interrupted looking at the prisoners. 'Now listen up. Palak, Ghoring stand aside and come on out and show yourselves!' The two men that Gildesh had talked about earlier, walked sheepishly towards the jail door.

Mr Teshi limped one step forward with his stick. He was surprised to see a foreigner. 'Who? Who is this gentleman? In the cell. Might I ask?'

'Oh,' replied the Sheriff. 'That's Mr Alfi. Mr Alfi Singer. A journalist. One of those writing fellas. Just visiting here and he got into a little trouble.'

'A journalist? Writing? What trouble?' Teshi questioned, as Ronson led out Palak and Ghoring.

The Sheriff gave the two a firm look. 'Looks like your friend Mr Teshi here, wants you to leave. You can go. Run along now.' The two men sided up to Mr Teshi.

'So what's happening with this...Mr Alfi?' Mr Teshi persisted.

'Oh, don't worry. He'll be leaving town,' replied the Sheriff.

'And do you mind if I ask, what is he writing about?'

'Oh nothing, nothing really. He came here about Gumbrans. But he hasn't seen one, so he won't be writing about anything. Hey Mr

Alfi? You won't be writing. We just need to finish up some reports, get his motorcycle repaired, and he'll be on his way.'

Mr Teshi began to exit with the two prisoners but looked back. He was still a little unsure about Alfi.

❀ ❀ ❀

The Sheriff lent both elbows on his desk, clasped his hands, and turned to Alfi. 'So, tell me. You now want *me* to make an insurance claim for *you* huh? For your lost wallet?'

'Yes. That's about it Sheriff,' replied Alfi calmy. 'It's the only thing we can possibly do in the circumstances. It's a simple insurance claim.'

'And then, you'll be on your way? You promise? Promise me you'll leave me, you'll leave this town alone with your new wheel - once we get it some sky?'

'Yes, absolutely. It would just help if I could get a simple police report. I'll send off a claim when I'm back in Kathmandu. It's a small thing. A formality really, and that's all Sheriff. So, tomorrow, I'll be gone. You'll be free of me. I'll be out of your hair! What's left of it.'

The Sheriff thought for a little while and called back to his Deputy. 'Ronson!'

❀ ❀ ❀

Alfi, the Sheriff and Ronson paced slowly down the street. It was the same dusty old avenue that Alfi had arrived in, just a couple of days earlier. The older villagers were sat, as they always seemed to be, looking out from their slow rocking chairs, their bodies swaying in and out of the shade. On seeing Alfi - this time with the Sheriff and his Deputy - their eyes cocked up with a fresh, inquiring look about their wrinkled faces. Skipping behind was Dundram, as ever playing his conch shell and almost making a tune. It all added to their entertainment.

'I don't understand?' Alfi protested. 'You have to come back to my hotel to make sure I've lost my wallet?'

'I told you Mr Alfi,' said the Sheriff marching promptly ahead. 'It's protocol. I've consulted "*the book*" and you really are taking up a lot of my time by the way. But if we have to send reports down to Du for your insurance, it's a precaution we have to take. To make sure we aren't making mistakes. Then, we'll give you your police report. When we make reports like this, it gets official.'

They entered into Alfi's room where the Sheriff half nodded to Ronson to begin his search; lifting bags and opening drawers as he went. He picked up a credit card from a table. 'What's this?' he asked.

'Oh that. It's called a 'credit card,' replied Alfi indifferently. 'Something I'll probably need in the future. But not up here.'

The Sheriff flicked a finger to Ronson to look inside Alfi's main bag. 'Hopefully, we can get this over and done with real' quick,' he said.

Ronson rummaged deep into the bag, taking things out, one at a time and laying them on the bed respectfully. Digging deeper his hand then suddenly stopped. He felt around with his fingers a little, and eventually drew out a wallet. He held it aloft in the air, as if it was a prize exhibit. The Sheriff's chins dropped. 'A wallet,' he observed. There was some obvious pain in his voice.

'Yes. That's a wallet,' said Alfi. 'But it's not *the* wallet. Not the one I'm talking about.'

'Is this your wallet?' the Sheriff asked sternly.

'It was a gift Sheriff. A souvenir wallet. Not the one I lost last night. I met a lady...look I really don't need to go into the detail, but she was leading goats on the way up.'

'You met a lady leading goats?'

'She sells them. Wallets that is,' added Alfi.

'A woman leading goats was selling wallets? I've had enough of this,' snapped the Sheriff.

'Look there is nothing in it. There's nothing in the wallet! Go ahead. Have a look! Inside there's no cash. Nothing. Not a bit. I'm not using it. It's not the one I've been talking about.'

The Sheriff didn't reply but instead paced slowly to the window. He looked out, over the houses and the hills, watching some smoke lifting from the chimneys, and gave out the longest of sighs, sounding like a deflating balloon. 'If I may say so Mr Alfi?' he said, still staring out of the window. 'With your fancy Western ways and talking. In this...little...town. Can I keep things very simple? May you allow me? I am a quiet, simple man who doesn't like complications. And we all, I think *even you* must agree...we all have limits. A breaking point. Where the sheer, if I may say so, lunacy of certain individuals can drive a man to contemplate the joys, the relief even, and uplifting permanent escapism, of suicide. A journey over the hill, from where there is no return.' Alfi was impressed at how the window had inspired such poetry, as the Sheriff came back to earth. 'Now, we'd like you to answer things real straight. Ok? Real straight - and slowly. Is this your wallet? Does it, Mr Alfi. Does it belong to you?'

'Yes. Yes, it does officer.'

The Sheriff exhaled. 'Disappointed.'

'Sorry?'

'So you claim you lost your wallet. And here, on inspection, here it is. We find your wallet. Which you claim is a gift from some *herdswoman* in your room. And, I have to put all this down into a report. Into head office, and look like a fool. A *fool* Mr Alfi! Where we have some serious people working down there, who take their jobs real seriously in Du. They don't take kindly to games Mr Alfi.'

73

Alfi sniffed, he was not sure if he was intelligent or surrounded by idiots. 'It is my wallet, but not *the* wallet,' he said.

'It's such a shame really. A great pity,' continued the Sheriff. 'I feel let down that, with all the patience we've given you, that it's come to this. I now have to follow protocol and so Mr Alfi.' The Sheriff glanced to his Deputy. 'Handcuffs please.'

'What!' called Alfi.

'I'm afraid we're going have to make an arrest. Again sadly. And as they say in high American literature, take you *down-town*.'

'What? What for? What for this time?'

Ronson struggled to unclasp a pair of scruffy looking handcuffs from his rear pocket until he eventually dangled them into the room. 'Do you mind putting your hands behind your back?' he asked, as he clasped them over Alfi's wrists.

'Insurance fraud,' exclaimed the Sheriff plainly. 'You say you lost a wallet and here we find your wallet. You're not making my life - or your life - any easier are you? What is it with foreigners? Read him his rights Ronson.'

Ronson cleared his throat and started speaking. 'We are arresting you,' he started. 'And anything you say...' he scratched his head failing to remember the proclamations. 'Anything you say. Might be...taken.'

The Sheriff interrupted. 'Ronson!'

Ronson continued. 'Down, down in evidence?'

The Sheriff interjected. 'Ok, what he meant to say was *anything you say might be taken down in evidence and used against you in a court of law*. Ronson might lack in the verbals here, but I can assure you he makes up for it in security.' The Sheriff pointed firmly at the small crossbow on Ronson's hip as his deputy unclipped it; a demonstration no doubt, the two of them had done many times before. 'He's a fine shot you know' added the Sheriff with a punctuating sniff. 'The best in the business.'

Why Ronson actually pulled the trigger we will never really quite know. It might had been some nervous reflex, a twitch perhaps, or the highs in demonstrating his gift for the first time to a foreigner. But nevertheless, the arrow immediately made its short, swift journey - firmly and accurately - into the Sheriff's upper thigh. It sent him buckling with a moan to the knees, in a kind of untidy religious genuflection, accompanied with several of the most unreligious of phrases.

❁ ❁ ❁

In their chairs from their porches, the villagers watched as the procession went by. Alfi, in handcuffs, was being led by Ronson who had a sheepish disposition of someone not quite sure about their future. He seemed to be in a world of his own, as the two of them walked kicking up the dust. Behind them, two diligent looking villagers carried the green military style stretcher. The arrow had not yet been removed and stood firm from the police issued beige trouser leg. Its shining blue feathers bristling in the breeze. Dundrum was skipping at the tail end - this time without a tune - as the Sheriff, still wearing his Stetson, stared to the sky from the canvas and declared defiantly. 'What we have here is an *inability to assimilate!*'

# CHAPTER EIGHT

The Poisoned Chalice

The box camera crackled, the flashbulb popped, as it was cranked up each time by a very concentrated photographer in belt and braces who was taking Alfi's photographs. Alfi's fingers, one by one, were rolled firmly onto ink pads; his prints pressed onto old parchment paper, as the Sheriff sat calmly observing, his bandaged leg stretched outwards and supported by a wooden stool.

The Sheriff sighed, leant awkwardly over his oval stomach and picked up a document from the desk. 'So,' he said, flicking through the papers. 'What we have here, is the damaged remains of a Gumbran - what you call a Yeti, a drunk and disorderly charge at Bleaches and now this, insurance fraud. You have been arrested three times Mr Alfi. In two days. That's pretty good going.'

'They say things come in threes officer,' replied Alfi, preoccupied as his left profile was being blasted.

'They also say this kind of thing can happen a lot,' added the Sheriff.

'What?'

'Well,' the Sheriff said rifling with the papers. 'Some of the bigger towns, a lot of it in Du, according to the manual. Travellers trying to make a fast buck. Saying they've lost things when they haven't. So basically, you've got two choices. Two choices when you get into that courthouse.'

'Courthouse?'

'Two choices Mr Alfi.' he reiterated. 'And I think you're lucky.

'Lucky?' snapped Alfi.

'We've trial day today. It happens just once a month up here and you happen to be visiting at the right time. At least you got something right! Otherwise, you could had been waiting up here, transferred to a small prison of ours up near Madrakani creek, for another 30 days. Gets a little uncomfortable. Crowded up there, after a while, especially with the smell of urine. Plastic buckets overfill real' easy. No handle either. It's a poisoned chalice Mr Alfi. So this morning, bless your lucky stars, you're going to court. And then we'll have you leaving, definitely. But you have to help us first.'

'Help?' enquired Alfi.

❀ ❀ ❀

From his stretcher the Sheriff turned sideways as he was being lifted to the courthouse. 'I am not guilty!' Alfi screeched. Ruben was in his ochre cloak trailing behind. 'And I'm not pleading guilty either!' The monk nodded in agreement, for he admired Alfi as he made life interesting.

'I've explained before,' opportuned the Sheriff trying to get Alfi onside. 'You might say that. But let's forget about your country for a little while, huh? 'Cos' its fancy and all that. But over here we get trials over real' quickly. Real quick. And we don't have this playing around, all this talking, and toing and froing, and just earning lawyers' money, like you do in the West. I advise, from a Himalayan perspective, that you plead guilty.'

Alfi looked down to the Sheriff's face that seemed to be resting a little more contently in the canvas. 'But I didn't do anything!'

'If you plead innocent,' the Sheriff persisted, 'you'll need a lawyer, which ain't easy up here, and would cost a lot of money. And it takes time, to get a lawyer up these mountains. Up over that hill, someone professional: at least three days by mule or that old bus, and they don't like coming up here too much. Especially anyone, any good. Which puts you into, as they say in high English literature...*in a bit of a pickle*...doesn't it? A dead end. *Up the creek without a paddle,* as your bards say...you'd be back in that jailhouse, enjoying our hospitality for another month - waiting. And I don't think you want that very much. And if, after all that, you're found guilty, after pleading innocent, the sentence, well...that can be a long one. They don't like people wasting time you see. Put it like this, you have to lose the battle to win the war Mr Alfi.'

Alfi looked glumly. 'A sentence?'

'Digging,' replied the Sheriff. 'They've got a big quarry ten miles out. And we can get some pretty hot days up there. It can break a man. They say strong men have collapsed to their knees up there. Nothing left to give. Not an ounce. And we know, and you know, that all we want - is for you to go home. Get yourself back to Du and forget that all this ever happened.' The Sheriff adjusted himself in the canvas, feeling he was on a winning streak he sat up a little. 'And besides Mr Alfi, I don't want you...in the way. You would have noticed Mr Teshi, you met at the jailhouse. He might be a quiet man but he's a powerful one too. There's no need to go into that any more. Let's just say that you going, you leaving here, as a writer and all that, is for the better. For you, for him, for everyone. Just plead guilty. It's the easiest way.'

'I told you, I'm innocent.' Alfi retorted.

The Sheriff spoke reassuringly. 'Now, now. The most you'll get is a little fine.' Something you can pay with that little plastic card of yours, we can ring up Du to do it. Ronson will put some sky in that motorbike and you can forget you ever came.'

Ruben tapped Alfi's shoulder. 'Maybe Sheriff is right? It is better way.'

'This holy friend of yours makes some sense,' grinned the Sheriff.

❀ ❀ ❀

The large wooden ramshackle courthouse was packed to its rafters with a jostle of expectant spectators. There was a hum of conversation and it seemed to be the town's monthly - and probably only - entertainment. Sitting quietly on long wooden benches and facing the gallery was Alfi's jailmates. Even Horse was there, dozing with his head propped up against a window, despite the fact that he wasn't being charged with anything. Alfi had been positioned in the centre of the courtroom where Ruben sat behind, as well as an overawed Dundram.

Ruben leaned into Alfi's ear. 'Don't worry,' he whispered. 'Don't worry, not too much. The yeti bones are ok. We nearly fix them. No one notice. Gumbran good as new, even though it is three-hundred years old.' He tapped Alfi's shoulder reassuringly.

On a high platform in front was a simple tall backed judge's chair. Elevated - like most courtrooms over the world - for the accused to be judged from above. Behind it on a wall was a painting of a gowned character standing nobly next to the same chair with a heavy-looking book in his hand. An inscription on its cover read "In Sky we Trust."

Alfi glumly surveyed the scene. The audience in anticipation. It dawned on him then, the mess he was in and far away from home. To his right, the Sheriff had placed himself agreeably with his leg across two chairs. Ronson was alongside, ready and waiting with an open notebook and pen. Alfi looked opposite, where at a slight angle and facing outwards into the courtroom, were three prominent looking rows of benches. Sat on these, he counted eleven sullen vacant faces - men and women, the women still in their top-hats and smoking, and a tethered yak at the end. The animal appeared to be the most astute of the lot - despite the fact that it was chewing the cud.

He turned back to Ruben. 'What's that? Is that a jury?'

'Yes,' Ruben replied excitedly. 'Sometimes, in some cases they need jury. They on stand-by.'

'What's with the Yak?'

'Oh that,' said Ruben. 'He's part of the jury. It's a great tradition up here. By local tradition we believe the Yak can smell truth.'

'How do you know? When he smells truth?'

'He begins to sniff,' replied Ruben.

'What about if someone's lying?' asked Alfi.

'We've got a shovel and mop at the back.'

There was a stir around the room as a judge appeared from a concealed door behind the tall chair, a door that he was having trouble closing again. He was dressed similarly to the character in the painting behind him; black gowned with a grey ringleted wig, blue cravat and holding a stare that demonstrated the height of solemnity. An anonymous voice called out from somewhere at the back of the courtroom. 'All stand!' and everyone stood. The judge took to his chair, fidgeted with some papers and ushered indifferently with his fingers for everyone to sit. A voice called out from the back of the room again. 'All be seated,' and everyone sat.

The judge spoke without lifting his eyes from his papers as if being a judge in Madrakani, was probably the most dreadful job in the world. 'Alfred Singer please rise!' he said. Ruben looked with pride as Alfi stood up slowly. The judge continued wearily. 'Alfi Singer, you have been charged with insurance fraud, trying to pervert the cause of justice, and it says, in an addendum here, being a complete nuisance. On the 27th December, you claimed you lost your wallet.' The judge stopped unexpectedly and studied his paper-work again. 'Oh,' he said. 'Today's your birthday.'

Dundram stood up stiffly and sounded an elongated note from his shell. There was a flutter of applause from around the courtroom. The judge struck his hammer. 'Order! Order!' he yelled and then continued. 'Then on inspection of your room by our temporary Sheriff and his respected Deputy, Deputy Ronson - the latter I believe, then shot the former in this case - they found your said wallet. Before which, you had wanted to make a sizeable insurance claim. They had reason to believe therefore, that you were partici-pating in making a fraudulent insurance entitlement.' The judge stopped and gave out a large outtake of breath. 'And so, how do you plead?'

Alfi paused and then began to mumble. 'Inno...' before stopping.

'What?' The judge asked abruptly.

Alfi mumbled a word again that sounded like a new, welcome addition to the lexicon. 'Inno-guilt.'

'What did he say?' Speak up man!' called the judge and there was a buzz of confusion around the building. The judge sounded his hammer again. 'Silence! Please! What is your plea?'

'Guilty,' Alfi finally ushered, as if he'd just witnessed the sinking of a beloved ship into the Bosphorus.

'Oh,' paused the judge, before adding. 'Oh. I see.' He glanced again at his papers giving the impression that he was now faced with all kinds of dilemmas. 'Considering all the facts and evidence, presented here, before me. And the defendant's plea. I find the defen-dant...guilty as charged.'

His hammer was struck, when suddenly there was an unhealthy sound coming from the direction of the yak. It went on, uncomfort-ably for a while, hushing the room, a silence that was only broken when an anonymous voice called out. 'Permission to retrieve mop and shovel sir?'

'Granted,' replied the judge matter-of-factly and added. 'Would you like to say anything before I pass judgement?'

'I'm just...disappointed,' said Alfi to the sound of a shovel scraping, the splashing of water and mopping.

'Given you have pleaded guilty,' the judge declared. 'And had not wasted this trial's time. And that you're a foreigner, and new to this town. Um. Let me think. What would be, could be, a suitable judgement?' He hesitated. 'I'm going to be lenient on you Mr Alfi. A $2,000 fine and you leave Madrakani as soon as your bike gets some air! I hear from the Sheriff, that this is very soon.'

'$2000!' retorted Alfi. '$2000!' The judge struck his hammer again as Dundram blew a high, single pipping note to conclude the matter.

'Not so bad,' Ruben leaned forward. 'Not so bad.'

# CHAPTER NINE

*All Things Must Pass*

It was a bright morning as prayer flags carrying their mantras danced over the street like kites, sending their prayers to the heavens. Alfi glanced up admiring their colours as he swung his luggage onto the bullock cart. A cheerful Ruben followed suit with his flimsy saffron knapsack, there wasn't much in it - such is the life of a monk.

'So, you're giving Ruben a ride to Kathmandu too?' asked the Sheriff, as he limped a foot forward, steadying himself on Ronson's shoulder who was holding an innertube and pump. Dundram came skipping behind

'Yes. Why not,' Alfi said, and they climbed up on board.

Placing some weight on the wrong leg the Sheriff winced. 'I hope you've enjoyed your visit here,' he said, and there was some fondness in his voice. 'And that you don't get into any more trouble. My advice, for whatever it's worth, is you forget this whole thing, and that your visit here to this town, ever happened. Put it down to experience and enjoy your ride down the mountain.' He gave a half smile and looked to his Deputy. 'Ronson, you make sure you *see* them leave this town - once and for all - and that Mr Alfi gets some sky into his bike. You hear?'

'Yes sir!' he replied willingly.

Dundram blew his shell to Alfi, who lent down from the carriage and tapped the boy's shoulder.

'It's been very interesting having you here,' the Sheriff added. 'Very interesting. You're the first foreigner this town has ever had. They're not all like you - are they Mr Alfi?' And before Alfi could answer he continued. 'You take care now.'

'Goodbye Sheriff,' concluded Alfi. 'And thank you.'

Ronson looked lively, hoisted himself onto the driver's seat and with a flick, goaded the bullock into action. Its tired legs clopped forward making a sound on the stones as Alfi waved back to little Dundram who was just standing.

The boy stared. Just stared at him, empty looking. So young, he'd never tasted loneliness or the emptiness of its defeat. Soon, they would disappear around the side of the hill, down and out of view, and the little boy would never see them anymore, as if they no longer existed. Such melancholy of a last farewell was new to him, it captivated and even lured him. His conch shell was hanging precariously by his side - just dangling by the fingertips. He had nothing left to say.

❀ ❀ ❀

Ronson and Ruben watched in silent fascination as Alfi worked the foot pump. It was strange for them to see a foreigner do physical work. Up and down he pressed, his foot occasionally slipping off the pump. It was a fascination that was only broken by the sound of another engine - a black jeep, as it hurried along an upper road above them. It turned sharply, leaning in a plume of rising white dust before straightening again. Yet even amongst the dust that hung in the air like a cloud, Alfi caught sight of Stodge turning the wheel with Mr Teshi in the passenger seat, and two other figures behind them. 'They're in a hurry,' Alfi observed good-humouredly, as he continued with the pump and the car was gone.

He gave it a last few heavy presses and squeezed the sides of the tyre. 'Well, that's about it,' he said, handing him back the pump. 'And thanks Ronson. It looks as good as new!'

'You take care now, Mr Alfi,' beamed Ronson. 'Both of you. And good luck. I liked meeting you.' And with that, Ronson leaped up into the carriage again and flicked the reins. The bullock's head turned, its long dark eyelashes giving the slowest of blinks as it plodded away.

Alfi took to his bungee cords and began strapping his luggage as tight as he could. Yet with Ronson barely out of view, an elderly man suddenly appeared. The man stumbled a little as he walked towards them. His modest little figure seemed to have stepped out miraculously from behind a large powdery rock. He was white, and looked quite west European, yet his head was shaven in a Buddhist way. He wore an orange tunic, the colour of an ascetic, with a matching pair of large round orange glasses. A gnarled stick was held loosely over his shoulder, and in spite of the slight stumble, he walked, seemingly, without a care and gazed at the two of them in a friendly way. 'Nice bike,' he said, admiring the machine and looked at them - up and down.

'Thanks,' replied Alfi, still wondering where the man had come from. But he knew from his past experiences of meeting lonely travelers, that he'd find out soon enough, without the need for asking.

And so the man spoke. 'I walk around here, you know,' the little ego within him enjoying their bewilderment. 'These mountains. They have become my friends. I can name every one of them. People used to come to worship them - but not anymore. Now they're just rocks, to most people. Just rocks. Such is the modern ignorant age.

Mountains, oceans, they don't really have names, anyway - do they? It's only people who name them.' He kicked up some loose stones by way of punctuation, looked up at the higher hills and tutted. 'But nature is alive you know, even the stones. I wander here and there. Mainly there, rather than here, really. I have a great affinity with solitude you see. It can become your friend if you let it. I recommend at least an hour with it, every day. Whereas loneliness, loneliness is a different matter - isn't it? It's not a choice - and the worst of it can be found within the crowd. It can hang around and never go away, with a sting in its tail and bring a man down. But in solitude you can listen, and be yourself. You're away from temptations, and there must be not one single distraction, not even a thought. Not so many people can do that - can they? Escape the hum of their own noise?' The old man gazed up to the hills before speaking again. 'Left on its own, some say the mind can become morbid as it needs distractions. But purgation, illumination, communion with God - isn't that what the Christians call it? Or God nature, however you want to put it. Maybe *you* will see it one day?'

'Me?' asked Alfi.

The old man smiled. 'Maybe. Maybe, you'll see it. Freedom from your own mind. You'll find out soon enough. How to step out of your Self and not look inside. Ah,' he sighed. 'All this...it's just conversation...isn't it? Conversation, it's all talk.' His mood shifted and he became lighter. 'So where have you been? And where are you going?'

'We've just left Madrakani,' Alfi answered.

'Ah Madrakani.'

'And now we're heading down to Kathmandu,' said Ruben gayly.

'Back to the city hey? Never been my cup of tea. The city life. Being busy doesn't make you successful you know. Just running around, following the tempestuous mind. Some live like ghosts and are servants to it. Without desires they'd have little else to do.'

'It must be hard. Out here,' said Alfi. 'Living like this.'

'I felt my old life had become too comfortable. With no challenges apart from the ones I had myself created. I had no family you see. Wish I had in a way. But it's difficult to choose - to see the implications of choices you had not made. I am a yogi by the way. Which is a kind of holy man or priest.' The Yogi looked at the bike. 'Would you like me to bless it? This bike.'

Ruben nodded with approval. 'It would be good Alfi,' he said excitedly. 'As we have long journey. And he is yogi.'

'Well. Will it take long?' asked Alfi.

'It doesn't take long really.' He reached into his tunic and removed a small wooden tub. Unscrewing its lid, he dipped a thumb into it and touched Alfi's forehead with bright red vermilion powder. He walked to the bike and began chanting. It was a low chant, that seemed to come from somewhere deep in the chest. He placed a forefinger and the red powder on the rear mudguard, the wheels, the saddle, the headlight - smudging it down the glass to make a little curved line - before pressing a thumb firmly onto the kick start as if he were anointing it, his voice dense in resonance. He then stood in front of the headlight like a matador to a bull, and bowing his head elegantly, rested on one knee. His voice then changed drastically, where he gave out a long, high-noted whine. A call that went on for too long, before it finally stopped abruptly. He looked at Alfi straight in the eyes. 'All done,' he said. 'That should be about it.'

'Oh, thank you,' Alfi said. 'Can I give you anything?'

'Oh no. No. Not really,' said the yogi. 'It's free.' He kicked up some loose stones again, his leg like a pendulum with one of his boots, and added. 'I live up there,' he pointed to a forest on a far-off hill. 'Amongst the nature, some trees. It gives me peace, being a holy man. I am not one for noise.'

'Oh. What do you do with your time?' Alfi asked.

'Well, I pray. I go and offer pujas, offerings, to temples in villages. I meditate...the life of a holy man.' He tutted in recollection, turned as if about to leave and then slipped, tripping down a small slope to his knees. Alfi and Ruben rushed to help him.

'Oh, it's ok. I'm ok don't worry,' he said, getting up quickly and dusting himself down. 'I'm always doing that, always making mistakes. Accident prone. You know I blessed a cow in a village near Kargal once and two weeks later the animal died. Collapsed, out of the blue. Sad really. When it happened a second time, to a prize bullock, I was asked to leave the village.' He scratched his head at the thought, and asked. 'You don't know where I can get some Ganja do you? My supplier has died.'

Not expecting a reply, the yogi began to walk away again, slightly slipping as he went. He disappeared as quickly as he'd come. Alfi hadn't even asked his name. He wondered - did he have one?

❀ ❀ ❀

Alfi kickstarted the bike and they were away. It was good to feel independent and free again. They rode down the hill playfully, weaving their way along the dropping twisting turns of bleached white stones - all the while with Ruben doing his best to hang on. Further and just ahead of them, a dark figure of a woman was shepherding a small herd of goats, motioning them to the side of the road. Alfi remembered Rita. He smiled to himself which prompted him to think. Was it possible to transcend the human experience? To escape fully from it and become something entirely else? What else would that be? What was "the freedom from your own mind" the old man had been talking about? He watched her figure as they passed - caught within the shining metal frame of his mirror. She had the crooked stance of a woman much older. It wasn't Rita. He wondered, had she existed at all? The *child of light* as she'd called herself, of a dream, and of the hills.

'What is it?' Ruben called out.

'Oh nothing,' replied Alfi loosely. 'That lady, she reminded me of someone.'

They drove one descending bend after another, where the white rocky turns became tighter and dropped more steeply. Hours passed and Alfi, so attuned to his motorbike, began to hear the engine missing a beat. It gave out the occasional splutter and was telling him something, to slow down, so he rode more gently. Then it sent out a final wisping gasp and the pistons had no energy behind them. There was a silence as they freewheeled down the hill. Ruben lent his chin onto Alfi's shoulder. 'Maybe it was the yogic?' he said. 'The blessing? The blessing that did it.'

Further down they freewheeled, where there was a cluster of wooden houses and surprisingly at one side of the track, a vendor was waiting to sell fruit. He looked out from behind his tall pyramids of apples and oranges, trays of mountain apricots, raising a hand to his brow to make them out in the glare of the sun. Alfi touched the brakes a little and coasted towards him. 'Hallo!' he said, before finally stopping. 'Do you know, do you know, if there is a place, a garage or something? Somewhere where I can look at my motorbike? We're having a little trouble.'

The vendor considered them - surprised by the foreigner. 'You have fuel?'

'Yes, we have fuel, I think it's something else. I'd like to look at the bike, maybe there's a mechanic around? Somewhere?'

'Over there,' the seller pointed to a large, dark makeshift shed, just down the hill that was open to one side.

❀ ❀ ❀

Alfi knelt in the half-darkness aside the motorbike. The owner of the shed, who spoke no English, was sympathetic enough to even offer some tools and left him alone to do the work. Eventually, after working a half-hour, he stood back from the bike and announced to Ruben. 'I think that should be it. It was the carburetor, as well as the air filter. Dust. Easily happens on these old machines up here.' He lent in again and in the half-light tightened a last screw, handing the screwdriver to Ruben.

All at once there was a fierce sound of another engine. They looked up. A jeep came speeding into the shed, it lurched forward then back again with a jolt, stopping with a roar and a skid. Instinctively, the two ducked down behind the motorbike, only to see the black bonnet of Mr Teshi's jeep that had passed them earlier. The doors swung open. Alfi and Ruben sunk deeper in the darkness.

Stodge was out first, stepping out heavily followed by a rather stiff looking Mr Teshi and two other characters from the back. Alfi knew the two immediately. Their timid little sunburnt faces. It was Goring and Palak who he'd spent the night with in the jailhouse. Holding his cane and hobbling to the rear of the jeep, Teshi turned to Stodge. 'Ok Stodge,' he said, pointing with his stick. 'Would you be so kind?'

A diligent looking Stodge opened the hatchback door, leaned in and began to unravel a thick Himalayan blanket. A row of small golden irregular nuggets shone back at him - lighting up his plump face. He gazed at them for a while in admiration, did his usual count and lifted each one into shoulder bags and onto the backs of Goring and Palak.

'This time,' Mr Teshi said, addressing the two. 'This time, can you try to be more careful. No more mistakes. Please? I do hope you understand.'

'Yes Mr Teshi,' replied the two of them obediently, adjusting the straps on their backpacks. 'Yes, this time, we' be careful.'

'Sometimes I wonder why I can never get anyone to work properly for me?' Just follow the rules. The instructions. Is it a lot to ask? Is it? No one listens to me. Do they Stodge?' There was no reply. '*Do they Stodge!*'

'Oh yes, Mr Teshi,' said Stodge agreeably.

'I am just trying to make a simple, dishonest, living,' added Teshi as he watched Palak and Goring getting ready. 'Nothing more. Nothing less. Now listen, *please* you two. You should be down in Kathmandu in a few days. Across country this time. Keep away from roads. Please, *do not* speak to anyone. Do not mix with anyone and sleep outside. No villages. Keep away from any living soul. This way, it makes it easier for all of us. You got that?'

'Don't worry Mr Teshi,' said Goring looking back at him vacantly.

'All will be ok,' added Palak quickly.

It was then, perhaps due to the unfolding drama or the sight of an illegality, that for some odd reason the usually calm Ruben lost his grip on the screwdriver. It fell with several bounces onto the stone floor and caused all heads to move in their direction. It was such a disappointment to an open-mouthed Ruben who ducked down further - next to an even more disappointed Alfi.

'Who is it?' Mr Teshi called out. 'Who is that?' Stodge removed a revolver. 'I know somebody's there. Come out. Stand up!' said Teshi.

'It's over there Mr Teshi,' added Stodge. Pointing with the tip of his gun. 'Over there.'

And so, eventually in the dimness, Alfi and Ruben emerged, elongating themselves in slow motion from behind the motorbike, hands in the air, like a child at school pretending to be a tree.

'I was just praying,' muttered Ruben limply.

'And I...I was helping him,' added Alfi.

'Oh,' said Mr Teshi in disappointment. He closed his eyes and opened them again hoping the sight would go away. 'If it's none other than that journalist gentleman. A visitor friend from our town. And his holy friend. What's the name? Mr Alfi? Alfi Singer, isn't it?'

'We just came in to fix the bike.' Ruben butted in nervously.

'Yes,' said Alfi.

'And we didn't see anything. 'No gold,' supplemented Ruben, as he thought this might lighten the mood.

'Gold!' said Mr Teshi sharply.

'What?' asked Ruben.

'You said *gold!*' said Teshi.

'Did I? Did I really? I might had said it. Maybe I said that. But I definitely, and I can categorically confirm, I did not say smuggle.'

Alfi interrupted quickly. 'Look. We're just here fixing my bike. Minding our own business. Two simple people, me and my monk, and my bike. And we'll be on our way. To Kathmandu.'

Ruben beamed in agreement as if this all could be over very quickly. 'He's right you know. We know nothing about your business.'

'Nothing?' Mr Teshi scratched his head. 'It's a big problem now. Isn't it? You two knowing *nothing.*'

'Problem?' asked Ruben. 'What? What do you mean?'

'Well,' said Teshi. 'Letting you down to the city.'

'When we leave, we leave, don't worry,' assured Alfi. 'We'll absolutely forget everything. Not a word.'

'Yes,' said Ruben. 'Everything we ever heard or saw. And we have bad memories. Really, really, we do. Can't remember a thing. Keep forgetting things. You know the number of times I've walked into the monastery kitchen, opened the refrigerator, and forgot what I came in for. Total blank! And there's not much in there anyway.'

'He's right,' Alfi assured. 'They're very ascetic.'

'I forget to pray sometimes. I do,' added Ruben eagerly. 'And I'm always losing keys. I think I need to write things down and put things away in the same place each time, so that I don't forget them.'

'It's a good idea,' agreed Stodge.

'What?' snapped Teshi.

'To write things down so that you don't forget them,' said Stodge which annoyed Mr Teshi, who was now gazing at the shed ceiling for answers.

He then stared at Ruben squarely in the eyes. 'You know, I have a brother, a much older brother. Who was just like you.'

'He forget' everything?' enquired Ruben.

'No. He was a monk,' Mr Teshi said.

'Oh, that's nice,' Ruben replied brightly. 'Good monastery?'

'But we don't talk anymore.'

'Oh,' said Ruben.

'Now, what to do?' said Teshi. 'You know...I know a lot of people, not only up here, but in Kathmandu and all over Nepal. And for me, it's really, very easy, to find anyone. No one can ever really hide or run away. And I like to keep my business...well private. And you two, now present a problem. Hey Stodge?'

'I'm sorry sir?' questioned Stodge.

'So, we really can't have you going down that mountain,' continued Teshi.

'We're not?' Ruben asked. 'Going down that mountain? We can't go to Kathmandu?'

Stodge shook his head as if the idea was all his.

'We can go *up* the mountain then?' Ruben suggested. 'Up's ok.'

Suddenly, there was an agonising screech at the barn door. All heads turned to see billy goats, bucks, nannies and kids all scattering in, in every direction. They were confused, as was the old herdswoman they'd passed earlier. She ran in with her stick, stomping her ground, shrieking, whipping and threatening to whip. 'Jau!' she yelled twirling in circles, her voice thrilling. 'Jau! Chalo, Chalo!' Stodge and Mr Teshi just looked - utterly transfixed, whilst Palak and Goring were about as confused as the bleating nanny goats.

Alfi swung a leg over the saddle. 'Let's go!' He kick-started the engine.

'My knapsack!' Ruben grabbed it and leapt behind. And in a wild acceleration they skidded in a deep grinding half-circle that created a mad clearing amongst the shouting animals. And they were out! The herdswoman watching them go with her stick. Out into the blistering sunshine and weaving their way madly down the hill.

'Get to the jeep!' Mr Teshi yelled. 'The jeep!' But the flock had them surrounded. They were too late. They couldn't move.

Alfi and Ruben were gone.

❀ ❀ ❀

It was sunset, and as the day began to fade, the bike made its final climb over a ridge. A ridge that would drop down again sharply and into Kathmandu valley. Soon, the sounds of trucks, buses, bullock carts and motorbikes would be bounding about them and they would be more or less consumed within Kathmandu's traffic. It was sublime to be hidden amongst the noise as Alfi eased off the throttle and leant back, sitting more upright on the bike. He lowered speed along the city's ring road until later, under the guiding hand of Ruben, he turned off the road and up into a rutted steep hill.

They climbed upwards, from where they began to overlook the thousands of silvery grey and ochre shanty buildings. They were high above the gold of the temples, and beyond the large white domes of the holy stupas that were now sunken in the city's haze, so much so, that the people and even the boisterous traffic, were now barely visible. Eventually, the bike halted beneath two gigantic wooden gates. Ruben dismounted. He was happy to leave the saddle and be home. Clutching his backpack with both hands to his chest, he took a deep breath. 'This is it!' he said, and then added brightly. 'And are all foreigners like you Mr Alfi?'

'Most have quieter lives,' Alfi replied. 'Maybe a quiet life is a good one.'

It was then, just then, that Alfi finally captured a thought about Ruben. For at last he'd noticed how his monk friend, with all his questions and few opinions, seemed always to possess a sympathy, an interest in others, and the world. Perhaps he should had seen it sooner. Ruben could never suffer the illness of envy, disinterest or boredom - or it seemed, worry. Could self-absorption, heavy intro-spection, be the plight of man? How Ruben took such great delight and gave the kindness of his time to other people. And how it would reward him so. The sharing of their happiness, an empathy of the other perspective with a broader, more satisfying view. It resulted in being liked too. The act of being kind was indeed resplendent.

Ruben responded, taking Alfi out of his dream. 'Mm, but where will you go now? I am ok. I'm a monk. No one can ever find me here behind these gates. No one can enter the monastery either and we monks, we all look the same.' Ruben smiled, amused by his own observation. 'But you, Mr Alfi? Where will you go? And you heard what Mr Teshi said. He knows everybody in Kathmandu and Nepal, he'll find you. And that man...the one with him, he had a gun. Maybe it's better you go somewhere else? You go home, back to your country? And end your journey.'

Alfi stared back at him. 'Perhaps there is only one place I can go?'

'Where?' asked Ruben.

'A long, long way from here,' he uttered softly. 'Maybe Rita was right.'

'Rita?' said Ruben. 'Who's Rita?'

'Maybe, I was always going to the end of the universe.'

'Where? I cannot always understand you Mr Alfi. What universe?'

Alfi gave him the warmest of smiles. 'You take care of yourself Ruben,' and started his bike that began to move.

Ruben called out after him. 'Wherever you go. I hope...I hope we can meet again Mr Alfi! Maybe one day, I can meet you there too? At that universe of yours?'

'Maybe,' said Alfi. 'Maybe,' and his head dropped for this was another farewell. Alfi was gone.

# PART TWO

# CHAPTER TEN

## Mindgarten At The End Of The Universe

Dark shadows stretched behind the mountains that faced the last gold of sunset. Black tapered clouds crept over their peaks and reclined themselves within a liver-coloured horizon - and all the Himalaya went black. The mountains looked down on Alfi that night - giant, silent, as he and his bike became lonely figures. He climbed steeply into them and over the hills, and within the crisp night air they began whistling; his silhouette was now across the face of an ascending moon.

Hours passed and the track rose further, until the only thing above Alfi was a sea of blinking stars. He drove along the high rugged ridge in the darkness, and rounding a turn to the other side of the mountain, a new valley revealed itself to him, more than a thousand feet below. A tremendous flatland; a patchwork of fields and colours; lilac, pale green and yellow, all shimmering under the opaque light of the now fully risen moon. This was cultivated land that stretched so far out that their edges became invisible. He drove further along the tip of the hill where the road began to descend, down the valley and towards the fields below. Half way down and the homely smell of woodsmoke came in passing wafts. In the distance and still far below him, he could make out clusters of white buildings, all dotted about; some reaching to the base of the far-off white mountains on the other side of the valley.

Nearer still, and in the distance, he could see what looked like manicured gardens and lawns. There were lines of perfect rectangular pools, one after the other, shimmering black water that carried the white rippling beams of moonlight. This was structured human habitation. Further, and there were lanterns perhaps? He could not be sure. Clearer now and yes, he could see them shining on their cozy porches. And all around was the terrific wall of the Himalaya: protecting, encircling - a boundary between this and the outside world.

He turned excitedly down one plunging bend after another, eventually reaching the valley floor. It was after midnight as the road flattened and he picked up speed across the stones. Ahead of him was what looked like an old wooden sign hanging high over the rugged track. He tensed his lips, his arms were tired, as he drove on towards it. Glancing up, were the deeply carved, golden letters.

*'Mindgarten at the End of the Universe.'*

❀ ❀ ❀

A disheveled Alfi in hiking boots and dirty motorbike gear was led along a glittering, multi coloured corridor by the Frenchman holding a candelabra who had a strong drawling French accent.

Alfi considered him for a moment; the long wavy hair that hung over his shoulders. He wore a purple top, probably hemp, and baggy trousers over his narrow legs. Around his neck and wrists were a collection of beads, dozens of them in fact, necklaces and bracelets, that must have doubled his slight body weight, and on his feet were brown leather scuffed sandals with black polished toe nails peeking through them. Around one ankle was a heavy looking silver bracelet with small bells on it that jingled as he moved. It reminded Alfi of a domesticated yak.

'Mm,' drawled the Frenchman, as he opened a door at the end of the corridor, peering in with a candle. 'This is it. You can stay here as long as you don't have sex.' This ridiculous comment jolted Alfi as he gazed into an even more colourful room. It occurred to him that his host had the unique ability to be both helpful and unkind at the same time. He gave a French drawl again. 'Mm. Sometimes, not often, we get adventure seekers here. They just come for a short time, look around, do some meditating, and then move on. They treat this, as they treat their life, like a shopping list. Consuming experiences, things just to be done. Then they go away and boast about it. Is that you?'

'No, no.' Alfi repeated quickly, wanting to get the Frenchman onside. 'I don't think so.'

'So how long do you expect to stay then?'

'I was kind of hoping this could be my last destination. At least for a while.'

'A while?' the Frenchman raised an eyebrow.

'A long while.'

The Frenchman ignored this last comment and rearranged some small lit candles on, what looked like, a makeshift little shrine. 'Whether you stay or not, is not my decision,' he said as he moved the candles needlessly. 'You're given a month. Call it probation time, if you will. We call it *Green Bird* and then our leader 'Thay' decides. If you can stay on or not.'

'Green Bird?' asked Alfi.

'Truth time. You'll find out. By staying one month we'll see your true nature. You might want to leave too. It's not a place for everyone.'

'Have you been here long?' asked Alfi.

'Nine years. It could be longer, or shorter. We don't measure time after Green Bird and the seasons don't change very much up here neither. We don't encourage people to measure time or know their age too. It's an obsession in the West isn't it. There are no birthdays here.'

Alfi tried to win him over with some humour. 'Saves time buying cards I s'pose.'

But his host wasn't having any of it. 'It makes no difference,' he retorted. 'Some die young, some die old. Death can come at any time, don't you think? What is the use in worrying about it, or age?'

Just then there was the sound of thunder and the Frenchman looked upwards. He held up a finger for silence. 'Hush!' he said. 'We have omens.'

'The thunder? What does it mean?' asked Alfi.

'Rain,' came the nonchalant reply and Alfi scratched his head. 'I run things around here,' he continued. 'In terms of the Green Bird. So we'll get you another room from tomorrow. Something...more permanent. You'll work and you'll pay rent. It's not much.'

'What kind of work?'

'I set the work; you'll see. I'll be looking carefully at you. Mr?

'Alfi. Call me Alfi.'

The Frenchman took a deep disappointed breath and looked into the room without any feeling. 'Here's your bed,' he said, directing Alfi's eyes towards a green shapeless bean-bag lying abandoned on the wooden floor.

Alfi examined the room in more detail. It was full of colour and cosy in its own way. A little alcove had been decorated with dangling crimson beads that sparkled from a myriad of candle flames. The walls were adorned with images too - mostly of figures meditating - as Alfi remembered Brother Iblan and his friendliness - which gave him a little comfort. The monk had taught him that when meditating, the

Buddha used hand gestures to communicate thoughts or feelings: known as 'mudras.'

A palm facing vertically outwards, meant the act of teaching and reassurance, one that he'd seen earlier in Madrakani. The tips of his fingers pointing towards the earth conveyed diligence - the gift of truth or even enlightenment. The one that Alfi particularly liked was a more common one: the intertwining of both hands, resting and facing upwards from the middle of the lap. Brother Iblan had told him that, while this was a simple mudra, it was a very significant one, and he'd dreamt that one day Alfi would see in a more *"significant way."* He'd said it had meant "Gone Home" and although Alfi couldn't see this mudra in this room at the time, he considered, could this be his new home? Or could the words "Gone Home" be interpreted differently?

The mudra depicted on a wall above the Frenchman was a very different one - the 'Targanj Mudra,' meaning threat. Alfi wondered if the threat was from him or the Frenchman standing before him, who turned and jingled towards the door. 'Someone will come and fetch you in the morning,' he said coldly.

'What's your name by the way?' Alfi asked trying to move away from the perfunctory.

'We don't use original names here,' he replied. 'Everyone, after Green Bird, is given a new name for a new life. We've over 2,000 residents, families and children, all with Mindgarten names. The people will decide your new name - if you stay on after one month - or if you make it Mr Alfi. If they like you, they usually give you a name related with the beauty of the Mindgarten: the name of a flower or a tree or something, something of nature. They use their imagination. It depends on how much they like you. Otherwise, your name will be more obvious.'

'So what is your name?' Alfi asked.

He paused. 'Frenchie,' he said, and his indifference did little to mask some subtle resentment as he jingled along the corridor and out of the door; his ankle bells disappearing into a chorus of chirping insects, and into the night.

Alfi turned to face his room. He had arrived in the 'Mindgarten at the End of the Universe' and didn't quite know what to expect.

# CHAPTER ELEVEN

## The Differential Void

There was a timid knock on the door that next morning. Alfi opened it to discover a short, demure looking smiling monk called Lobsang looking up at him with a brazen smile. 'Go feck yourself!' he said.

'Sorry?' asked Alfi.

'Oh, I'm so sorry,' the monk waved the back of a hand to his lips by way of an apology. 'I suffer from what we call 'sting-tongue.' I think they call it 'tourettes' in your country. It means that sometimes I say wrong word. I get influenced. And this past month, I watch a lot of cooking on television. English Chef. He swear' a lot. It is affliction. Sod off!' he blurted out again and held his mouth in embarrassment. 'Sorry again. And welcome to the Mindgarten by the way. Don't worry after a while 'sting-tongue' will calm down. This is first time. When I meet new people it's worse. Nervous.'

'Thanks,' said Alfi, and as it was daylight, he noticed some beautiful gardens over Lobsang's shoulder that he hadn't seen the night before.

'Carrots!' the monk cussed before continuing. 'Thay, our venerable leader, has been expecting you to come. But he did not expect you so early.'

'Expecting?' replied Alfi. 'But nobody knew I was coming?'

'Of course,' said Lobsang as he looked ruefully towards a row of white flowerbeds that danced delicately in the breeze. He then drew his face up to the sky as if it was telling him something, before he spoke some more. 'But you know, a farmer can look to the air and like animals, he can smell the rain and know when it's coming. It is just a matter of knowing the signs and learning the skill. Most people cannot see the signs. But Venerated Master Thay, he can see.' Before Alfi could reply, Lobsang blurted out. 'Christ! This sauce is rotten!' He slapped a hand to his lips again before composing. 'Sorry, I really *should* watch much less television. Come, we must go. Thay will be very pleased to see you.' They walked alongside one pretty garden then another as Lobsang continued. 'But you know, it will also be sad for him to see you.'

'Sad?' asked Alfi. 'But why?'

'You coming here. It has come early. It could mean the "expiration" he told me about is coming. Such is life. Difficult really. There is never enough time and yet so many of us, unlike Thay, do not do much with it.'

'Expiration?' enquired Alfi but Lobsang didn't answer.

They walked past neatly kept flowerbeds, row upon row of colour, until they reached a fountain in the middle of large pond that sent sprays of water upwards and in the glittering morning haze, it had created a rainbow. Around them, and walking along several wide-open thoroughfares and pretty little pathways was a scattering of people; men and women, many dressed in white, going calmly about their day. Everybody it seemed to Alfi, was in a state of serenity and sublimely at ease. Some young children were busy playing: running around in circles, chasing each other and giggling in their dizziness. Alfi eventually spoke. 'It's lovely here. These gardens, the flowers, the air, the people. Everything. How big is the Mindgarten?'

'It's big. Big place. We have schools here. Hospital if sick. Many nice places. Venerable Thay started this place sixty years ago. He was the oldest son and his father give this land to him.' They walked further before Lobsang added. 'Thay has much younger half-brother, but this brother no good. He gets jealous as he was not given this land, so he live' far away from here. And Thay make this beautiful place. With Russian lady.'

'Russian lady?' enquired Alfi.

'Ha, you want to know everything in the first moment!' Lobsang laughed. 'She was a beautiful princess from long ago in Russia. But she take drugs and go to parties in Europe many times. Then she come to Nepal on hippy trail, do you know it? Hippy Trail? Many came here to Nepal on Hippy trail in 1960's. And she met Thay. She had German boyfriend then. But he died - drug-taking. This is why they call it *Mindgarten,* the German way. Anyway, she start' Mindgarten with Thay. But she, the Russian princess, she also expired now. You know people, who came on hippy trail are now very old. There are not many left! Some are here in Mindgarten, but there are many more younger people here too.'

They were interrupted as a ceremonial bell sounded softly from a tannoy somewhere. This was followed by a short play of charming music then an announcement. "Addiction to safety, stepping out and taking risks session, will be held in Augustine Flower Bed Nine. Twelve noon." A gong played lightly again.

'You'll see!' said Lobsang.

Alfi asked. 'What's that?'

'We have many daily programmes here. Very clever people here. They decide. They do whatever they want to do. Many programmes to help improve the mind, or anything else. You'll see.' The two of them continued to stroll as Lobsang muttered. 'It's undercooked.

Raw! It's bloody not good enough!' He shook his head, baffled again. 'Sorry,' he said.

❀ ❀ ❀

The large room was richly decorated with saffron coloured walls and a gold painted ceiling that was embellished with fine looking Tibetan motifs - dragons, eagles and angels with sharp eyes, looked down on the two of them as they entered. Along the walls were small portraits. These were of benevolent looking holy people; gurus or teachers that also watched Alfi as he stepped by. And in the very centre of the room, surrounded by an array of eclectic chinoiserie old furniture, was a large inviting sofa draped with a throw of purple velvet, facing a Tibetan-looking red wooden table. Several candles were lit - where the whole mood of the place was something of a sanctuary. Alfi caught sight of a writing desk that had been placed neatly against a wall, with a little chair tucked into it. Above this, was a large framed photograph of a striking looking western woman in Himalayan dress. He guessed this must had been the Russian princess that Lobsang had spoken about.

Alfi stepped back. He was startled. As just beyond the sofa and sitting on the floor atop a gold thick cushion, was a lone male figure. He was shaken he hadn't noticed the figure sooner. The stillness of the form, also dressed in saffron, seemed to blend into the furniture and disappear like an apparition into the room. It was the venerated, shaven haired, Thay - who was sat there - and utterly still. The Rinpoche, the perfect one, with his eyes closed in the silence; he didn't even stir as Lobsang held out a second cushion and ushered Alfi to sit next to him.

Alfi sat and waited where a gentle sound began to radiate from Thay's lips. At first, it had a deep resonance to it, but it soon became lighter, eventually morphing itself into a hum. Alfi fidgeted not knowing quite what to do. Then, he had an inkling he could hear a melody. It became clearer, and surprisingly he made it out to be the tune of Irvin Berlin's *"There's No Business Like Show Business."* Louder still, from a motionless Thay until, suddenly, it stopped. Thay opened his eyes, turned and looked to Alfi carefully. There was a soft satisfaction in his face that broke into a smile.

'I love that song,' he said. 'Such a lovely, boisterous melody,' he paused before adding. 'Now let me look at you. Ah,' he spoke pleasingly. 'They say you have come from America?' He coughed a little mid-sentence and Lobsang appeared with a glass of water. Alfi was surprised at how quickly such an eccentric introduction had become so casual.

Lobsang bowed. 'Would Venerated father like some water?'

'Thank you, Lobsang,' came the reply as Thay sipped.

Lobsang lent forward again. 'Would you like your pillow? The six-inch velvet sir?'

'They'll be no need.'

'Right you are sir. Some biscuits?'

'You have biscuits?' Thay asked.

'No. No, I don't,' came the reply.

'Then no biscuits,' sighed Thay.

Lobsang continued. 'Grapes sir?'

'I've told you before, not to keep calling me "sir" and stop giving me lists.'

'Right you are.'

'That'll be all Lobsang.'

Lobsang took a step backwards before asking. 'Permission to speak sir?'

'Not granted,' said Thay before adding again. 'That'll be all Lobsang.'

'Right you are sir. Feck you.' Lobsang turned in military fashion and stomped away, slightly elevated from the room.

'I do apologise,' Thay said. 'He has an affliction you see. Nobody else will employ him. In the villages they think he's possessed by someone, possibly their notion of a demon or something, or in his case, that chef of yours. What's his name? Gordon?'

'Ramsey,' Alfi offered.

'Yes,' said Thay eagerly. 'That's him. He watches too much of him in the television room these days. I thought the meditation would help with his sting-tongue but it simply doesn't. Of course, it's impossible for him to lead any of our meditation classes. The sudden jolt of foul language, throws people from their stillness. Sometimes I see no end to it. His cooking's no good either.'

'It must be very difficult,' replied Alfi feeling more comfortable.

'He's even started using food as a fashionable substitute for swearing,' Thay continued flabbergasted. 'Only last week, he came into my room, completely unannounced, yelling the word *scallops*.'

'I'm sorry to hear that.'

Thay paused and changed tact. 'So, how was your journey? Mr... Alfi?'

'It was a long drive to get here.' Alfi said happily. 'I was given a map by Brother Iblan in Kathmandu.'

'Ah, brother Iblan,' Thay replied with a cheer. 'You know, when he was a novice, a child monk, I taught him.'

'He said you two were friends.' Alfi, was now completely at ease in Thay's company. Thay then paused the conversation, as he noticed a small vase containing some burning incense. He was disappointed at his own thoughtlessness and leant forward to put it out with a pinch of water. 'This is better for you Mr Alfi,' he apologised. Alfi was surprised that he seemed to know about his aversion to incense.

Thay continued. 'You know just a few hundred years ago, the world was not overpopulated and we were at *one* with nature. If you wanted an apple, you would just go ahead and pick one from a tree. But today? Today, there are too many people. So, to fulfil our needs, we go against earth's nature. We build factory farms, give suffering to animals and take the wild from them, to make crops. There're power stations, there's pollution. Most of it caused by over population. The desire to have so many children? I don't quite understand it? If we could just temper that a little. The world would be a better place. There's too much consumption, don't you think?'

'I do my bit,' said Alfi half apologetically and then with a hint of humour. 'I am thirty-nine years old and have absolutely *no* children. Not even one. I feel blessed. I can leave my lights on and have long showers.'

Thay chuckled before his reply. 'I know children can be a great source of happiness,' he said. 'Perhaps moreso for women. And whilst a person who is capable of remarkable achievements will find gratification in their work, for the many with unremarkable talents, nature's impulse may dictate to have more children, as their highest form of significance. You have to feel a compassion for that. Yet I wonder if, in some cases, the joy of parenting can have diminishing returns? At least for some. No doubt, love to a helpless infant comes naturally and has no bounds. But with the growth of the child's independence, could this create frustration or even conflict? Oh, I don't know. I've never had children.'

Thay smiled again. 'Some of the modern teachings of the West tell us, I think it was Mr Darwin or Wallace, that within the animal kingdom, population multiplies faster than food, so that they must compete to survive, and that nature acts as a selective force. Killing off the weak, and forming new species from the survivors who are fitter to their environment. But with human kind we have the ability to make more food.'

'There's the bigger question, I agree, we call it Malthusianism,' offered Alfi.

'Mm,' replied Thay. 'Malthusianism, a new word.'

'It suggests that human population growth occurs exponentially to birth rates. Thomas Malthus...We have a propensity to use abundance of food or money, to increase population rather than maintain a better standard of living.'

'Very good,' said Thay. 'And if you're not careful, marriage and children can distract you from higher pursuits. And the problem is, once you go away from the flow of nature, you make more problems. I think the Japanese call this Shintoism.'

'But here?' asked Alfi.

'Ah here, in the Mindgarten, we're not Japanese, but we try to balance ourselves with nature, we do not deplete or industrialise our resources.'

'You know, when I walked here with Lobsang, I was struck by how beautiful it is. The gardens, the buildings, the trees. It really is something.'

'Maybe, you have come home Mr Alfi?'

'Home?' Alfi hesitated. 'Well, it's certainly nice to be here. It's also strange. Lobsang also gave me the impression you were expecting me?'

'Did he now?' Thay added wryly, giggling to himself. 'He talks too much, does Lobsang. Maybe it's that sting-tongue of his. It's true. I did expect you. But not quite so soon.'

'He also said that it's *sad* that I came to this place, now. I don't understand?'

The words obviously touched Thay, but he did his best not to show it. Instead, he glanced to the framed photograph above his writing desk before giving out a sigh. 'It is, I suppose sad, that could be true. But perhaps it's a little selfish of me to say that...that I was hoping you would come later. Everybody hopes it will come later, don't they? You see Mr Alfi, sometimes I have the ability to see the coming and going of things. But my images are vague. I can only visualise them imprecisely, as if a figure in the mist. But leave this subject for now. For a little while anyway. Let's not ask questions about that. We must be patient, and you must be tired after your long journey.' Thay tapped his own thigh to punctuate the end of the topic. 'You must have many questions, about this place?' he added.

'Yes. Yes, I do. Can I ask? Is there a religion here?'

'Ah,' Thay smiled knowingly. 'One of the first questions people ask! Here, we don't practice any one religion Mr Alfi. People can follow, or not follow, whatever they like.'

'And you?' enquired Alfi. 'If you don't mind me asking.'

'Well, for me? Look around Mr Alfi! From the marvels of the human body to the design of the Universe - how planets circle one another...the wonder of nature, the migration of birds, the change in the seasons to the pollination by bees, photosynthesis; physics, chemistry, the list goes on; it gives us all glimpses. I personally believe there must be a *Divine* origin or grand *Design* to it. The planets have been arranged so well - don't you think? The sun, any further from it, and we could not sustain life. Closer and we would incinerate! The moon, just the right distance to affect the tides, to avoid stagnant water and give life. The speed we turn as a planet - any faster or slower and we would not survive. Even Jupiter, the scientists tell us, is perfectly placed to stop us being damaged by asteroids. An amazing coincidence don't you think? Oh, I don't know. For others, perhaps atheism gives people a sense of empowerment - which is what some of them need? But how can we just shrug our shoulders and say it all happens by chance? An accident, as if from nothing? But what it is, I do not know. So, I cannot preach about something I do not know about.'

'Mm,' was Alfi's only reply.

Thay continued. 'That's only my thinking and I like to think, like Buddhism, based on logic. People can sometimes be cynical about religion I feel. In that they think they're being manipulated or are being taught the wrong answers when they find out more about it - or some other evidence suggests it's untrue and that a God cannot exist. But with science, when we learn that old discoveries or theories might had been based on incorrect assumptions, we adopt a new science - we do not abandon science altogether. Like science, we must approach the spiritual path with learning and invention. Faith is also believing in something without understanding or knowing fully about it. We are only humans after all.'

'A silent God does have its limitations,' offered Alfi.

'Perhaps the God cannot speak to us - or we cannot hear it!' Thay said teasingly. 'The problem is, that the believer has to explain something that is essentially non describable, when the non-believer needs words. But one day, I hope to listen to Him, to hear him talk to me, in some sense. And there are limitations to what the human mind can understand you know. If you saw a pig staring at a page of writing and trying to read, it would be a pitiful sight, wouldn't it? But because a pig cannot read or even see words, does it mean that words do not exist?' Thay laughed aloud. 'But even a pig, has senses that we do not understand. That are beyond us!'

He held his small hands out demonstratively. 'We cannot see gravity Mr Alfi, you cannot touch or hold it, yet we know it's there and we feel its effects everywhere. Think about the mind too, we cannot pin-point where it is, like we can with the heart or the lungs - or is it, as some say, inside the brain? It's not tangible. But we know it is there. How could anyone deny the existence of it! We feel with it. We think we're happy or we're sad with it.'

Thay hesitated and then added. 'And another question, whilst on the subject, is this...does the mind control the body, or the body control the mind? It's an interesting question. When we have an impulse for example, such as hunger, you would assume the body is dominating the mind, but what about self-control or other actions? Is the mind then not the discipliner? Do these interchanges oscillate? Is it a case of a sparring between the two? Such things are complicated and no one yet, seems to know the answers. Spirituality for me, is a little like the mind, or gravity. You cannot see the spiritual but you can feel its effects everywhere, of love too. Particularly for those who are sensitive to it, and can tune in. Yet the intolerant choose to ignore it. They have no faith; they must see it with their own senses.'

With that, Thay got up and walked to a glass cabinet. Turning with a smile he offered. 'Now a conversation should not always be a competition of one particular view over another, and over complicated. Would you like some whiskey Mr Alfi?'

'Whiskey?' Alfi was surprised.

'There is nothing wrong with enjoying life,' he responded playfully. 'We're not a monastery you know!' He reached into the cabinet, selected two fine glasses and turned. 'Drink can be a most enjoyable mind-altering state - and sometimes much more easily accessible than meditation...in moderation of course.' He giggled to himself and held up the glasses pleasingly. 'You should visit our Epicurean Gardens one day. Do you know Epicureanism? It's one of the many theories people like to consider here. One that I like too!'

Alfi began to recite. "A greatest good is to seek moderate pleasure in order to attain a state of tranquility, freedom from fear and absence from bodily pain."

'Very good!' Thay clapped. 'You know your subject well Mr Alfi!' Thay began another recitation. "Whilst the pleasure of the mind can sometimes come from contemplating the pleasures of the body, the absence of pain, rather than the presence of pleasure should be a source of happiness." He broke into sweet laughter again as he poured the whiskey. 'We should constantly remind ourselves about this! Health! Mr Alfi. Health!' They held out their glasses and sipped. Thay chirped. 'The absence of a stomach ache far outweighs the pleasures of gluttony! Now, to answer your question, I think there is a God. But perhaps we've made the mistake of thinking that God exists purely for us, the human race, and that it has two eyes, a nose and a mouth, just like us, because we want to be identified to it, to be loved by it and feel safer by it. This could well be true, and God may or he may not love us. It is our ego.'

Alfi added his own tease. 'But look at all the places of worship we've built?'

'Precisely,' Thay responded. 'And as far as I'm aware, no other species does this. They have the misfortune or fortune of possessing little sense of reason!' He giggled. 'It does make one wonder though, doesn't it? Whether, in the act of praising, at least for some, is it sincere at all? Or are its origins in fear? Are we hoping to get something in return? It's human nature I suppose. We like to gain merit. People say "I love you" and wait for the other to say "I love you too" back. Perhaps we should just get on with life like all other creatures on this planet. Yet, I still marvel at God or God nature or however you like to put it. I do praise it for its sheer majesty and feel a love from it, it must be said, and for the moral way it guides me. So I am confused. But look at it this way. Whatever form God exists, perhaps we are no more important to it than a flea.'

'You could've picked something bigger?' joked Alfi.

'Like everything else, we all suffer from disease don't we?' Thay supplemented. 'Oh, I don't know...it's nature's, God's way of things. This is what I *think* I believe - but people are free here to believe in whatever they want, and I'm not foolish enough to think I know the answers, or that my feelings will never change. If there is a God, we've only got five senses Mr Alfi, and we will need a lot more than these to understand the nature of it. We've a lot of spiritual teachings going on here in the Mindgarten. These are not compulsory. But you should try some! Being spiritual gives one a great sense of comfort.'

'I will. Thank you.'

Thay beamed. 'There are only two rules here in the Mindgarten. One, that people do not harm others - with bad speech, bad intentions or bad actions. And the other, that we show compassion, understanding and kindness to each other. And from these two simple rules, everything else will follow. We do not try to manipulate others.'

'And you...are the leader?'

Thay broke into laughter again. 'Oh no. I'm no leader. It's true, I did create this place with Alexandria. And I offer some instruction or advice, practical teachings, once in a while if people want to listen, you'll see. But it's not compulsory. People come here to find things out for themselves. We are no cult Mr Alfi! But a place for rebirth to find the true Self.'

'And where? Where are people coming from, who live here?' Alfi asked.

'They come from all over the world and are in a process of recreation - to start life again. A life anew. Just because people are born and have developed into the way they are, doesn't mean that they cannot change. Many come here because they are suffering from what we call - the *Differential Void*. It sounds complicated, doesn't it? The Differential Void. Fancy words. What it means is, that they have everything, all material comforts in their world and according to their tribe, a good existence - but they feel they have no purpose. Life has become routine and they're lacking something. Perhaps they've a feeling too, of insignificance.'

'I know that feeling,' Alfi added.

'So they've come here to find meaning in their lives. But the trouble with a traditional monastery is that the monk's view is, like many views, ultimately subjective. Those who enter monkhood at an early age have no experience of outside life. Apart from thinking about it,' Thay laughed as he swirled the whisky about in his glass. 'Before they discount alcohol for example, surely, they should experience the bliss of it! Or in other things. They should taste the explosion of romantic love and all the anticipations and failures strung out along life's journey. How else could they comment on living with any authority?' He took a large, happy swig of his drink but then added somewhat dismally. 'I suppose, ultimately, there is no real meaning to life at all! For most of us.'

'Um?' Alfi was surprised.

'Unless,' Thay added. 'Unless perhaps for the few; if you're an eminent engineer, scientist or one of a small number from public life. Most of us cannot leave anything of any significance behind, apart from more offspring to go through the same cycle again. A child will study at school for example, to pass examination A to get to B, to obtain a good education and in turn a better occupation to provide more wealth and security, and perhaps support a family or whatever else they might like to do. To get from A to B to C to D, and so on. But whilst these are purposes and however good, they should not be confused with meanings, and if you followed this system to its logical conclusion you would end your life with Z, and still wondering what the meaning is! The key is to find meanings, try to find higher purposes along the way. Alas, much of life is mere entertainment,' Thay added with a wave of his hand. 'And with it ultimately being trifling and insignificant, it can be a source of frustration and unhappiness - if you let it be. But if you look at it another way Mr Alfi, its fruitlessness can become a liberation! We should enjoy life and love those around us, without being too wistful or sentimental about it. Desires for wealth, honour or fame are futile in the end, because they can make a man restless, when he could be contented.

'But...authenticity!' Thay continued dramatically. '*This* is the first thing we need to consider when we come here to the Mindgarten - and its attainment should be a constant reminder to ourselves. It is the foundation from where everything else flows. Who are you Mr Alfi? Who is the authentic you, *really?* It will be the basis for all your development! In your life so far, have you been the origin of your own actions or are you just rolling along, being led by your mind and what society expects? Are you living too much of your life by chance? I'm preaching questions to you Mr Alfi, *not* answers.'

He continued jollily. 'Sorry about that. It's difficult to know isn't it! Who are you? And we have another problem to consider. Yes, another problem!' Thay chuckled childishly at the thought. 'And what I like to call, *mind-body coalescing*. I talked about the mind and body earlier, but my thinking is that many of us might also be defining ourselves simply - by how we look. A simple propensity like that! The mind could mold itself you see, and be manipulated to partner with the physical image that we carry, even as simple as the type of face we have, and to a certain extent, what is expected of our behaviour in the outside world. A beautiful lady for example, may result in her mind becoming quite feminine, light or trivial, rather than shaping its outlook more seriously say, as if it were inside an anxious professor or bald little monk like me! Not to mention the brain being a physical organ of the body, and therefore manipulated by hormones and so on. So, to some extent, with this theory being possible, the mind is shaped, our behaviour can be shaped, at least partly, by our physical selves.

There are other outside influences too, like your environment and your interactions with the world. All these experiences affect our behaviour. Who would you be Mr Alfi? If you were born female or with a different skin colour, and in a different country? From this perspective would you be different? And if all the above is correct, that we're merely a collection of influences and experiences and who we are physically, then humans as we think of them; as self-contained and self-shaped individuals, *do not* exist!' Thay paused, as his thoughts were getting ahead of him. He then added more gently. 'Yet I prefer to believe in *essence*. Is there any *real essence* to you Mr Alfi? A soul? Independent of your surroundings, your body and its mind? And if there is such an essence, what about the mind that controls it?

Is it you? Or is your mind something else? And is it really your friend?'

Alfi nodded thoughtfully as Thay continued to speak.

'We must also not treat ourselves as if we're causally determined by outside things that happen around us, that we have no responsibility for. Instead, we must take ownership of our lives and engage in the process of self-becoming. Of self-making. Of flourishing. Our lives - and who we become - must be our life project!'

'Authentic?' asked Alfi. 'That might mean 'not fitting in? You could end up being a misfit.'

Thay laughed. 'To be the authentic you, will result in you living very comfortably within society. The key is, when you're faced with life choices, you have to assess whether these choices are actively what you want to do, and whether they are consistent with who you are, or who you want to be? And to do this, the first step is to discover your real essence. Whilst some may disagree. I believe that *essence precedes existence*, and not the other way round. Call it your soul if you will, handed down. It's our pure foundation. The real "Self" is harder to find than we think.'

'Is it selfish?' Alfi asked. 'Just to be yourself?'

'An authentic person does not have to be selfish,' replied Thay. 'In fact, authentic selves are often more compassionate. They've realised that they must move away from the ego of their mind, and instead enjoy caring for others. They try, as we all do here in the Mindgarten, to be understanding and compassionate.'

Thay stood up, went across the room and returned with a small dark glass jar filled with little oval white pills. He unscrewed its lid and with a small tong, carefully removed two of them, placing them on a little white saucer in front of him.

'Ok,' he said. 'One small lesson. Now we are here Mr Alfi! Just say I have kept these pills for you! Many believe that the goal of life is to find happiness. That all you have to do is find happiness - and all will be satisfactory, we will be contented. And they believe that happiness must be found internally. Within themselves. Within the 'I' the 'Me.' He held out the plate. 'You see these little pills?' he said. 'What would you say, if I told you that they were completely harmless to your health, and if you were to take just two of them, right now, that you will be happy for the rest of your life? Would you take them?'

Alfi hesitated. 'Well. No.'

'Precisely!' said Thay tapping the table with gusto. 'It would not be real! The goal of life should *not* be to find happiness Mr Alfi! The search for happiness in itself is inadequate and futile. Our aim should be to find purpose, real purpose - fulfilment...and as a consequence, a true happiness may, or even may not follow. And to find purpose the first step is to be authentic to who we really are! To find our real passions and where our life should be going. You must have seen those who have a passion for something? They have drive, hard work and enthusiasm - but are they happy? Not necessarily so. It's secondary and less important. We can find many meanings in life Mr Alfi simultaneously. They do not have to be high-minded. A woman who tenders her garden up here and crops for the limited seasons, or teaches others and expands her knowledge, these are all meanings. It is logic, that the more things a man or woman is interested in, the more chances they have for finding meaning - and in turn happiness or moreover; satisfaction with their life.'

Alfi interrupted. 'Brother Iblan said that busyness is a good thing.'

Thay chuckled in agreement. 'Ah, the idle rich,' he said. 'If you don't mind me saying, they can be very unhappy. I for one believe, that once you've lost the compulsion, the need to do anything, the necessity to work, then you've lost a major source of purpose - and potential happiness. Some may substitute a lack of purpose with pleasure - fill their time with pleasurable things - but it is never the same, it will never do. Some sense of progress, of moving forward, of development, is essential, at least for those with a modicum of intelligence. But there can be a lot of cynicism in the West I feel. This has come from a combination of perhaps comfort, together with a feeling of powerlessness in the wider society. Powerlessness makes people think that very little can be changed in the wider society and comfort makes this feeling just about tolerable.'

Thay walked to the window, drew open a curtain and peered outwards. 'Another source of *unhappiness* is the inability to be interested in anything unless it offers some profitable importance to the Self. This is a tunnel view. The world is a fascinating place Mr Alfi, with lots of fascinating subjects and people within it.' He turned to face Alfi squarely. 'One of the secrets to happiness is this: let your interests be as wide as possible and focus on these interests with zest and imagination. We get one chance to live - so why not make the most of it!'

'So,' began Alfi. 'How? How do I become authentic? How does anyone find their real self?'

'It takes time,' replied Thay. 'Think of a person as in layers. First there is the conscious layer, where we think, then the subconscious - a reservoir of previous thoughts, habits, character - and how we usually do things, this will inform the conscious. And then there is the third layer - the mind, which controls the conscious and the subconscious. But the mind can be manipulated and it can be manipulating. It is still *not you* Mr Alfi.'

Thay leaned forward secretively. 'But there is a fourth layer. Another existence, the essence I have been talking about, Some may call it the soul - and where the authentic you actually resides; sitting quietly behind the mind. Most people never reach or experience it, but if they do, their feelings become extraordinary. Even if it is for one fleeting moment. Your true self can also guide you. Like a kind, wise parent. Tempering your own mind and the messages, prejudices and feelings it possesses, and dealing more creatively with all the trials and all the opportunities that life places in your way. This is something it can do. It will go beyond what you consider as being human.

But the question is this. If you reach it, your true self, should you return from it - this enlightenment? This type of existence? As to stay within it, outside of your own mind as if a man in space, it is a darkness and is it not an oblivion? To step out of yourself - are we not more comfortable and safer even within the mind's own constraints? Oh, I don't know. This is something I feel *you* will have to toil with Mr Alfi. And sometimes, in finding your true essence, it will give you visions too! Insights into the past and into the future.' Thay stood up not saying a word - suggesting the end of the topic. Eventually he spoke more casually. 'Oh, all too much to talk about! Far too much on our first day.'

Alfi was exhausted in thought as Lobsang busily entered. 'It's time for dinner sir. Bastard.'

'Ah, time for some more bad food,' resigned Thay. 'You know there are a lot of activities here in the Mindgarten that you can learn from.' He paused and added sadly. 'But there will come a time when I will not want to speak anymore, or perhaps time will not allow it. When all that is to be taught or to be said by me, is done. Besides, there're far too many opinions in the world don't you think? They hang about us, as numerous as the leaves on the trees. Even the Buddha once said that opinions were things that "just bothered other people." He was right, they can also create a lot of anguish. Too much noise!' Thay leaned forward enquiringly. 'You will of course visit "The Orb" Mr Alfi?'

'The Orb?' Alfi asked.

'This will be your gateway Mr Alfi. To the fourth layer I have spoken about! The real you.'

# CHAPTER TWELVE

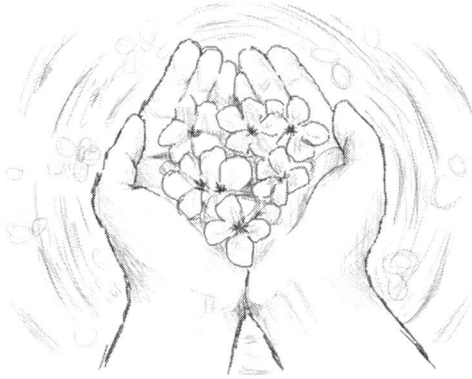

*Lily*

Lily planted the little flowers and sang a lullaby that hovered effortlessly from her lips. Her long pale blue dress hung in deep shadowed folds over her white baggy trousers as she knelt where, beside her on the grass, was a punnet of strawberries. Alfi heard her delicate voice and was drawn invisibly towards it - her face finally coming into view. The olive skin, the deepest brown, black oval eyes, her lips full, and her dark hair - shimmering and dressed back tightly, glimpses of her glittering white teeth - as she sang the words as if in a dream. For him, after such a long journey, this simple scene had all that was gentle of the world. It was peace. Why would there be the need for anything else? He stood captivated, as she pressed down the last seedlings and sat back to admire her display. Still humming her words, Alfi waited for the right moment. 'They're beautiful,' he said.

Startled, she ceased to sing, looked up, and in an instant her face softened as if seeing a friend. 'Yes. Yes, they're beautiful,' she said. It was as if she'd always known him. 'And forever will be, if you look after them. You have to give the flowers space, don't you? Not any two plants too close together. Like you have to give people space too, don't you think? A person with no space - who is crowded - too busy or too much controlled, or a person with too many things to do, how can they ever find happiness? The secret is to have less things to do, and to use time wisely.'

He was surprised how she took such a simple observation to such a degree. 'It's a shame they don't last forever,' he offered.

'But then new flowers come along and grow again,' she said wistfully. 'It's like everything. Just a cycle. You're new here, aren't you?'

'I've just arrived.'

She gave a smile. 'Then you must be tired then. I remember, when I first came here. By special jeep, not me driving of course and it took several days and I was tired too. But you have time here. We all have time here. Having time is a great comfort isn't it? She lifted the punnet. 'Would you like some?'

'Thank you. My name is Alfi.'

'And mine's Lily.'

'How long have you been here?' he asked.

'Oh, just around six weeks. Not long. I had trained as a nurse but now I teach the younger children here. English, mathematics, other things. I've just developed a story to help them. Help the younger children learn to read. "The Alphabet Wars" I call it. Want to hear it?' she asked playfully.

'Alphabet wars? Yes,' said Alfi.

She sat upright readily. 'Children have to learn how to construct words. So I've created a story where there's a kind of civil war within the alphabet. The vowels firstly want control - as they're a kind of an elite - and refuse to give over power to the consonants, the more common ones, although they're outnumbered by them. They have the belief that there should *not be* a democracy you see. The less informed, the ignorant, should not have the vote, as their leaders expose their ignorances with false proclamations that appeal to their prejudices. They see democracy - and handing over influence to the mob - as a poor compromise against a more informed type of governance. But in being led by the elite, this leads to another type of corruption, also taking advantage of the mob's ignorance, and so the consonants want to fight back. The H's? Well, they're marginalised, silenced, in so many words, and feel they're not listened to at all - like a second-class citizen. And so they move away from the others and form a small gorilla group and cause all kinds of trouble. The Zeds fight against the S's for recognition in some words, and so on - and before you know it - the whole alphabet falls apart. There is a civil war.'

'What happens?' asked Alfi.

'A silent world with no words. No letters coming together and no books. No more children's stories. The world becomes a very quiet and unhappy place. The letters do not even begin to understand each other, and they're separated - but they're fighting for nothing you see, and making misery for themselves. It's all based on fear and no understanding. So eventually, after many soldiers are killed, they decide that it's better to come together again. To talk to each other, and to listen to others. They make peace, and once more, little by little, we have words and books again. There's no more fighting. There are still differences of course, but like my flowers, they learn to give each other their own space, to live and to grow. Accept differences, rather than trying to make everyone the same.'

Alfi looked at her good-humouredly. 'I'd hate to see how you teach mathematics.'

She smiled at this remark, and just then her head pointed upwards to the bluest of skies. A vividly green parakeet swooped overhead. It dropped quickly, its wings holding back like arrows, and then it rose again, flapping with no real direction and catching the wind. Alfi watched her angelic face following its flight and eventually interrupted. 'Is this...?'

'Green bird.' she said. 'A parakeet.'

'Ah the green bird, smiled Alfi. 'I also met Frenchie the other night.'

'Oh, Frenchie,' she said faintly.

Alfi continued. 'And he told me something about the Green Bird, that I have a month where I go through the Green Bird period.'

'Something like that,' she replied. 'Then you can begin your new life, whether it is here or outside.'

'You seem to know a lot already. Do you like it here so far?'

'I feel safe,' she replied. 'I can be myself here. The trouble is outside, if you leave.' She pressed down some last flowers before continuing. 'Right, that's it. Pat them down, water them and let them grow to the best of their ability. It's no more complicated than that, is it? It's important, very important, to let them grow their own way towards the light, but guide them too.' She admired the plants again and turned to Alfi. 'Would you...would you like to go for a walk? To join me?'

They strolled between manicured gardens and across the lawns. The crisp, fragrant air carried perfumes from the flowerbeds and the smell of freshly hewn grass. Droplets of early morning dew hung on the blades like diamonds. They continued silently, there was no need to entertain one another, nor even the need to speak. Instead, simply to enjoy the other's company. They came to a neat pathway, one that curved its way into an emerald forest. Below the tall trees, the forest ground flickered with the morning shadows and the angled beams of the sunlight. Alfi saw a man and a woman sitting on a bench together. At last, he spoke to break the silence, a silence that could had comfortably lasted forever. 'Do people get married here? I guess with all the families, the children?'

'Some of them might had been already married,' replied Lily softly. 'Before they came to the Mindgarten, but they don't really encourage marriage here. Tying people within a contract it's not so romantic after all, is it? If people truly love each other - they just stay together. Contracts are for businesses where there is mistrust and implications, and it's more difficult to get out of.' She laughed a little at her own cynicism, but was disappointed if it sounded callous. Tenderly she supplemented. 'Here they practice Heart Palming.'

'Heart Palming?' Alfi asked.

She began to demonstrate and held her left palm outwards. 'This is hand-palming,' she said. 'A greeting that those who have entered love together, give to each other. You put your left arm out like this, with your hand, your palm facing upwards to the sky. And the other partner cups their palm gently inside it, on top of it, both palms facing upwards. Like this.' She demonstrated. 'They make this commitment to grow together. To support each other intimately. Just like this.' She began to almost sing her words. 'One palm inside the other.' There was a fluttering dance in her voice. 'And every time they meet. This is their gesture that shows this commitment to each other and to other people.' She then looked towards some moving trees and became regretful. Some of her hair caught a breeze, the locks falling over her forehead. She brushed them away thoughtfully. 'But one day, it might mean nothing.'

'What do you mean?' asked Alfi.

'Maybe,' she continued. 'One day, my dear beautiful husband, beautiful to everybody, the perfect man, might come here and take me away again. And I will have no choice but to go.'

Alfi was struck momentarily at the beginnings of a story he did not know about or understand. He wondered "what did she mean?" as they continued through the forest. It was becoming evident to him that conversations did not really need to form conclusions - to have an end. Instead, they could simply suspend themselves in mid-air, and disappear as quickly as they had come in a wafting breeze. The pathway meandered out of the trees again, where now they were surrounded by open fields and a sea of wild flowers.

In the distance was a row of neat looking, identical white marble houses. About ten of them. Each with their own portico with unusual pyramid shaped glass roofs, that sparkled in the sun. They walked further, until they reached a tall black onyx signpost staked in the ground at a point where several other pathways met. Written vertically on it, in gold shapely letters were the words "Philosophy Rooms" and on top there were carved wooden arrows pointing into different directions, not unlike those used in tourist look-out points that give the distances to far off places. "Existential Flowerbed 10 minutes. Doism Stream 25, Plato's Symposium of Roses 15, Epicurean Garden 20, Calliope fountain 30." Alfi was surprised by the sheer number of places.

They continued, where orderly looking, perfectly rectangular ponds, stretched out; one after the other, into the distance. Inside each, were exotic fish of every colour and description imaginable. These swam from one end of the pond to the other in easy relays, feeding amongst the reeds, tailing around rocks and communicating with one another. Up and down; living their lives completely and obliviously to the world above them - utterly ignorant that they were being watched from above. Alfi thought, was God like this?

Arranged everywhere were more flowerbeds. One profusion of colour after another; stretching around and between groups of houses and to the base of the far-off mountains. Brightly coloured birds darted about; some sat on branches admiring the scene below or tweeted happily to one another from behind the leaves.

After a while they turned to the very centre of the Mindgarten, a wider thoroughfare, where Lily pointed to the most gigantic of all the white marble buildings. At its front was a grand-looking baroque staircase that led to a richly decorated gold entrance. 'Over there,' she said. 'Is the Great Hall. You can come there at six each evening if you like. But you'll have to get your robe.'

'Robe?' enquired Alfi.

'We all dress the same for the Great Hall,' she smiled. 'You have to go to Miss Chan's to get it. A Chinese lady. She has a shop in Tabiki, the nearest village to here. You'll find it.'

'Oh. Ok.'

'And over there,' she pointed at another row of attractive white buildings. 'Over there, are the session buildings. They do all kinds of things there. Sessions to improve our mental health, a lot on philosophy. Maybe this is why they call this place the Mindgarten. We always feel we're growing, progressing spiritually and possessing more knowledge. A person must flourish you know, otherwise what are we doing?' They treaded further as Lily pointed to another line of white buildings. This time their designs were much simpler, small cubist architecture; not fancy in any way at all. 'They call these the "Stoic Rooms," she told him. 'Can you see what it says over that building - the sign?'

She smiled to herself, as he walked over to read the words. *'Disappointment has no place here. Expect the worse,'* he read.

She chuckled. 'People go there when they have too many expectations. They are the Stoics but you can study all kinds of other philosophy here in the other rooms.'

They walked on, where the land rose a little and it became wilder - not tended in any way at all. They were on an escarpment now, isolated from the rest of the Mindgarten that was behind them, and ahead in a stiffening breeze were the foreboding far-off mountains of the Himalaya. Along the crest of a short nearer hill and facing the mountains, was a row of small, white domed buildings, perfectly replicating one another. To Alfi they looked like igloos. 'What are these?' he asked.

'Oh those,' she replied as the wind grew stronger. 'We call them "Solitude Cleansing Pods." I've never been. But some believe you can find yourself through solitude.'

They trekked nearer for a closer look. Alfi reached the first one, where a small wooden sign was hung by a rusty chain swaying from its roof. There was an inscription on it. *"I've never found a companion that is so companionable, that is so much good company, as solitude."*

He thought back to his luscious rides on the motorcycle, as well as the old man alone, he'd met on the mountain. The inside of him agreed...how he never felt alone in his solitude. He walked to another dome to read. *"To be oneself, you have to know what oneself is."*

'All these pods have got their own names,' said Lily brightly. 'The pod up there...' she pointed. 'Is called *"Breathe,"* this one's called *"Self."*

They walked to the last pod of all, and read the words. *"To be or not to be, that is one hell of a question."* Alfi smiled at its humour and walked around it, studying the stonework with his hands. A small instruction was written into the wall. *"Please cleanse for the ability to think."*

'What do they mean by cleanse?' he asked Lily.

'Oh, I don't know,' she said.

'There seems to be no way in?' he felt the walls again, the brick-work, with his palms. 'No sign of a door or anything?' He stood at an apex that appeared to be an entrance - but there was still no door. 'It's strange. No way in?'

'What's this?' she noticed a half open wooden box under the shadows of the apex. Inside, was a carved ligneous object that looked like a sitting bird. 'In the wooden box?' she said. 'Look. It's a bird. An owl or something?' She studied it clinically. 'Maybe it could mean wisdom or something?'

'Yes,' Alfi half agreed, and pressed his hands against the walls again.

Instinctively, she reached up and removed the owl from the box, which triggered the sound of something turning. There was a low thud, followed by, what appeared to be, the sound of gears meshing. And that was it. The wall, where Alfi was leaning with both hands opened sharply and sent him falling into the pod. It closed again quickly after him, and he was gone!

A deep message rang out. *"Cleansing phase one"* and with that, the entire pod began to shake. Lily in desperation, put the owl to the floor, stretched out and held on to the walls. There was a strange hissing, and after a minute or two, it all stopped. Everything became quiet.

Timidly, she called. 'Are you alright? Are you alright in there? Can you get out?' There was a muffled reply paired with the sound of him tapping. A second recorded voice began.

*"Second phase cleaning to begin in one minute."*

She heard Alfi catching his breath. 'Now listen! Listen to me very carefully Lily,' he called. 'Put the owl back into the box.'

'What do you mean?' she asked.

Alfi cleared his throat from inside the pod and began to speak more clearly. 'I cannot make this instruction any simpler Lily. I want you to put the owl *inside the box.'*

Lily followed his instruction, picked up the owl and placed it carefully back. The sliding wall opened, and with a swish, Alfi was standing there: his dripping hair, shirt sodden and heavily waterlogged trousers. He looked comically pathetic.

'I guess that's what they mean by *Cleansing* Pod?' she said, but before Alfi could open his mouth, the wall closed again, and in a snap, there was another recorded message. *"Second phase cancelled. Beginning enema. One minute. Please align boots with foot pads. It is vital to face in the correct direction."*

Alfi called quickly from inside the pod. 'We now have, what I will call, a *situation*. Now listen carefully Lily. You listening?'

'Yes.'

'Where?' he asked pedantically. 'Where now, is the owl?'

'It's in the box,' she replied.

There was a silence. 'Ok. Let me think. Ok Lily, take the owl, as quickly as you can, *out of the box.'*

'Out of the box?'

'Yes, out of the box. Let's take a chance on this.'

She did this and the wall suddenly slid open again. This time Alfi took no chances and leapt out, falling clumsily into Lily's arms.

And that was it. This was the moment! As with all such moments, and with their faces close. That their eyes first caught the sight. They looked to one another - and they were lost. As if nothing around them existed. Not even the fields, or mountains, or the Himalaya that engulfed them. Time did not matter. And then, as quickly as it had come, within this beautiful place where they were almost one - it was gone again, and they were brought back to earth, for the mind to take over from the soul. And as they stood there, they hesitated and broke into a nervous laughter. Perhaps inside, they were still shivering from the place that they had been. And all the while, in the distance, Frenchie looked over at them. His heavy eyes, there seemed to be suspicion in them. Or was it the thought for something he had lost, or could never reach.

# CHAPTER THIRTEEN

## Sense or Sensibility

It was the next morning as Alfi stood on his wooden veranda leaving his new room and locking his door. 'So, the new guy, moved in next door?' a happy voice called out. He turned to see Lester, a short, chubby, mostly bald man, approaching the door next to his. Lester beamed with a smile, held out his hand and they both shook. 'I'm Lester, Lester Wannaburger,' he said.

Alfi was surprised by the name. 'Lester *Wannaburger*?'

'I know. I know,' Lester said shaking his head. 'Terrible name isn't it? My father had the family name changed after he opened a string of burger joints. His idea of marketing. Spent my youth flipping burgers and with a name like that, school as you can imagine, wasn't kind my friend. Funny thing was our original name was McDonald. Ironic isn't it? But after Green Bird it's names anew! I'm looking forward to it! A new start, a new life, and all that. And a new name...' Lester grinned openly and Alfi immediately liked him.

'I'm Alfi Singer, pleased to meet you.'

'So how are you finding it so far?' asked Lester brightly. 'I guess you're feeling your way round?'

'It seems beautiful here, the people are friendly,' replied Alfi.

'So it looks like you haven't met Frenchie yet?' Lester said, still with a bright grin.

'Oh him. I guess he's alright really. I guess getting to like him - you'd call it a slow burn.'

Lester raised his eyebrows. 'Yea, a slow burn. That's one way of putting it. The truth is, they say he doesn't like single men coming here very much. Very few...very few make it through Green Bird. The last three male singles? Well, they disappeared. Just nine days in. Not a trace. Last I heard, one of them was sitting on a beach somewhere in Goa. Almost crippled. Hatha yoga. The other two: still not found, probably up in the hills somewhere.'

'Really?' offered Alfi.

Lester looked outwards from the veranda where other Mindgarten residents were quietly going about their day and added. 'Life can give you some difficult turns my friend. But we'll be ok. What's four weeks anyway? Hey? Four weeks, then we're free. I've only been here a few days myself. Like you. Just breaking in! We're pretty much 'off the blocks' at the same time.' He placed his key into his room door but was having trouble turning it. 'This lock, been trouble ever-since I came here. Maybe it's the humidity?'

'You seem pretty settled in here already?' asked Alfi.

'Well. You know. I talk a lot,' replied Lester with a smile. 'Something I did with my old job. Door to door.... Sales. It's my bag. Getting along with people. I'd sell this and that, you know: just about anything to get by. In the old days it was the staples: curtain rails, household utensils, peelers that type of thing. But you try selling kitchen knives door to door - in the States - my friend! It isn't easy. Halloween was low season. So, I moved into encyclopedias, Britannica mainly, then the internet came along, and door to door selling... well, it was finished. People don't like people knocking on doors anymore. People stopped reading too. Technology! It can be your friend or it can be your foe. So, I used my experience of door-to-door. I became a doorman at an upmarket hotel for a while. I liked that. Meeting people. Good people, with class, but then technology caught up with me again. Yes, always on my tail. They installed automatic doors. Now I'm forty-three years old and life seems to be passing me by. You know, every time I see a door opening automatically it still upsets me. Kinda rubs it in. Maybe, I'm washed up? Forty-three years old and possibly, with just thirty good summers left ahead of me - before they start putting a shawl over my knees. Just thirty summers! It's not much is it? And what if we get bad weather?' Lester stopped himself, realising he was talking too much, and asked. 'So, um? What about you?'

'I've been in Nepal a little while,' said Alfi. 'I was a journalist. And one, complicated thing led to another and so I find myself here. A long story. I'll go into it another time.'

'Another time,' repeated Lester agreeably and tapped a wooden rail surrounding the veranda with gusto. 'Everybody's got a long story to tell my friend. And we've a lot of time to tell it. Me? I can tell you. I first came to India before Nepal - but it wasn't under good circumstances. My wife, well, back in the States - we got married six years before. We lived in a town - a small town, where people did a lot of shopping and still pointed at airplanes.

She got to know me - more personally of course. You know, the way people do when they move in together. It's different, the veneer wears off. I like to call it *pants on the radiator* syndrome. But I was good around the house. I was helpful, but she didn't see it that way. And did what any self-respecting, honest, intelligent, woman would do. She left me. Well, asked *me* to leave. Not that I blame her mind you. Hate to be self-deprecating and all that, but I thought it was a measure of the intelligence of the woman.

She was always thinking forward you see. She could see the road ahead my friend...and she didn't like it. She was the type of girl who knew what she wanted to get, rather than what she wanted to give - she's probably on her second divorce by now. People never learn do they? Before that, before she asked me, well, told me to leave, she became embittered - and quite spiteful of course. Many women do. That's the way the cookie crumbles. Funny, isn't it?

She had wanted kids. Kids! Well, maybe earlier, that was possible. But I've always thought kids are like farts. You put up with your own, just about - but you don't like other people's. Luckily, we didn't have any anyway. That's what relationships can do to some people. One extreme to the other. They love ya. Then they hate ya. Funny isn't it - that it can swing that way? She took the house, the car, even the dog, Sandy.' At last, Lester then paused, and looking out from the veranda, he became quite wistful over some recollection he was having, eventually he continued. 'You know, when I look back, at the good times we had together. And there *were* good times, you know, I can tell you. I can still see her eyes. You know, the way she sometimes looked at me. It's funny, isn't it? The little things you remember. It's never the big things. Just the little things. Walks in the park, even in the rain; the happiness, the sheer simple joy...letting her off the lead.

Then my friend. I figured I'd follow a childhood dream, to see something new of the world and come to India - that's one of the advantages about having nothing: you've got nothing to lose. It gives you a freedom I suppose. Besides, being a developing country, I figured they'd have fewer automatic doors. Maybe there would be an opening? You know, I've always thought, in the modern age, it's best to stay just behind the curve. I was hoping to come out here and find myself. Quite a cliché, isn't it? Finding yourself. When in reality there's nothing to find? At best, all we can hope for is some kind of cure, some direction, I suppose. After this - it's Lourdes.'

'That's one story,' remarked Alfi sympathetically.

Lester fiddled with his key in the door again. 'Ok I gotta go. But listen. This is important. This Frenchie guy, I think he's a kind of filtering system. My strategy, the best strategy for whatever its worth, is not to let him know that he's breaking you down. It will only make things worse. He's only got a month. Just one month to bring us to our knees, and then we're free. So don't give anything away. Don't show any sign of weakness! That kind of guy only needs a hint of it, and he digs in. You know what I mean? We just have to get through this. Just one month. Stay positive. Focused.' Lester eventually turned the key and began pushing at his door. 'Show him we're strong,' he said. 'And that we can stand on our own two feet. We're going to work together my friend!' He pushed the door and tripped into his room.

❀ ❀ ❀

Miss Chan called out in her *Chinglish*. 'I'll need you to take your down pants and show me your penis!'

Alfi stood in her store in the village of Tabiki - just outside the Mindgarten. Village was an optimistic word for Tabiki. In fact, hers was the only building along a dust-track, beyond which was nothing - except a large empty barn down the road beside a little flowing stream.

She looked up at him expectantly - her short, middle-aged rotund figure, kindly Chinese features and tied back, black shining hair with red and blue ribbons. In the background was her elderly, and also short, husband Belan, who was dressed impeccably, very much like an English tailor, in dark pleated trousers, a pressed white shirt, bright bow tie and braces. Draped around his neck was a faded measuring tape with several numbers missing, rubbed out, no doubt, by his thumbs over the years, but still waiting for action. Miss Chan stared into Alfi's baffled eyes.

'What? Sorry?' said Alfi. 'I, um.'

She gave an infectious giggle. 'It is Chinese tailoring expression!

Don't worry. A mechanic needs to see under bonnet! You no understand yolk?'

Alfi looked at her blankly.

'Ah foreigners,' she mocked, waving her hand before adding.
'Follow me.' She broke into more laughter and led him along a
corridor with Belan trailing quickly behind. Reaching a fitting room,
she dramatically yanked open a curtain and yelled out. 'Belan!'

'Yes Angel,' came the reply, as her husband came trotting forward
and equally dramatically whisked his measuring tape from around his
shoulders as if he was about to lasso something.

Miss Chan studied Belan with some exasperation - the way a
parent would to an unruly child. She removed a pad and pencil from
her apron pocket, which was Belan's cue. He began measuring Alfi's
limbs and calling out dimensions as she quickly jotted down the
details.

Minutes later, Alfi found himself in muted disappointment, as
he faced a mirror wearing a garishly multi-coloured tunic with Miss
Chan smiling admiringly at his reflection. She reached forward and
tugged a seam. 'We need 'peece' off here. Just little peece.'

Alfi plucked up courage. 'Is the colour quite right?'

'Oh. Don't worry. Don't worry about colour,' replied Miss Chan
reassuringly. 'This just for sizing. Come. Come. Come to "front of
house." We need fabric! We need colour!' She yelled flamboyantly as
she marched Alfi back along the corridor. 'Belan!'

'Coming Angel,' came the trotting reply.

They entered the main shop area again, where Miss Chan had
positioned herself behind her counter. Behind her, were countless
shelves of neatly packed material in clear plastic, stacked all the way
up to a twenty-foot ceiling. In front of this was an old-fashioned, tall
wooden ladder that could move sideways on rollers.

She allowed Alfi to take it all in, she was proud of her stock. 'I
know everything about Mindgarten,' she said. 'I was here at the very

beginning. Very beginning.' She smiled in recollection. 'I can remember when Thay first come here, with beautiful Alexandria, the Russian lady. She was a quiet, gentle, listening woman. Not like the ones that talk too much today. It was such a pity. A great pity. She always had a smile on her face, Alexandria.'

'She did,' Belan recalled fondly.

Miss Chan continued. 'She had boyfriend when she first came - but soon after they arrived - he expired. Thay was very young at the time. But he was also the eldest son of rich family. So when his own father expired, he inherited most of his father's money to buy this land. It was a very nice, exciting time. After some years, Thay's much younger brother came back here. I think, he was a half-brother from different mother.' She sighed. 'Such are the affairs of Nepalese marriages! Thay's young brother was a very angry man because he did not get any money. I never liked him - he' jealous. And so, the young brother moved away again. So Thay stayed here with Alexandria and built the Mindgarten. But some years later Alexandria, who became very holy, she became a nun, she also expired. It was a terrible time - so many people loved her. So Thay just continued alone. Alexandria's ashes you know, are above the Mindgarten, deep in high forest, called 'Nine Muse Gompa.' You should go there one day. Very peaceful, but it is hidden and hard to find.' Miss Chan hesitated, her mind resting in some sadness. She brought her thoughts back to the task at hand, and turned to her husband. 'He needs better fabric.'

'Yes Angel,' Belan replied.

A large dog dashed out and dived towards Alfi. 'Oh, this is Brandy,' she called out and came from behind her counter to ruffle the dog's neck. 'Don't be afraid. Don't be afraid. If he sniffs your rear, it is a sign of respect! This is how dogs greet each other you know - even in China. Each ass is different. Looks like he likes yours!' She yelled to the dog. 'Brandy - go to room! Go to room! Leave ass alone!' With that, the dog leapt towards the door of a laundry room, cleverly pressed the handle open with a paw and disappeared still wagging his tale. 'He always sleeps in laundry room,' Miss Chan smiled. 'For him nice and warm. Now, what colour you wan'?'

'Um,' said Alfi looking up at a bewildering array of choices stacked neatly upon each other and, in a flash, Belan had already climbed half way up the ladder and was busily rummaging through the wrappers.

Miss Chan shook her head. 'In former life he' monkey.'

Belan called down from the steps in crisp English pronunciation. 'Would sir prefer darker shades? We will be entering the autumn months soon you know, and one should not appear out-of-step with the seasons.'

Suddenly, with a clang, he missed a step and slipped outwards as a right arm and leg swung out like a pendulum. He regained his position quickly back to the ladder. 'Balan!' Miss Chan yelled out. 'He always doing this! Hold both hands Belan! Both hands!'

'Yes Angel,' came the feeble reply. He then asked calmly, as he came down one step at a time with a parcel of fabric under his arm. 'Can I ask, for the trousers, if sir dresses to the left, or to the right?'

'How many times I tell you! Hold, then reach. Hold, then reach. Never stretch with both hands!'

Alfi interrupted. 'I really don't mind climbing up there myself. I can get the fabric.'

Miss Chan ignored this remark, and carefully watched Belan's position.

'Thank you Angel,' Belan said. 'I do apologise sir. A lapse of concentration, something, sadly more common these days...in my golden years. But quite frankly, sometimes I wonder what is "golden" about them? Often, I climb the ladder and wonder what I came up for. It plays havoc with my knees.' Belan came down shakily, sighing with relief as he finally returned to earth.

He placed the sample of cloth in its plastic wrapper on the

counter, bent down to retrieve a yak tail from beneath, and briskly brushed away some dust with it theatrically, as if this was the upmost sign of professionalism. 'Brown,' he said with pride. 'Good quality brown. You cannot beat it.' He gave it a few more noisy whacks with the Yak tail. 'Good quality.'

'Yes,' said Alfi. 'I need it for the Great Hall.'

Belan stopped midsentence, and looked with some disappointment. 'The Great Hall?'

'Yes,' replied Alfi.

'You need it for the Great Hall?' he questioned again, shaking his head and walking back to the base of the ladder. Leaning against it with all his small might, the wheels began to creak as the ladder rolled sideways.

'I really don't mind going up' offered Alfi. 'If you could tell me where to look.' This was again ignored.

Belan puffed. 'The Great Hall. Sir will be needing white! White, white, white.'

Miss Chan observed with a degree of pleasure. 'Belan, he very good tailor,' and lowered her voice. 'He has pride. He well-polish'. Trained in England you know.'

They watched trepidatiously as Belan climbed the ladder and rummaged through the plastic wrappers again. Alfi thought then, of the bond between Miss Chan and Belan. Behind them there was a photograph of a pink lotus blossom on the wall - a flower that represented purity in the East, rising in all its beauty, from muddy or murky waters.

'White, white, white, white...' Belan muttered.

They had, Alfi considered, become accustomed to each other, in such a way that only time, years of habit, of familiarity could bring. Miss Chan's countenance of bridled affection, broke frequently into a pride and admiration, caring deeply, sometimes in a show of amusement. Belan meanwhile, his disposition low in moderation of the senses, with an exceptional heart and a show of warmth, cherished and depended on her so. They were the perfect combination. Was then, devotion indifferent to love? Were they two parts of the same thing - or would the kind of love change? Had there been any initial fire of it, in those first timid moments in the fresh of their beginning? Or did this matter at all? Was theirs the action of *sense or sensibility* - or a coming together, a union of the two? Marriage was after all, an old-fashioned and practical institution.

Belan over-reached and she bawled. 'Belan, I told you! No reaching, no reaching. Stop it. Go up, one step higher.'

'Thank you Angel,' he slipped his footing again. 'I've always thought white a poor choice for the Great Hall,' he said to himself as he upped one more step, reached and added. 'At my age - it's more beige you know.' He carried on the conversation with himself as he climbed. 'You cannot go wrong with beige. They say in England, that when a large tribe of elders are coming, it is indeed like "a sea of beige." Quite impressive really. And I should like to see it one day.' Belan selected some fabric and began his descent.

'I want you to come down very, very, 'lowly. Very 'lowly.' Miss Chan instructed.

'How are my feet?' asked Belan.

Miss Chan studied him as he moved. 'Left down, left down. That's it. One step, now right step down, 'lowly. 'Lowly as you can. Now, now, 'lowly.'

Belan eventually reached the ground. 'Here you are sir,' he said patting a plastic parcel with pleasure. 'White, no beige!'

# CHAPTER FOURTEEN

## Eudaimonia
### To live well and to flourish

With its dramatic domed roof, colonnades and gold entrance the Great Hall stood magnificently in the very centre of the Mindgarten. Surprisingly, inside it was the very antitheses of grandiloquent; simply decorated with polished marble floors and plain walls that reached up to a tall vaulted ceiling. From this, a spectacular silver chandelier hung from a singular thick silver chain. It shone light over the packed congregation below who sat on simple white chairs. In front was a stage with a small, amateur looking, cinematic screen on it. The crowd's mood was jovial, in a hum of excited conversations, so much so, that Alfi felt a palpable bounce to it as he sat down with Lester.

The hall gradually ushered down to silence as Thay appeared from a side of the stage. He clutched his Tingsha in both hands - the little Tibetan symbols which gave him so much comfort. Once chimed, they would punctuate his mind to lead him through a gateway into meditation and knowledge. His small figure came to rest on a little wooden chair to the right of the screen. He looked down to his feet without saying a word as the silver canvas flickered and a video began to play which surprised his audience. In it, a confident, middle aged American celebrity - within his own auditorium somewhere in America, possibly California - pontificated to his own awestruck crowd.

'People often ask, what is the secret of my success?' the celebrity said. 'I knew, that if I worked hard, and never gave up, never gave up on my dream, step by step I would get there. I believed in myself. No one was going to stop me. And yes, there were many doubters along the way! But you know what? I never gave up on my dream! I kept climbing that mountain.' The celebrity paused, his square jaw facing his audience evangelically - as he was being vindicated. Alfi considered, was the character ridiculous? What culture and value system had he inherited? For this figure on the screen seemed trapped within himself, with no way to escape, or no exit to find bliss. The celebrity continued. 'You just need to set your goals, work hard and go for it. You need to be strong, to bring to the universe your unique talents, your abilities, and you can change the world. Don't listen to anybody else, just follow your dream.' The crowd, in the film at least, erupted into a rhapsody of applause, yelps and cheers, for he'd given them hope and an affirmation - that they were on the right track. His celebrity and his success, had presented absolute proof, as he gazed at his admirers.

Thay's head dropped. The film ended and the screen turned black. He touched the symbols gently together; their beautiful chime, stood up and rested them on his chair as the Great Hall stayed silent. 'What is success?' he asked with a pause. 'And why is there a need to do anything? Anything at all? What do we all need to achieve? What is it about the human condition that conjures up the need for the achievement, especially if it is for the fruitlessness of impressing others? The successful ones tell us, but do they offer logic? They tell you to follow your dreams but the truth is, that there were a thousand others; just like him, with equal or better talents. But they never made it, even though they worked just as hard, or even harder. The ego. His ego, with his highfalutin language, will not account for luck. This is logic...and he is just an entertainer. The least important, yet best paid, of life's talents.'

Thay giggled, and there was a timorous murmur of agreement as he continued. 'Do not listen to people who tell you to "follow your dreams and never give up and you will be successful." Try of course, you may be lucky as he was, but give it a limited time and if it does not work, try something else. Otherwise, your life will be wasted chasing something that cannot be achieved. A fool is it, who does the same thing repeatedly and expects a different result. The problem here is *hope*. There are two kinds of hope. There is good hope and there is bad hope. A good hope can be used to motivate, to action things - to bring about change, a change in the circumstances. But a *bad* hope is one used incorrectly, to wait, or try misguidedly, or to do nothing, to lead to inertia. This is the wrong path.'

Thay eyed his audience carefully. 'Now, if you're lucky in this world, there's a lot of good work that you can do. And remember, that there are many people who do not have the opportunity to do interesting work. Their work is full of toil, with no opportunity for change or no way to escape, or very boring too. But if you have the chance to choose your work, good work needs two things. It must be enjoyable, at least to a certain extent, and there must be the feeling that the outcome of your effort has some importance to the world. That the outcome is tangible. If you have these two things, then you have good work.'

He hesitated, sizing his audience somewhat and walked wearily to the centre of the stage. 'Mm,' he said, surveying a sea of faces. 'Now for a moment, let us consider two negative emotions...jealously and envy. You should *not* look at what others have, but what *you* have. What you do with *your* life. Do not compare with others. It is fruitless. And no one has the perfect life permanently - however they may seem.'

There were mutters of agreement across the hall as his gentle voice continued. 'Now...competition. Only be competitive to a limited point. It does have its uses you know! But *all* your life - to be competitive - this only leads to fretting, worry or even aggression and conflict. There'll always be someone better than you. We all know that. Also, do not seek recognition as a reward for your life. For recognition is short lived. How many people do you remember from a hundred years ago? Or even five years ago? And don't expect others to take as much interest in you, as you take in yourself!'

The audience laughed a little at this, and Thay chuckled along with them. 'Now, back, back to work,' he continued. 'Some people are defined by their work, that's ok to a point, if their occupation is their passion. But for most people their work might be only fairly fulfilling, and for money of course. Let us be honest, it is a compromise. So, if your occupation is not your passion - then make the most of it and be creative! Try to make it at least agreeable. In work - as in life - do your best and then try not worry about it. Generally, after doing our best, we must resign ourselves to fate. Once you rise above the notion of worry this will be a recipe for success! Do not allow your mind to become trivial...or cynical.

So, if we work in something that is comfortable and to some extent challenging, we can at least obtain some sense of fulfilment. And money? You know it can be a great source of happiness! Forget what the ascetics say! It can create comfort, security and peace of mind. And with a sufficient surplus of it – it can create freedom. It can help others too, and you can have a lot of enjoyment spending it!

But too much money can lead you astray, if you let it. Do not be obsessed with getting it.'

There was an inkling of glee about Thay's face, as he often enjoyed the surprise within an audience when, in being a monk and an assumed ascetic, he spoke about the joys of spending money.

'You must create as much autonomy in your life as possible,' he continued. 'And the best way to do this - is to be different. Do not copy, do not be derivative. Be agreeable but different. To fulfil your potential as an individual you must be inventive with yourself!'

Someone in the crowd called out in agreement as Thay continued.

'Hobbies, fads and pleasurable things will not be a source of lasting fulfilment, but they'll give you a temporary respite from which you can bring joy and energy into your life. So enjoy these things - but a continuity of purpose and achievement in weekly life, is an essential ingredient for happiness. This all takes effort, self-introspection and the ability to look forwards.'

Thay lent forward and asked rhetorically. 'So, what are the fundamentals of happiness?' The fundamentals of happiness are simple. They rely on a friendly and sincere interest in people and the world around you. Take a *genuine* interest in other people and not just on the stimulus they can provide. Your feelings must be authentic and not fixed to the value systems of others or the tribe around you. And for fulfilment, you must take ownership of your life, develop it, and develop yourself in such a way, in any way you can, otherwise your life will be wasted. But remember this. Do not have too strong an ego. For it will become a prison from which you cannot escape!'

The congregation gave a light flutter of applause.

Thay coughed, caught his breath and spoke quietly. 'Happiness, contentment, depends upon external circumstances and your attitude to them. And similarly, being too reliant on external circumstances, particularly on those that you have little control over for your happiness, will increase stress and anxiety.

Consider this; two men can walk up a muddy path - one can dislike it and the other can find much enjoyment in it. One might see his feet getting caught in the mud, the other: his thoughts of rain and nature, or even the joy that he does not need to walk the same muddy path tomorrow! The walk remains the same, it is about their attitude to the path. *The mind is the source of all experience, and by changing the direction of the mind, we can change the quality of what we experience.*

The 'I', what we think of as ourselves, is constantly changing too. Look in the mirror and you'll see lines and wrinkles that were not there yesterday. You might wear spectacles that you didn't wear before, or have a different hair colour, or no hair at all! And so, your inner perceptions are also changing, you are not the person you were before, and never will be. Now look at this as an opportunity to change how you view the world and those around you - without being stuck into old patterns of thinking and old habits. This will give you far more opportunities to explore life in the future and to have new experiences.

In a personal matter, in your relationship with someone else too, you might say *"Oh, he always does this, or she always does that,"* but you can change your own perception and reaction to that person, and therefore change the outside flow and eventually the circumstances.

Health, love, successful work and respect from the herd, are some of the essential ingredients for fulfilment and if you want; you can call this happiness. So direct your passions outwards, not inwards. You cannot always be happy and fulfilled, that is impossible. It is the condition of life. But your attitude, your internal thinking is something you can change, to cope with it. You need to discipline your ego and calm your mind.'

'Hurrah!' called out the crowd.

'Fear, envy, a sense of sin, or self-pity or self-admiration, all lead to *no* genuine interest in the outside world, but only on how it may serve, injure or fail you: how it may feed, or not feed the ego. This is a recipe for *unhappiness.*'

'Yes,' some voices called out.

'Happy people live objectively not subjectively. The happy person resigns themself, where possible and with good humour, to the things he cannot change. He or she, has wide interests and a friendliness that wins affection and interest from others. Their life work spurs them on, with a sense of satisfaction and progress.'

The audience cheered again.

'Do not wait for opportunities to unfold. You must make opportunities unfold for yourself through your actions. Becoming who you are from your virtues, skills and passions. This is your life project.

But what are life goals? Are they futile or misguided, are we not just like *all* other living creatures after all? This is something you must wrestle with. Ultimately what is worth doing and what is not, is something that must be constantly decided. We can always stop - and just *be*, like all other living creatures. Do not let the mind, with its wild notions, wants, incantations and desires, conquer you.

And remember, to be very careful with desire for it can turn against you! If you desire something terribly and you cannot satisfy that desire: then give it up! Let it go. It's easier to extinguish the desire, like blowing out a candle than trying to follow a desire that you cannot fulfil, or one that demands too many sacrifices. When desires are accomplished, their appeal becomes diminished anyway. They turn out to be much less important than they started out to be. And with people, remember most of all...that a person should *not* be an object of desire, but an object of your compassion.'

Thay settled back resignedly onto his simple wooden chair and wafted a hand across his face. 'I am getting old now - and tired,' he said, and smiled warmly to his audience. 'The ancient Hindus believed that for a happy, contented life, you should have three things; virtue, success and pleasure, in what measure I do not know, but I would also suggest kindness within all these three things. Kindness occurs quite naturally in virtue, but it can be ever-present in success and pleasure too! One rarely sees those who are kind to be unhappy. A *happy* life is the same as a *good* life. Fashion your life as a garland of beautiful deeds.'

'Hurrah. Hurrah!' the audience chanted - and Thay's words were over.

He bowed his head, and Lobsang walked onto centre stage and waved an arm. 'Sod off!' he shouted, and the audience broke into a chorus of laughter - and with that, Thay had disappeared behind the screen.

❋ ❋ ❋

'Well, that was something!' Lester said, as he and Alfi walked happily down the steps of the perron and out of the Great Hall.

'Yep, it really was,' replied Alfi, he was still a little lost in thoughts.

The throng of Mindgarten residents brushed by them. There was a warm, slightly euphoric friendliness in the air, as the people spread across the main square and treaded along the different pathways, around the gardens and away, into the lowering light and into the direction of their homes. Eventually the crowds became diluted - just figures dotted about here and there.

Lester noticed a woman in the distance. Like everyone else that evening, she was wearing a white tunic that flowed elegantly around her. She glanced back at him. Her long, thick auburn hair and attractive hazel eyes; she turned away, then to him again; her graceful female figure. 'Oh,' said Lester. 'Was that...a look or a stare?'

'What?' Alfi replied. 'What do you mean?'

'The woman. The woman over there. Was she...looking at me, or was she...*looking* at me? And what kind of look? It's the laws of attraction my friend. Tis a pity I don't have the courage. And that we all place so much emphasis on face-value, isn't it? How we look. Well, for me anyway. What do we *really* want hey? If looks are so important?' Lester kicked up some dust and was a little frustrated, but it wasn't in his nature to be angry. He spoke again. 'Yes, it's the laws of attraction my friend. There's a big difference between a look and a stare - I can tell you. A stare is a lot longer than a look, and a look is just a notch up from a glance. These things, these subtle things, really matter, they make a difference. Although in truth, a stare, at me, in my case anyway...is not always positive.'

Alfi giggled. 'So you're looking for someone, huh?'

'Aren't we all Alfi?' Lester watched solemnly as the woman began to disappear, soon to be out of view. 'I'm like anybody else,' he continued. 'I just want to be with someone. I just want to share my... empty life.' He scratched his head and added flippantly. 'Maybe it was just a glance anyway? People glance all the time.'

'There's only one way to find out,' offered Alfi.

'Nah. I'm giving up rejection for lent,' Lester sighed. 'But you know what? Out there...there are a lot of women, a lot of women they say, who secretly go for the short, chubby, bald type - with little or no life prospects. We're less likely to stray you see. As we're afraid we won't find anybody else to take us in. We're loyal. And that kind of loyalty attracts a lot of people. It's rare. You can't bottle it my friend. It means something.'

'It's a point,' said Alfi.

'The problem is,' continued Lester. 'Do I really want to go out with someone who's desperate enough, to want go out with me? It's a *"Catch 22"* my friend. All the women I *really* want - are unobtainable. Life, love, is just one big compromise I suppose.'

'By the way,' Alfi interrupted brightly. 'They've got this thing going on tomorrow night, I saw it advertised in Cicero Flowerbed 9. It might interest you. It's called "*A Soul in the Dark.*" Apparently, you go in. To a big dark room and just talk to people. It's pitch black in there, so nobody knows what the other looks like. I guess that kind of thing might attract a lot of single people.'

'Really?' said Lester enthusiastically. 'Cicero Flowerbed 9? Now a gaze? That would really be something.'

# CHAPTER FIFTEEN

*Self*

Foxglove stood on the lawn surveying the gang in front of him. There was a hint of disappointment in his eyes as he looked at Lester on the grass. In fact, he had a hint of disappointment as he looked at all of them, sitting there that morning; Alfi and the two others - an elderly woman called Agatha and a serious looking Sikh man called Ramesh who looked like he wanted to kill someone.

Foxglove's robe was more stylish than most. It was drawn in at the waist, by means of a false diamond studded belt that blinked occasionally in the sunshine. He wore matching sets of glittery silver bangles that jangled all the way up both arms, and elaborate silver rings on all his fingers including his thumbs, topped off with multi-coloured fingernails.

'Good morning everyone,' he said in an effeminate, affected English accent. 'Ladies and gentlemen. Boys and girls,' as the group looked between them for any sign of youth, of which there wasn't any.

Foxglove massaged his smooth chin, over-dramatising a pause for thought. 'I'd like to begin today, by talking about the *chakras*,' he said. 'Opening your chakras...okay? Chakras. Oh...chakras, chakras, chakras...This will aid spiritual growth and most of all balance.'

This introduction left the group fidgety, until Agatha looked up from her folded knees and uttered in a tired, croaking voice, 'Balance?'

'Yes balance,' replied Foxglove defensively as Ramesh held up a hand to ask something which was ignored. 'But first,' Foxglove said, raising a forefinger. 'Let's talk about the breath. The breath everybody. And why do you think, we need to concentrate on the breath?'

The group looked to each for answers before Agatha spoke again. 'To stay alive, to breathe?'

Giving her a displeased look, Foxglove pirouetted gayly to the others. 'Anyone else?'

Lester called out meekly. 'To relax?'

Foxglove looked at the group. 'In a way, I suppose. You're on the right lines. The right vibe.'

'Vibe?' questioned Ramesh unashamedly.

'Yes. Vibe!' Foxglove snapped, and swept back his long wavy hair and flicked back his head. 'Anything more?' The group fell silent feeling they'd reached their limit, until Foxglove spoke again. 'The breath is connected intimately with our mind, and breathes differently - based on our thoughts. When we're excited, when we are anxious, when are depressed, when we are exasperated...'

'That's me,' interrupted Agatha.

Foxglove fluttered his eyelashes. 'When we breath quickly, shallowly, these are not good breaths; they are bad breaths.' Lester looked to Ramesh. 'And all your feelings, affect your breathing in a different way. We breath differently when our mind is in a different condition. So, we can turn everything the other way round, and let our breath control our mind. If we breathe calmly, our mind will become calm and so on.'

'Makes sense to me!' said Lester cheerfully as Alfi nodded.

'Also,' Foxglove continued. 'Also, we can only breathe now, and in the present, we cannot breathe in the past or in the future, and so by concentrating on the breath we are bringing our mind to the present. You will not worry about the past, or the future.'

With that, Foxglove stretched his arms upwards high into the air, in a kind of proclamation. 'Now, chakras,' he said in the breeze. 'If you sit on the floor concentrating on the breath - in the meditative position - your chakras may open. There are seven chakras you know.'

Lester interrupted shyly. 'Do you mind if I ask...'

'What?' said Foxglove brusquely.

'What exactly *is* a Chakra?'

Foxglove put his arms down. 'An energy flow.'

'Thanks,' said Lester.

Ramesh butted in. 'How long do we have to sit for the chakras to open? Will it be long? On account of my knees.'

'Thank you for reaching out with the question,' said Foxglove.

'Reaching out?' Questioned Agatha.

Foxglove continued melodramatically. 'Chakras cannot be set by time.'

'Oh,' replied Agatha disappointed.

'About ten minutes,' added Foxglove matter-of-factly. 'Give or take.' With that, he seemed to notice something invisible hovering above Lester's head and trotted up to him. Bending down, and grasping Lester by both shoulders, Foxglove then started a whining chant - that sounded like a feline calling from a surprisingly narrow drainpipe. The sound, after thirty seconds or so, mercifully stopped, as he considered Lester carefully with wide eyes. 'I see a lot of tension,' he said. 'Tension in your eyes, your shoulders and tension in your mind. Your spirit. Now tell me, what time do you bathe?'

'What?' asked Lester gingerly.

'Cleanse? Clean your orifices?'

Lester looked to the others uncomfortably.

'Orifices?' asked Ramesh, a question that was again ignored.

'Well,' replied Lester. 'Usually in the morning.'

'Yes,' said Foxglove. 'More...'

'And later. At night. Night time.'

'Avoid full moons,' Foxglove instructed.

Lester replied meekly. 'Full moons? How? How...how do I avoid full moons?'

'Stay indoors if you can, change latitude on a full moon night every two hours, just to keep ahead of it. Keep moving the position of your bed all night, and never, ever, wash under it - a full moon that is. Under any circumstances. You could become agitated, especially around the tail bone. The location of my favourite chakra by the way. It's such a shame we have to sit on it.'

'Ok. Gotcha. Full moons, keep moving,' agreed Lester, eager to end the topic.

Foxglove shook his head. 'And your chakras. I'm sad to say... they're clearly misaligned. So misaligned! Tell me, do you walk straight?'

'Yes,' replied Lester.

'Straight as a dye!' supported Alfi.

Foxglove was baffled. 'Mm.'

Lester added. 'Can we move on? Do you mind?'

'We just have to hope,' offered Foxglove and he tilted his head backwards, towards the sky again. 'Now,' he called out. 'The Universe. Ah, the Universe! It's a big place. Isn't it? Lot of space up there. But there are some people you know, who believe that our universe is indeed miniscule. And, even inside our world there are many other, smaller universes, like protons and neutrons, orbiting around a nucleus of an atom. Coincidence, isn't it? It's just a matter of size. I had a dream once, that our universe was inside the testicle of a giant.'

'Could be worse,' Alfi whispered.

Foxglove closed his eyes, breathed in audibly and raised his hands slowly for them all to stand, like one would to a magic carpet.

'Please stand. Arise!' he announced grandly.

'He led them on a long walk, so far off, that it took them to the very edge of the Mindgarten. The wind rose and began to sound, where ahead were only tall, wild swaying fields, taller than any man, and a wilderness that disappeared to the far-off mountains. Foxglove pointed to a narrow track that cut its way through high bronze grass. They followed silently in single file, as the path sloped downwards. Then gradually it rose up again, where ahead Alfi could make out something shinning in the distance. The tip of something - it looked like the summit of a dome, that blinked to him like a jewel.

Closer, and as the track descended again, it began to appear. A perfect and enormous sphere, three hundred feet into the air and presenting itself like a silver moon that had descended to earth. Indeed, to Alfi, and to all of them who stood there that morning, it could had been from another planet. Around its surface, were perfect and symmetrical octagonal indentations, as the whole structure shimmered in the sunlight. Foxglove sensed their awe. 'Here it is,' he said, looking up with a grand pause. 'Majestic, isn't it? 'The Orb. A very special place and unique to the Mindgarten!'

They continued forward, dropping down to a flat and surprisingly neatly cut field. A granite pathway had been laid that stretched all the way towards the Orb's base, as if it were a red carpet. Foxglove stopped the group once more in a half circle and pointed to the top. 'Magnificent, isn't it,' he said. His long hair blowing about in the wind. 'And there if you look! At the very top of it! You cannot quite see it, there is a mirror which tracks the very movement of the sun. It's run by a computer you see,' he smiled at their interested faces. 'And at the given time a small door at the top of the Orb will open and let the sun's rays in! These rays will be guided downwards by the mirror and onto a huge *crystal pyramid* that is inside, at the base of the Orb. Indeed,' he said dramatically. 'The crystal pyramid is the *very power* of it,' he shook his head with a mixture of admiration and disbelief. 'And from this pyramid the sun's beams will be radiated outwards to light up the entire Orb! You will feel the powerful energy from it. From a planet ninety-three million miles away! A blinding light. Not bad hey? And you will sit and meditate. Meditation is a form of tuning in. You will concentrate on the breath amongst the bright white light. You *will* need to close your eyes tightly of course.' Foxglove began trotting forward. 'In case you go blind.'

They reached a small doorway where Foxglove bent down and opened a white wooden box. 'Take these,' he said, leaning in and handing out small torchlights. 'We'll walk slowly inside, and take off your shoes. It will be very dark at first, before it all begins - and then we'll walk up onto a higher platform in the middle. I hope you're ok with heights? Depending on how receptive you are, you might have some insights, even on your first visit.' Foxglove was reveling now that his audience was both fearful and captivated, and whispered expectantly. 'You might even see visions of who you really are - or even your future.' The group clenched their lips. 'Now,' he said grandly. 'Come with *me* everyone! And remember inside the Orb we must have complete silence!' They followed, removed their shoes, bowed their heads and entered in.

The walkway that spiraled along the inside walls of the Orb surprised Alfi. Quite narrow, it was laid with white feathery carpet, so deep in fact, that his feet were barely visible within it. Foxglove guided them by the lights of their torches with Agatha walking slowly at the end, until finally, near the top, he ushered them to stop. The next section would be tricky, as they would need to balance themselves along a suspended platform up high in the very centre of the Orb - one that would sway a little as they walked. Foxglove sensed their trepidation and raised a forefinger reminding them to be quiet. They balanced themselves along it, and once in the middle, he pointed for them to sit.

They sat quietly, and a cool air circled their heads that reminded Alfi of his long undulating rides in the mountains. 'Lights out,' Foxglove whispered, and as the last of them fiddled with their torches, they were in complete blackness. They waited. The minutes passed. Until their eyes were drawn upwards to a sound from above. A light flickered from the Orb's apex as a little door, no bigger than a small window, slid clumsily open. Now fully ajar, it revealed the bottom part of a large mirror, tilting itself backwards towards a brazen blue sky. It revolved slowly in jagged movements. Until it stopped, and tilted back further. It was as if it was waiting for something. It lent awkwardly backwards a little more, shaking a little as it went, then after several smaller tremors, the mirror halted again and was completely still. Foxglove felt this was the time and ushered. 'Close your eyes. Close your eyes! Tight!' And so, they all waited. Their eyes closed with a fear of the unknown about their faces. And with a roar it came.

The mirror trembled as it caught the first golden light. Thick beams of sunlight drove down past them. The entire Orb shivered, as the beams came down like lasers and into an enormous crystal pyramid at the base - one they'd not seen earlier in the darkness. All at once, blinding lights shone out in all directions, moving like white phantoms, caught, trapped and confused; turning and changing their shapes in a now howling wind. And so, their mouths were drawn open. Helpless, they creased their faces. And then, suddenly within a crisp sharp beat, as quickly as it had come, Alfi was out of the light and into blackness again. Complete blackness with nothing for the eye to see. Where was he now? He was moving...

He was being pulled in deranged movements. Up, down, and along, into a deep lightless tunnel that was uncontrollably taking him in. Which way was he turning? He felt the cool wind rush through his veins, and then suddenly, his body had become spacious, without limit or even substance. Then, in a wild assassinating flicker, he was no longer within himself, but outside, and facing an oblivion of darkness. He looked back, and caught sight of himself from above, sitting there with the others.

Was he mistaken? Seeing himself sitting there with them? Was he just like them, like any other sentient being after all? Did he really exist as he imagined himself? Was there a Self, a real essence to him, or was he just being manipulated? Was he a mere alchemy of circumstance and experiences? Or did he have a soul?

Then he heard mutterings from within his own mind, of voices that came from before. In previous incarnations; a man or a woman? What words, what languages, did their mouths possess? And within this dizzying haze, a gossamer cloud came between him and the view, and when it lifted - like a morning mist - he could see...was it his future?

A figure alone. Abandoned to the wilderness, amongst the parched, dusty mountains, who was *to cease to be*. Yet, it was too distant. Was it Alfi? Was it him?

Yes. It *was* him. Leaving the Mindgarten. Pitiful and alone.

# CHAPTER SIXTEEN

# Calliope

It was early evening as Lily and Alfi reached some old stone steps that climbed into the pretty garden. The only sounds, apart from their footsteps, were of songbirds that called out invisibly to one another from behind the trees. They entered the circular garden, where white and pink ivy clung to an old stone wall that encircled and enchanted them. In front, was an emerald pond with, in its center, a tall statue of a woman reclining on a rock and playing an ancient Greek instrument. And as she played the lyre, a fountain behind her sent water upwards until its delicate spray hesitated, before coming down again, rippling the water as the low sun sent shimmering gold across its surface.

'Here is where I come at eight, every evening. Just to think.' Lily said, staring at the statue. 'She is one of the *nine muses* you know.'

'Nine muses?'

'The muses inspire creativity, particularly in music or the arts, but I hope they can inspire other things too. Life is a kind of art, don't you think?' she said dreamily. 'An art to living, of creating something beautiful. Calliope, they say, was the greatest of all the muses.' Lily smiled at the thought before announcing enthusiastically. 'And this is her fountain. Calliope Fountain.'

They sat on a weathered stone bench that had been etched with black and grey colours over the years, and faced the figure. A silence followed, one in which they found comfort. She watched as a dragonfly skidded quickly over the water before rising and disappearing again.

'My story, Alfi. I want to tell you. I came from a village. A long way from here in the west of Nepal, a place called Dankuta. My culture, our culture in Nepal, is very different to yours, I think you know that.' She sighed gently to give Alfi time to understand.

'For one,' she said. 'We consider less of ourselves, and more of the family and those around us. I got to an age where it was time to marry and, as a daughter, you only bring expense to a family. Whereas a son stays with his parents, he becomes married and looks after them, as do his children. He is more useful. So I began to feel the time was coming and I would have to go. You feel a kind of heaviness about it, without anyone actually saying it.'

Lily watched the water falling. 'My mother started looking for a suitable man, a nice man,' she said. 'But I thought, how could I marry a stranger? My mother loved me and she understood this, and she had gone through this too, when she was young. In my culture we believe that within marriage respect and understanding will come first and love will come after. A love of security too, I suppose. Love, as you have in the West, is less important.

So, I would cycle to other villages some days, just to be free, just to be away from it all. And I remember thinking: "What would a *love marriage* be like?" To meet someone you choose? We knew these marriages often do not work in the West. There are many failures, divorces; perhaps because there is too much independence in the women, and a marriage needs a dependence from one to the other, from which the other will enjoy the love of giving. Some say that marriage for women is the commonest form of lively hood... maybe so, but it's also like the interlocking of a jigsaw puzzle don't you think? They are equal, but if they are the same, they will not fit. So I wandered. And I began looking for someone - at least this was an idea in my head. I was silly, cycling around, between villages, like a child living in a dream and hoping I would find someone. But there wasn't much to choose! And then, like a miracle, a man came along from another town a long way away. He was doing some errands and visiting a friend near my village. We began to talk...and then, every day by phone, he began to love me.

He was educated and he had a visa for a job in America! A work visa. I told my mother about him and I *thought* I fell in love with him. But maybe I fell in love with the idea of him and what it would bring? He was such a kind, sweet man. My mother and father were not so sure but he gave them $1,000 to help them if he could marry me and said he would go to America, and eventually he would get me a visa for me to join him. He was going to live in New Jersey. You know this place?'

'Yes,' Alfi half smiled in recognition. 'I know it.'

'So, we married, he went back to America. My parents had never seen a love marriage before but allowed it and I waited with them in Nepal. After some time, he got my visa and I went over to stay with him.'

'What was his name? Your husband in America,' asked Alfi.

'Thakur. He had a good job. In computers. I did not know exactly what he did. All I knew was that he sat down, stared at a screen all day and they gave him a lot of money. And when I got there, he already had American friends. He was a nice man Mr Alfi. So loving, and so supporting of me. He said he wanted to give me his life! He would do anything for me.'

She paused and her voice slowed. 'When you think about it, even if there is no love in the Western sense, all a marriage really needs is *one good* partner who is kind, loving and reasonably attractive,' she laughed gently at her superficial thinking. 'And has the ability to bring in money and is loyal and understanding. Then the other partner will think "why would I ever leave this person? How would I ever find better?" It's not complicated. All he wanted was for me to be happy. I think, even then, he knew I was beginning *not* to love him. Love is a very strange thing, isn't it? You cannot control it. You can't make yourself love someone, even if you try.'

Lily looked emptily down to her feet, for she'd reminded herself that she'd broken someone. 'It hurt him of course. He felt it, that I did not love him, but he waited. When I first arrived, in America. I stayed inside a lot. I felt uncomfortable in this strange country. It seemed to me that money; money was everything. It defined who you were, what you could do, and even who you would spend time with. People with money, made friends with people who had money. People who were poor talked with people who were poor. There was no mixing, not like in Nepal where everyone is a brother or sister. Thakur, he tried to help me a lot, and wanted me to go out and meet with the other wives of the people he knew. There's a sense of owner-ship, don't you think, when someone pays your bills, especially if you live in another, strange country. I felt I must follow him. And follow his instruction.'

Lily thought back and could see every dulling minute; her disap-pointment of life in America. The nights sitting alone in cheap, empty cafes and not wanting to go home. The vacant Formica seats and watching the rain in the darkness and staring. Staring at the beads of condensation on the inside of the window, glistening from the car lights outside, and moving slowly, clumsily downwards, her sorrowful black eyes reflected in the glass.

'And so,' she continued. 'I stayed in New Jersey. Thakur, my husband. He was a good, kind hearted, gentle man Alfi. He loved me and all he wanted, was a future together. Simple isn't it? Life would have been much easier - wouldn't it? If I'd loved him. But my heart, it let us both down. I didn't want to leave, as I felt, I felt...pity for him. He gave me everything and I did love him in a certain way. I loved him for having the most pure, giving of hearts. I was being honest, honest with myself, and I loved him for loving me I suppose. Maybe many people do this, without actually knowing, or are too scared to admit it, but it was not romantic love, and so I felt empty. Lost with no solution. I could not be happy with him or be excited. But I was also not happy with the thought of leaving him and letting him down either. And then, you know, you know what I did? One day, I just got up and ran away. What a fool, and how cruel, I've been.'

'Where? Where did you go?'

'I found a refuge. For women, women from broken homes. Mainly women who were escaping from cruel husbands or violence. And I was running away from a loving one! I'd let him, I let all my family down, and his. My brother, he helped me. He sent me money for my flight back to Nepal. So I flew back, but I knew, I knew I would never be able to go back to my family. There was no home for me there. And the shame I'd brought, the shame to Thakur's family too.'

'So you came here?' Alfi guided gently.

'Yes. All this...all this trouble, over a stupid thing called love. And most people... well eventually anyway, learn to live without it, don't they? Marriages can last a lifetime - but they move on differently, where their love is exchanged for togetherness, a reliance, a routine. Better than the alternative of being alone. So, why did I need the initial fire of it? When we all know it will fade anyway? So yes. I came here. I walked and caught buses and trucks to get here to the Mindgarten. And that's my story.'

She looked to Calliope and then to Alfi. 'So now you're thinking, poor Asian girl? One day. I think he is going to come here to take me. Take me back. And back to our families and culture. Maybe I will have to go with him because I have no one else. You don't understand Alfi that in my culture a woman needs a man, without which, life is very difficult. Such a need of a woman, when caringly answered by the husband, becomes the strength of a relationship.' She stopped, for she thought she'd said enough, as Alfi's mind wavered in the silence.

They stared into the water as, unconsciously, his heart was telling him to do so. And so his hand moved hesitantly along the old stone surface towards hers until, finally, their fingertips touched. He followed her gaze towards Calliope, as their two minds became entwined. Their thoughts caressing one another from within the stillness. Eventually, he broke the silence. 'I wonder what song she plays?' But Lily didn't answer. Instead, she gazed on at the sculpture, her fingertips still touching his.

The solid figure played her unknown music to anyone who cared to listen. Her stone face captured half concentrated, the eyes hopeful, yet in the midst of something unreachable and too distant. The water continued to fall from the fountain above, creating a most perfect haze that had turned golden at the day's end. Droplets descended along Calliope's figure, weaving their way slowly along the folds of her dress until arriving at her stone feet, to fall singularly into the pond like foot soldiers.

'It's late now,' Lily orated the words as if almost inside a dream. 'I must go.' She stood up and walked slowly away. Away from the water, and away from Alfi and Calliope; and as she did so, as she disappeared down the old stone steps, her footsteps created echoes.

# CHAPTER SEVENTEEN

*Mother*

Foxglove stood authoritatively beneath the gold embossed letters *'Cicero Flowerbed 9.'* He was awkwardly balancing a large green ledger, as a line of men and women shuffled shyly by him. Among them was Lester, as Foxglove called out pragmatically. 'In you go!' watching them as they filed past. 'And remember everybody, you'll be given a number on the way in. Memorise it, and if you like a person, their *vibretic* connections, ask for their number too. You can easily meet up with them at the end.' He paused to check some more names on his ledger. 'Remember, beautiful people can make ugly marriages and ugly people, well they can make ugly marriages too. It's all about give-and-take everybody! It's important to remain optimistic - even in these times of the fluxation and confusion in the roles of the sexes, selfishness, people using each other, as well as the impending oblivion and suffocation a relationship can bring - as well as the need to flee.' He danced on the spot and began to speak quite poetically. 'Alas in life, we blossom to attract the bees and then we wilt. Sadly, to become old flowers. And who wants a withered daisy, hey?' He called to a lady who was straggling in. 'You're not going to meet any nuggets in here.'

Others passed timidly, making little effort to listen, and trying to get their entrances over and done with. 'Such is life,' he called. 'Do your best! You're going to find out that *the physical* - what you look like - is now completely irrelevant, to a point, of course. I've always thought personal hygiene is so undervalued these days!' He lent to the ear of a woman who was entering in richly pasted make-up. 'Vanity is unattractive my dear, and you know it's pitch black in there!' Before calling wildly to others. 'Just listen to the person! Let them speak!' And with that, Foxglove joggled about on the spot a bit, and hummed an obscure love song that no one could quite recognise.

❀ ❀ ❀

In the darkness a woman's voice continued with Lester. 'So, after Alan ended it all, rather suddenly I must say, I decided that perhaps I was having too many relationships. Maybe I just needed a break. Alan was my nineteenth.'

'Nineteenth?'

'I liked to socialize!' she said defensively. 'And, you know, spreading the net wide and all that. Finding someone is a game of numbers, isn't it? But people can lead you into a bit of a dead end. Behind their masks they're often, not quite what you expect them to be, are they? Not what they seem. You often see that gradually, more gradually with some than with others. What lies behind the veneer, it can be quite shocking.'

'Yes,' said Lester, listening.

'Alan was the quiet type, and he wouldn't mind me taking the reins - so to speak. And sometimes, I'd notice when I spoke with him, he would just stare, you know, without saying too much. Just stare. Not in a strange kind of way of course. Just blankly, as if he was just waiting for me to get all my words out and stop. Some people would call it glazing over, I suppose.'

'Yep, glazing over, I know the feeling,' replied Lester.

'And one day, he became unusually quiet. He seemed to have a lot on his mind. There's a breaking point for everyone, I suppose. I remember I was talking to him, telling him about our future, what I wanted, what we were going to do - and he just turned. Turned slowly and walked away in the opposite direction. Scratching the back his neck.'

'Not a good sign.'

'I never liked it, when Alan was scratching. I told him. It was one of those things - well the many things - that he did that annoyed me. Using certain towels in the bathroom, where he put things away in the kitchen, how he drove the car - I didn't like his accelerating too much - his braking too, too heavy footed - or the way he ate food at the table for that matter - too slow, and then sometimes too fast. And I told him, with scratching, he was *not* to do it. Unless it was absolutely necessary. He agreed to scratch less of course. A relationship is about give and take after all. But he never seemed to quite follow. I've always been fair but firm. But he never seems to listen. Then, shortly after, I think it was only the following week. He disappeared. Just vanished! Into thin air. Without saying a word.'

Lester's mind wavered, for he'd seen this bullying before. To placate the other and avoid confrontation, one would become more accepting - particularly over the smaller things, that really didn't matter anyway. To keep the other satisfied; to maintain their parasitic ego in check, whilst they, themselves, would shrink. The narcissist meanwhile so ignorant, too self-righteous, too eager to notice - and even seeing themselves as the victim.

She interrupted Lester from his thoughts. 'He didn't even take many clothes or many other things with him, for that matter. It was as if he was broken in a way - and in a hurry to leave, once he summed up enough energy, the courage to do it. I don't know why. Why I did it? It was an impulse for me. Maybe I took it badly, life wasn't good at the time,' she waited before adding. 'It's too late, isn't it? Later in life, to find someone - a new love - because it's not new love, is it? It's when we get older, I suppose. That we're stuck in our ways. It's difficult to adjust, isn't it? And we blame the other person. When the best love by nature, is the freshest of fruits and only for the young to taste. For those who come together in the frost of the seasons, it has to move on more quickly to the pragmatic and the ordinary.'

She had become too poetic and corrected herself abruptly - remembering too her many compromises in her bout with loneliness. 'Anyway,' she added, her head slightly dropping in the darkness. 'It was tricky. Not easy at first, getting the right kit. Loneliness is a terrible thing, isn't it? It's so...silent. And seems *never* to go away. Some get used to it of course. The sound of their own voice. But loneliness doesn't give you any warning, does it? It just creeps up on you and never says a thing. And there it stays, morning 'til night, and you've got so much time with it.' Her voice stopped, before adding straightforwardly. 'It's diameters you see. Trying to get the diameters right - to get a good fit. And you couldn't really ask a mechanic, could you? But I got it right in the end, and the only decision was the front or the back seat. Where to *go*, so to speak. So, it was in morning that I tied it: the hose to the exhaust pipe and waited.'

'Hose! To an exhaust pipe?' asked Lester.

'It took a while running the car engine - before sending me to sleep. Much like at the dentists. I've always had gas you know. I don't like pain.'

'You were going to end it? Go through with it?' Lester asked.

'In life, I've always thought you should never have regrets about things you *hadn't* done.'

'I know,' replied Lester. 'But suicide...'

'So I sat in my car. The sealed windows, and waited.'

Lester scratched his neck in the darkness.

'And then, twenty minutes later, sitting there, quite quietly in the passenger seat, the engine stopped. Just stopped. I can remember that sound as it kind of hissed to a halt. I'd ran out of fuel. That was Alan's job! I've told him a million times - a million times...fill up! But he never did. The tank was always half full. Half! I put it down to his character. Which saved me in the end. And then...that's how I met Richard; the petrol attendant at the gas station. That smile of his, holding the nozzle in his boots and dungarees. He was...a very simple man. He didn't want much, he was quiet, and that was what I needed. Just a bit of company. To be with someone - to do things. That's all you need, isn't it? It turned things around for me. And just ten weeks later. Just ten weeks! Richard attempted suicide in my car. Funny, isn't it?'

'Do you mind? Do you mind if I move on?' Lester asked.

'No, it's fine' she said. 'Do I talk too much? I'm a Pisces by the way. That's Latin for fish.'

Lester shuffled about in the darkness, sensing the closeness, the proximity of others, the humming conversations, yelps and affected enthusiasms. He wondered why humans needed to convey their stories, their opinions so much? It was like endless music, ideas needing to be vindicated or explored. Was there to be any end to it? He realised then, that in his life he would prefer a quiet person, and someone who he could be quiet with. That was the message that came sweetly to him from the darkness that night.

Later, he was being bombarded by a buoyant Antipodean accent that lilted, descended and rose up again like a rollercoaster. 'I love coming here,' she said. 'The Himalaya. The mountains you know. It's amazing.'

'Yes. it sure is,' Lester replied, his voice already beginning to dull, his disappointment invisible in the darkness. "Was there to be anybody out there for him?" he thought. A partner? It became obvious then - as if it were, some scientific equation - as her voice hovered over him and was disappearing, that a companion should be chosen reliably by a comparable intellect, a harmonised demeanour and with a degree of physical attraction. But how could the world conjure up such a thing?

'The people here,' she brought him back to the present. 'It's just...amazing. Really it is. Amazing.'

Lester conceded, his eyes dropping. 'Nice. Nice to hear that.'

'Did you go to the Orb yet? Amazing,' she said with another spring in her voice. Everything about her, even within the darkness, seemed youthful and vigorous. He wondered could he keep up with it? Keep up with the pretense, the game of it all. Her's, was a sadness dressed up in bright colours. Maybe he was just being too honest.

'The Orb,' she continued. 'It was so...so? What's the word I'm looking for? What's the word?'

'Amazing?' Lester offered.

'Yes, that's it. Amazing.'

And out came Lester's defeated reply. 'Well, it's been nice talking to you, very um...'

'You're going?'

'I've got medication to take.'

'Oh, ok. Yaa. Amazing,' she said brightly.

Lester thought of the door, an escape to the outside.

❀ ❀ ❀

It was late, as he raised a beer with Alfi and sat on the veranda looking out into a black, moonless sky. 'And then,' Lester continued optimistically. 'Then, my friend, I spoke to someone. A woman, who sounded interesting. We chatted for a long time. A long time Alfi! Initially, small talk, you know, this and that. She was quiet, and gentle in her way. And we talked about more...intimate things. There was a connection Alfi. A real connection. We really got along together. You know what I mean?'

'Yep. I know what that means, and what it feels like,' said Alfi sipping his beer.

'And you know what?'

'What?'

'She touched me.'

'What?'

Lester gave a big smile. 'She touched me Alfi! On my arm.'

'Oh, ok.'

'At first, I couldn't quite make out what it was. Was it a touch, or did it last longer? More of a stroke, you know. Or a graze even. Who knows? These things. These subtle things mean something my friend. They're mating signals, and it's all about length. Length of time.'

'How long was it?'

'Five, possibly ten seconds,' enthused Lester. 'Ten is more of a stroke. Illustrating affection. Up to five...is just a touch in my book. It's hard to say. At the bottom of the pile - is a pat. A pat can be used to send you off. Send you away. I'm not a pat fan. People do it all the time. And then I blew it.'

'Blew it?'

'Yes, sadly, I buckled.'

'What do you mean...buckled?'

Lester scratched his head. 'I couldn't think. I just panicked. I didn't know what to say! We were getting *too* close. I turned round and left.'

'You left?'

'It was moving too fast.'

'Someone holds your arm for five seconds and it's too fast?'

'Ten Alfi, and I'm more of a slow burn. I mean. Maybe I'm too much the romantic type? You know. I need chocolates. I like flowers.

Walks in the park. I didn't even know what she looked like. She could had been anyone!'

'That's the whole point isn't!' Alfi said frustratedly. 'It's about a connection to another person.'

Lester looked blankly into the darkness. 'A caress,' he added. 'Maybe it was more of a caress? When she touched me. And I never even asked her name? Can you believe that? Never even asked her name? All I knew was that she was Number Fifteen.'

'There you go. Fifteen!' Alfi checked his watch. 'You should go back. Find fifteen.'

'Nah,' sighed Lester. 'It's too late. Another one gone my friend - and there was never many of them. It's gone. The ships gone off into the night. It's left the harbour. Anchor's up, and it's pulled out slowly into the sea. Never to be seen again. Besides, Foxglove was putting the lights on half an hour ago.'

Lester took a regretful sip of his beer. 'We all want love my friend. Don't we? God knows, I tried in America after the divorce - with the miserable amount of money my *loved one* left me. The dating game, agencies...the newspaper. I remember my ad. "*Overweight bald man, low income and prospects, seeks beautiful woman with good sense of humour.*" No response. I kept trying of course. Maybe I was scraping the barrel too much, and have you seen what women are like my age? It's not pretty my friend. Sour, that's what it is. Life has battled them down, and you can see it in their faces. I've always thought non-aggression is such a wonderful trait...And I didn't even ask how old Number Fifteen was.'

'Does it matter?' asked Alfi.

Lester lent back in his seat. 'Why do we have to go for women our own age anyway?'

'We don't. That's just the West. It's obsessed with age,' replied Alfi.

'Back home they even want to know how old your dog is,' sighed

Lester. 'I thought we'd become emancipated? They're happy for us to marry with different skin colours, cultural differences, the same sex, but for some reason they don't like an age gap. But we're over that now. It's just a case of finding someone, the right person. I should look on the bright side - at least we've moved on from natural selection. Stags locking horns and all that. I would have done even worse with that. Not a chance. I'm not a fighter Alfi. Never have been. Nature had natural selection taken out to help people like me. Now it depends on what you wear on a Saturday night.'

'It's a good point.'

'But you never seem to meet the *right* person do you?' continued Lester. 'You know, I went to a Talk in Saint Augustin, Flower Bed Three, the other night. There was a recitation of the works of the romantic poet John Donne. He proclaimed *that spiritual and carnal love were inseparable* - but I guess he'd never been to CBGB's on a Saturday night.'

'Give it time,' responded Alfi.

'I guess you'd call my type...unlucky. Unlucky in love. There's a lot of us around my friend! Makes you wonder what's it all about, hey? Why go through all the heartache to meet someone. When being alone with good friends, and peace and quiet. Friends who take a genuine interest in each other, companionship - is under-valued.'

'It sure is.'

There was a long pause after which Lester's voice became less animated. 'You know my mother,' he said. 'She always wanted something, all her life. Always wanted *to be* something. She came from a normal, run-of-the-mill family. I guess for her, getting married was a way to escape, a way out. So she got married. She wanted to have children, so she had children; me and Lizzy. And then things started to change. Life started to disappoint her, I guess. Sure, she had some happiness along the way, here and there, but she was never *really* satisfied. Happiness, always seemed to be something just ahead of her, at some point in the future - just one step away. She wanted her children to have good jobs and to live in a certain kind of way. She wanted the perfect home, the perfect marriage. She *wanted* so much, all her life. She wanted things to just be as she'd envisaged them. And you can't have perfection Alfi. I now realise that. And then - she died. She just died. Suddenly.'

'I'm sorry,' offered Alfi and touched his arm.

'I remember, her lying there, in that terrible place,' continued Lester. 'With mildly helpful but condescending remarks from the nurses and thinking - how an elderly person could be brought to this? They weren't even beds really, looking underneath. Just mattresses on trollies, waiting for a nod from someone with a clip-board to be wheeled away. Just a number, a name, like everybody else. I remember feeling the last warmth of her fingers, under that dim orange light, her bedside lamp, that night, and realised, I'd never told my Mom, never told her, that I loved her. And now the words were too late. I saw her face. I remember it. My mother's last glance at life, to that plain ceiling, in that awful place. She had the face of a victim.'

Lester's mind turned inward, where he could see his mother's gaunt fingers that night. The hand that previously was so youthful, full of flesh and touching his. How vulnerable as a child he'd been, when he clutched those fingers for support. For the love, and protection they gave. And now, in her older years when she needed him - had he become selfish? For whilst love from a mother is never yielding, what form does it take from a child in its return?

# CHAPTER EIGHTEEN

*Ex nihilo nihil fit*
*Nothing comes from nothing*

Alfi and Lester stood in the trench. One of them holding a pick, the other a spade, as the sun beat down on their tired red faces. It was their first day where Frenchie had assigned them duties on a farm. Looking down at the two, and standing alongside Frenchie, was a tall, solemn looking white bearded man, in a long white tunic. 'You two need to keep going,' Frenchie said smugly. And added, 'how are you feeling? Hot?'

'It's pretty nice down here,' replied Lester with an affected smile. 'Close to the earth. The soil. Never felt better. Just the smell of it! And the exercise, it will be good for the heart and lungs. We love to dig. Hey Alfi?'

'It has its moments,' said Alfi.

'Yep,' agreed Lester. 'You can't beat the sound of the pick going in.'

'You're going to be hearing that pick going in for a long time,' snarled Frenchie. 'There's a lot of digging to do. And it will get hotter in a while. The sunshine. Mighty hot. Like Marseille on a summer's day.'

'Vitamin D my friend!' called Lester. 'Vitamin D. Good for the spirit. And just say the word *trench* and it's hard to resist! Hey Alfi. It's got a ring to it! Don't you think? Gets your blood going.'

'Good,' snapped Frenchie. 'I'm glad you like it. This irrigation channel needs to go all the way up this side of the field, and back around the other,' he pointed at the distances with relish. 'Stops it from flooding.'

Lester placed a foot on the edge of his pick and nodded towards the quiet bearded man. 'Who is uh?'

'Oh,' said Frenchie. 'This is Ramesh Gorbanaravan Costinova Tericona Singh.'

'Kind of rolls off your tongue doesn't it,' said Lester.

'He is the Guru,' snapped Frenchie.

'What does he do?' asked Alfi.

'Very little,' replied Frenchie. 'He just experiences. He believes that life is ultimately meaningless and that seeking recognition is pointless as it ends subjectively with death and achievement is there-fore bereft of any point. This, rather than being negative - is a release. He doesn't strive for anything and has a soft-spot for nihilism.'

'Nice! Does he fancy a pick?' remarked Lester.

'He likes to observe in silence,' Frenchie said. 'He hasn't spoken for twenty-five years. He was married once, to a doctor. He has a son called Polyps.'

'Polyps?'

'He was named after a cyst. By the age of fifty he'd said he'd spoken enough, and now he doesn't know how old he is. If he said anything else, he said it would just be a repeat of what he'd spoken about before and possibly a waste of time. The last words he spoke were "I would like some eggs." He stopped speaking at breakfast.'

'Oh,' added Lester.

'So now, he only uses his tongue for two things: adding moisture to his lips or for pointing.'

'Pointing?' asked Alfi.

'He points with his tongue - if he has the energy to do it. You might see it one day.' Frenchie stepped one foot closer to the trench as his voice slowed. 'Now tell me, have you ever stood at the top of a tall building and just paused for a while, walked to the edge, and contemplated jumping off?'

'Can't say I have,' replied Lester.

'Not recently. No,' agreed Alfi.

'Just diving into the abyss,' Frenchie continued somberly. 'That's his problem - the Guru here, he often has. He has and we call it, the *suction of heights*. A long time ago he was in a passenger truck, not far from here, around these high hills, and had the sudden compulsion to drive over the edge. Just turn the wheel, drive over the precipice and be done with it. End it all. Luckily for the other passengers he wasn't driving it at the time. He prefers to be cosmic these days. Sometimes he muses.'

With that, the Guru's head turned and he suddenly stuck out his tongue, pointing with it into the distance. 'There you are!' said Frenchie delighted. 'You see it! He did it! He pointed with his tongue! I think he desires you to dig to that tree. At least by the end of today.'

'What tree?' asked Lester. 'I can't see it.'

Alfi put a hand over his brow looking for it. 'That tree? Over there? Right over there at the very far end?'

'Is that in a different time zone?' added Lester.

'Yea,' Frenchie replied curtly. 'That's it. The thick one with the leaves. Dig to it, and he'll be very pleased. I'll send someone to pick you up later.'

Alfi stared. 'It's a long way. To that tree.'

'Distance is relative to velocity Mr Alfi,' Frenchie drooled back in his French accent. 'In your case, the velocity of the spade and pick. I'll be watching you Mr Alfi. Watching your progress.'

The two, Frenchie and the Guru, turned sharply, marched to the truck, slammed the doors and pulled angrily away.

❀ ❀ ❀

The sound of the old truck spluttering and skidding across the field was met by Alfi and Lester's expectant eyebrows over the rim of the trench. It was twilight, and finally the end of the day, as they loaded their mudded tools into the back, opened the passenger door and slid along the front bench seat to sit next to the driver. They were tired, too tired even for words, as the gear lever was pushed forcibly forward and they were off; on their way over the high hills and back to the centre of the Mindgarten.

Lester looked out wearily through the blowy open window as the truck turned this way then that, trying to gain traction at a ferocious speed over loose rubble and rock. Below them in spurts, was a vertical abyss down both sides of the mountains, sometimes just a finger's width away from the fast-spinning bald tyres. Lester turned inward again at a riveted Alfi, then to the fists clutched tightly to the steering wheel of the troubled, somehow soulless expression, of the Guru who was driving. The dusty windscreen above the never-used rusted windscreen wipers, captured all three of their dismal faces.

Relieved, the jeep finally arrived outside their accommodation with a decisive and violent swerve. Lester lent a hand out through the window, fumbled with the door latch, climbed out and dusted himself down to the knees. He was followed by Alfi, who slid along the bench seat and stomped out heavily, both of them still too exhausted to speak. They looked up. Crisply dressed and waiting for them on their veranda, was Frenchie. Lester's pace perked up immediately, he even began to whistle - a huge surprise to Alfi and even the Guru.

'What a day!' Lester called out. 'Great day. Couldn't have got a better day for it!' He began to massage the back of his neck and shoulders. 'The neck. That muscle spasm. Totally cleared! Totally gone. A miracle! I've had specialists look at it for years. The best! New York. And they never thought of a trench! Completely overlooked.' He looked up in mock surprise to see Frenchie. 'Oh Frenchie,' he said. 'Nice to see you! Been waiting long?'

But Frenchie was having none of it. Instead, he left the veranda and marched to the truck, all the while staring at the two of them over his shoulder with a candid bitterness. The Guru shifted the engine noisily into gear. The truck turned quickly, surrounded by dust spinning out from beneath its wheels, and Frenchie and the Guru were gone.

Out of view. Lester sank to his knees. 'I...I think I am not cut out for this. I know, I know, I'm not going to last. That's it!'

Alfi stared at him. 'Come on,' he said. 'We need to work through it. You said that. And you said that Frenchie was going to try to break us. The first days. We just need to get into the flow of it.'

'The flow of it! There is no flow! No flow Alfi. It's just one day Alfi. Day One! This whole thing is a disaster. Look at me.' Lester got back to his feet and began walking with a limp to his room door. 'And why did the trench have to be so deep anyway Mm? I mean how deep does an irrigation channel need to be?'

'We need to give it time. Pace yourself,' replied Alfi.

'My back is crippled,' said Lester leaning on the veranda. 'My vertebrae. My knees. I think, I think I've lost height. Height is important to me. I wasn't tall to start with. Every inch! Every inch lost, I lose my appeal!'

'You'll be ok. Ok in the morning. A good night's rest. I think they're picking us up early.'

Lester replied with doubt in his voice. 'Early? He's picking us up early? What does *early* mean?'

With that, Lobsang appeared, trotting over busily and stood looking up at the two of them on their porch. It was as if he were a Roman messenger. He studied them, up and down, the worn-out faces, the ruffled, mudded clothes, before he spoke. 'You look tired Mr Alfi. Both of you.'

'Keenly observed Lobsang,' called back Alfi.

'But Thay,' Lobsang added. 'He would like to see you tonight.'

'Tonight?'

'Yes. Can you come over about nine? After I have made his dinner. He is always in a quiet mood then.'

'Tonight? Does it have to be tonight?'

Lobsang gave a kind smile. 'Yes. Tonight. Feck you!' And skipped away as quickly as he'd come.

Lester asked timidly. 'Did he say thank you?'

'Kind of,' mouthed Alfi.

❀ ❀ ❀

Lobsang led Alfi along the red corridor towards Thay's apartment. Opening the door, he gave a gentle bow and ushered Alfi in. 'Thanks Lobsang,' whispered Alfi, where at the far side of the room, Thay stood looking out of the window.

Lobsang called respectfully to his master. 'Will there be anything else sir?'

Without turning Thay answered. 'No. That'll be all, Lobsang.'

'Right you are sir. Up yours!' came the reply as Lobsang stamped a foot to the wooden floor, turned as if on military parade, and disappeared soundly out.

'I see you have been making friends with Lily.' Thay said eventually, still gazing through the window. 'She's a good person.'

'Yes. She is.'

Thay continued. 'She's quietly strong you know. Remember, in life we all make mistakes. Some are brought upon us, and we can do little to avoid them, that is living - but we do not have to live by our mistakes. She's honest. And a good person like her can spur another on; making them, and her, a better person. She just needs someone to settle with, I feel. And I have the feeling that will happen soon.' Despite staring out of the window, Thay sensed Alfi's embarrassment and turned to face him, changing the subject. 'So. So how is Frenchie treating you?'

'Well, he's ok,' Alfi replied limply.

'Ok?'

'Well...the work is a little hard.'

'I'll ask him to try to give you - the two of you - other work,' said Thay circumspectly. He gestured for Alfi to sit. 'You know that when people are angry or unkind, what it really means is - that they're suffering. And for some reason, I can never quite work it out, they then want to bring this suffering onto others too? Angry people do not like others being happy. In truth - what the intelligent man should do - is take pity on them but avoid them as much as possible, as you would a dangerous animal!' Thay giggled. 'We keep Frenchie as a good example to us. He's an unusual case, as despite being here in the Mindgarten, he remains not quite at peace with himself, or anyone else for that matter. His mind is too stubborn to change you see. Maybe there is something in the nature of a person that will never go away - so you just have to leave it. He teaches us temperance.'

'I suppose that's one way of looking at it,' remarked Alfi.

'Remember Mr Alfi, it's easy to show compassion and kindness to a person who is kind to you. But try to show it to those who try to harm us, who attempt to upset us - that is another matter. If someone tries to cheat you or bring trouble to your life, yes, you can even show such a person some compassion, but it's best also to keep away from them. For in many cases, they might never change - and you must be kind to yourself, nurture and protect your own inner peace, and then you can be kinder to others. Your own inner peace is a very important foundation Mr Alfi, for how you live your life. So why waste time with those who seek to upset it? But in his case, you cannot put out fire with fire, only water. So we must not meet anger with anger, instead, just watch, as it unravels itself, it will dissolve eventually, unless he is mad. We are all suffering to certain degrees, that is my understanding - some more than most. And there also comes a time when you must just be quiet...and let the others be wrong. Maybe there's jealously or even fear in it, and he doesn't want you to get through Green Bird. And you should feel flattered - nobody kicks a dead dog you know!'

'Thanks,' Alfi said passively.

Thay entered into a long pause, the way holy men often do, quite comfortably. 'You know,' he said finally. 'There was once a Celtic priest, a linguist, a long time ago who noticed there were similarities between languages. The word 'mother' for example, has the 'M' resonance within it, in many other languages too. In ancient Egypt the word for mother is Mut and five thousand miles away in places in the Far East, it is Mair, this similarity stretches throughout the world. In India where it is 'Ama', Europe, Africa and beyond, even in South America. His theory was that languages may had been passed through trade. The Silk Route, for example. But how all the way to South America or Africa? Quechua; the isolated Peruvian language calls mother 'Mama you know! It's an interesting coincidence, don't you think?'

'It is,' replied Alfi, a little cautious as to where the story was leading. 'I never knew that.'

Thay considered him carefully. 'Do you believe in reincarnation Mr Alfi?'

Alfi stuttered, a little charmingly so. 'Well, if I'm honest, I can't say I do. Not that I want to show you any disrespect or anything.'

Thay smiled agreeably. 'Neither do I.'

'You don't?'

Thay clutched the hem of his ochre robe. 'Look. Look at my clothes Mr Alfi. Are these not the clothes of a monk? I look like a monk. In some ways I am a monk, but not a Buddhist one. Now, back to reincarnation. Maybe there is a mistake. If you live well, they say, you won't come back as a goat! This has given some cultures, somehow, the right to show disdain, to show contempt to animals!'

Thay began pouring two whiskeys, handing one to Alfi, and continued in a kind of whimsical wonder. 'Buddhists believe that when you die your soul goes on a celestial journey through the universe and is reborn somewhere, somewhere else - but my ideas are different. Besides, as I told you before, our populations are growing and there are more people alive today than have ever lived before, so with some logic, there are simply not enough reincarnated souls from the past to go around. Unless some of us are reincarnated goats!' He laughed playfully and added. 'Instead, I've been thinking of a theory of inter-connectiveness. Like that of the Celtic priest with his languages.'

Thay opened a glass cabinet and carefully removed an ornamental wooden 'Matryoshka' - a Russian doll. Placing it on the table he continued to speak. 'The older, cultured Russians, demonstrated something to us. Perhaps they didn't even realise it! But most of us agree, that inside our bodies we carry the genes of previous ancestors.' He opened the Russian doll and drew out a smaller figure inside it, then another - one decreasing in size after the other.

'Your parents,' he said. 'Their genes might immediately be apparent whether superficially so, such as the colour of your eyes or how you look, including perhaps, how you behave, your temperament and so on. But you're also carrying the genes of older ancestors handed down from generation to generation, your grandparents, great-grandparents, and so it goes, through thousands of years! A family tree, Mr Alfi, whose branches expand far and wide, so infinitesimal that only a fool would try to make sense of it.

So in fact, who you are, what constitutes what *you think* of as the *Self*, your tastes, character, abilities, what you like, and what you don't like and so on - at least genetically speaking - consist of a multitude of factors handed down through the ages and all coming together randomly. How is it that unmusical parents, or a mother and father with little idea of numbers, can give birth to piano prodigies or mathematical geniuses? Where does this talent come from Mr Alfi?' He lent closer. 'Now think about this Mr Alfi. As you can carry ancestral genes from previous generations...is it a great leap of faith to consider that you might also carry their *memories?* Memories from previous minds, from the past. Some genes are *immortal*!' Thay continued opening one Russian doll after the other, until he reached the very smallest one in its centre. 'Your genes, through random couplings in history, could carry complex connections from all over the world. I could be wrong, but that's what I believe. And sometimes these memories can come out. They can be coaxed out by chance. And when this happens, this is when those who believe in reincarnation, could be confused. When they see these recollections, they believe it's evidence of reincarnation. Am I making myself clear Mr Alfi?'

'Your theory seems to make logical sense.'

Thay pondered before adding. 'You know, my theory could be incorrect. I am only a man and have great respect for Buddhism, as I do all faiths. But I remember when I was a child, my father took me on a journey back to the town where he grew up. Just to show it to me, and for him to enjoy being there again. So, what about you Mr Alfi?'

'Me?'

'How you came here?'

Thay put the doll back together piece by piece and returned it to the cabinet, putting it on display again. He turned and added, 'Now, back to the Self. It's also true that your given personality traits intermingle with your upbringing; your environment and your experiences, they are unfixed and malleable through time. A person is therefore manipulated, ever changing the shape of their individuality. It is *not* the case of nature *versus* nurture, but nature *via* nurture - the two are not opposed. But even this, this is *not* the type of Self that I have been thinking about. The one that I've mentioned to you before. The Self that I have difficulty to find or to explain, stands alone and independently, and free of any influences whether genetically or environmentally. Indeed, it could be argued, that this type of Self does *not exist at all!* So in essence, *you* do not exist, at least independently. Am I confusing you Mr Alfi?'

Thay reached back into the cabinet and returned holding something wrapped in purple velvet cupped sweetly into his little hands. He rested it onto the table and unravelling it, revealed a small crystal pyramid.

'I hope you enjoyed your first visit to the Orb,' he said. 'And maybe it gave you some insights.' He held up the pyramid with both hands. 'This is the same, the same kind of pyramid that's inside the base of the Orb - although a much smaller one! And if you give it long enough, and gaze into it with the right mind, it will sometimes allow you to look deeper, and delve into the Self, perhaps a real Self I have been talking about. It has a magic about it that I do not understand! You can sometimes hear voices within it too - and it has given me images of the future. Although these images are often not clear, there are often clouds within them. For example, the images and what they tell me about *you* Mr Alfi.'

'Me?'

Thay carefully wrapped the pyramid back into its cloth and handed it to Alfi. 'Here you are. You must have it.'

'But...' Alfi attempted to interrupt.

'Wherever you go,' Thay insisted. 'You must take it with you. It will probably take time, but you'll be able to see with it. It will allow you to sit behind your own mind and watch it working. You will be able to oversee your own mind, and in turn, for you to become the governor of your Self. It will also help you to decide what to do. When the time comes.'

'What to do?' asked Alfi. 'What do you mean?'

Thay's mood changed and he glanced away from the pyramid as if he did not want to see it anymore, and became quite wistful. 'Sometimes Mr Alfi. I imagine you travelling a long distance from here and this makes me sad. Upset, that we have still not found the answers. And then, in other times, the pyramid tells me that this place will be run happily by a brother.'

'A brother?' asked Alfi.

'Maybe a brother from this life, or an ancestor one from before. From far away, who was told to come here.' He tapped Alfi's hand and spoke more casually. 'Oh, I don't know. But the pyramid tells me we have little time. So finally, remember this. If anything should happen to me, I want you to *wait and to listen.* Listen outside your window Mr Alfi, in the black of night. For when you hear the howl of a wind and there is no reason for it, and when you hear the whisper of my footsteps, you will know that the choice *you* have made, using this pyramid, is the right one. For I cannot speak to you from the other place, it is forbidden. But your choice would be the authentic one, and you must follow it, regardless of the consequences.'

Alfi wondered what this all meant, but before he had a chance to reply Thay had drifted out of the room.

# CHAPTER NINETEEN

## Quit While You're Behind

In the calm of the early morning darkness, Frenchie's short stick tapped an aggressive staccato along the middle of the doors. There was no reply at first until he hammered again and louder. Finally, a lock clicked revealing Lester standing unsteadily in his wrinkled pajamas, rubbing his eyes with a knuckle. He looked at Frenchie and the Guru next to him. 'Good morning,' Frenchie said sarcastically. 'Time for work.'

Lester wiped his eyes again. 'What time is it?'

'Four, forty-five,' replied Frenchie coldly.

'What a.m? Ok. Ok, come back in the morning,' said Lester. 'We'll be ready, bright and early. Does nine suit?'

'We need to you start work *now*. It's the best before the heat.'

There was another click, as Alfi's door opened ever-so slightly. 'I'm ok with nine too,' he orated through the gap.

'Good idea, that's sealed then,' quipped Lester.

Frenchie formed a disingenuous smile. 'The good news is,' he said. 'Is that I hope you two are artistic! Thay has instructed me to give you some different work - something gentle and creative.'

'Creative?' asked Lester. 'Artistic? What do you mean?'

'Gentler?' repeated Alfi.

Frenchie's voice became pretentious as if he were curating in some Parisian gallery. 'Arts, the aesthetics are such wonderful things, I'm sure you'll agree. How they can change the mood somewhat. Just the simple use of colour, the delicate hair of a brush, to create form, to affect the senses - as if from nothing. Have you ever done any painting before? The two of you? Do you have any talent for it?'

'Painting?' remarked Lester. 'Well, a little as a kid. 'What are we talking? Oils, water colours? I dabbled. Did some sketching.'

Frenchie scowled back. 'Emulsion. Be ready in thirty minutes.'

❀ ❀ ❀

The tall wooden building stood on a far outcrop of the Mindgarten that was cruelly exposed to the elements. The sun was already half way up the sky, as the two found themselves high up on a pair of aligned ladders, Alfi with a six-inch brush and Lester who had acquired a roller and tray, both with paint pots dangling by hooks from the runners. The bright yellow paint they were using glistened, sticky looking, in the heat of the late morning.

'Four hours in already,' remarked Lester as he pressed his roller into the tray. 'And did he say he wanted two coats? I mean, if we put it on thick enough...'

Alfi didn't answer, and it wasn't long before Frenchie and the Guru pulled up. They got out of their truck, slammed their doors by way of an introduction, and stood looking at the building for any signs of progress. Lester began a playful whistle as if he hadn't had the faintest idea that they were around, and called across to Alfi. 'At last! Great to have the sun on your back. It's warming,' he announced pleasingly. 'And I don't care what they say. You cannot. You *cannot* beat the roller.'

'I'm still with the brush,' offered Alfi flatly.

Lester replied. 'The brush? Detail yes. But the roller, it's a much wider proposition my friend. Stretching out like this. Good for the elbows. Never felt looser! It offers a much broader, creative experience. Transformational. This stuff spreads so well.'

An agitated Frenchie yelled out. 'You two better come down!'

'What?' asked Lester. 'Come down? It's only been a few hours! We're just in a stride here. In the swing of it. I was just finding my rhythm.'

'Never mind your rhythm,' Frenchie interrupted meanly, and then added with satisfaction. 'We've got a major blockage in Plato's Meditations. A problem.'

'Plato's Meditations?' enquired Alfi.

'Sewerage,' replied Frenchie with obvious satisfaction.

Lester looked to Alfi. 'Did he say sewerage?'

Staring upwards at the soles of their feet Frenchie drawled. 'We'd like you two to go and sort it out. The Guru has the rods.'

They looked to see the Guru holding rods in each hand, much like a Masai Mara herdsman.

'Rods? I see,' said Lester. 'Can I just ask?'

'What?' snapped Frenchie.

'It might be a...stupid question. Don't get me wrong here. But are we getting paid any for any of this?'

Frenchie gave out a long, affected laugh, the way people do when they want to make a show of it. 'Paid?' He shook his head mockingly. 'Paid!' Even the Guru bounced his shoulders a bit, and Lester joined in for the fun of it. Frenchie called out. 'There is no payment for Green Bird!'

✿ ✿ ✿

Despite being a formidable philosopher, the aromas from Plato's Meditations were not enlightening. Combined with the heat, the entire place had more of a liking to the philosophical works of Arthur Schopenhauer, who described the world and all within it, as miserable. The wet ground, squelching and sinking underfoot, did little to help, neither did the flies who were buzzing in, and then at the last moment, deciding to do U-turns.

Lester pulled backwards with all his might, with Alfi behind him, as they tugged and twisted at the rods which, for some unphilosophical reason, failed to move an inch. A dilemma, that even Plato would have mentally toiled with. The two stopped, Lester mopped some more beads of sweat from his forehead with his last remaining patch of clean elbow, and looked down the deep, dark hole. All the while, Frenchie and the Guru stared from above, like commandants about to signal a firing squad.

'Thirty-eight degrees,' Lester called out, as another droplet of sweat fell from his head into a puddle where he was standing. 'Couldn't had picked a better day for it! No breeze. Humid. Everything seems to hang in the air. On the bright side I think I've lost my sense of smell.'

'Lost mine half an hour ago,' said a pragmatic Alfi.

'Remind me if I'm wrong here,' replied Lester. 'But it might be a good idea to sniff some jasmine when we get home. You can't beat jasmine.' He crouched down, and with his hands on his knees looked at the bamboo rod that was hanging suspended from the hole, then up to Frenchie's boots. 'I've had jobs before,' he said, looking into the hole. 'But nothing, nothing comes close to this in terms of personal satisfaction my friend! I mean it! Not even charity work! We're helping people. Helping them to defecate without a care in the world. Do you know what that means? It's a wonderful feeling. Fulfilling.' He stood back upright, scratched his head and gripped the rod again. 'You know, I read somewhere that the sense of smell consists of particles of what you're actually smelling, floating upwards and resting on receptors inside your nostrils? I think they're called, in this case in question, floating defecation pheromones. Sometimes knowledge can be a bad thing.' He wiped his face and unperturbed, turned buoyantly to a speechless Alfi. 'You know, we might be working down here. We might even feel trapped. In a hole. In the proverbial, literally, so to speak. But inside....' he tapped his forehead knowingly. 'Inside, I'm as free as a bird! Free as a bird my friend. No one can box me in.'

Frenchie bawled down. 'Perhaps less talking and more pulling!'

'Yes sir!' replied Lester, as he and Alfi started to heave at the rods again.

❀ ❀ ❀

It was the end of the day as Frenchie's truck pulled in with a sodden Lester and Alfi. They were laying half-over each other like a pair of untidy sacks in its open back. They slid out legs first, their boots heavily touching the ground and walked towards their doors with Frenchie watching them seriously from the brow of his steering wheel.

'That really was something,' Lester called out as he plodded by the open truck window. 'You know, when that final rod came out, and that brown tsunami came right out at us, the look on your face... it was a picture. We could had surfed it my friend!'

'It was riveting,' agreed Alfi.

'Riveting,' said Lester flicking his head. 'That's the word. You can say that again. Riveting.'

Frenchie eyed them for a little longer, shoved the truck into gear and drove off. Being nasty and eminently bitter, absorbed quite a lot of his energy.

With the Frenchman gone and out of view, Lester slumped to his knees. 'You're looking at a beaten man my friend. Quite clearly...we should quit. I've said before, and I'll say it again. It's always been my life philosophy. Quit while you're behind!'

'Come on,' Alfi retorted in a lame attempt to be cheerful - he was cleaning his boots sideways in some high grass. 'We just need to give it time. More time. We're getting there.'

Lester clung to the handle of his apartment door. 'This is a total, total disaster. This whole thing. I'm not going to make it Alfi. I know I'm not! I've seen my type before. They fail...every time!' He pushed the door, slipped and stumbled inside his room.

# CHAPTER TWENTY

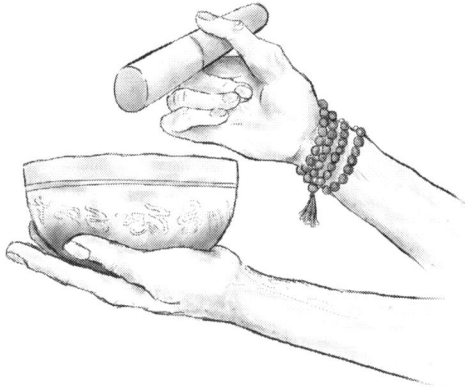

## Vanity and Suffering

Thay sat at his desk which was illuminated by a pretty arrangement of golden candles. Lobsang stood behind him, but despite his sting-tongue his lips were clenched lightly, there would be no need for words. His master examined the elaborate parchment paper placed before him. The calligraphy sketched upon it was beautiful, a skill in which he'd spent years acquiring, and its almost telepathic powers.

Leisurely, he lifted the pen from its inkwell and began to sign. Waiting for the ink to dry, he looked up at the framed old black and white photograph of the Russian Princess. It was as if, at this moment, she was watching over him, her eyes following his and telling him something. He folded and pressed the paper with red seal wax by the flame of a candle. It all seemed, he thought, the right thing to do. And touching the frame around the Princess's image it opened to reveal a safe. Reaching into a pocket he took out a small gold key and handed it to Lobsang who placed the paper inside.

❀ ❀ ❀

At twilight, Alfi would often walk through the Mindgarten alone. Perhaps it was the quiet, resigned way people behaved at the end of the day that appealed to him. Their energy depleted, where the whole of the Mindgarten seemed to fall into a lulling contemplation. Palm trees showed him the direction of a breeze, that carried the scent of wild-flowers, honeysuckle and jasmine; as people wearing bright colours walked into and out of his eyes. Children played in circles in the last lowering light, laughing as they went, and after all his journeying, Alfi felt a consummate feeling of ease. He was home.

He glimpsed back to his time in Kathmandu with Brother Iblan; the monk's light touch to the prayer bowl, where he'd been told that the Buddha considered much of life to be suffering; not just in the ultimate sense through disease, old age and death, but in the constant ebb and flow of the smaller things - the recurring need to take one's self from the unsatisfactory to the satisfactory, which would diminish again as the satisfaction was only temporary. The solution to this continual churning, was to extinguish many desires, to be liberated from them. A feat attempted too in other religions, such as Christianity, through virtue, self-control and wisdom. He'd also learnt in the Mindgarten about the desire for good things.

As the days went by in the Mindgarten, both he and Lester were even given more tolerable jobs from Frenchie. He smiled in recollection of the time with his new friend. They'd tended gardens together, bailed hay in high bronze fields and enjoyed lively conversations full of humour and vigour, as well as quieter deliberations at night upon their veranda. His mind's eye caught too, his now frequent walks with Lily. The calm contemplative strolling, hypnotic even, as if the world outside them didn't exist - they both drawn so effortlessly together. His time also with Thay, where their meetings had become more regular. A ritual and a meaningful kinship, where it never occurred to him for what reason their meetings had become. He'd felt a warmth from the other Mindgarten residents, his private audiences with Thay had not gone unnoticed and he was given a delicate reverence for it.

He walked on, and reaching the open windows of a brightly lit exercise room he peered in. Inside he could make out Lester, struggling to keep up with the others in a yoga class. Smiling to himself, he moved further. Past the glimmering gold entrance of the Great Hall, alongside the rows of ponds with their colourful fishes, and on to a scattering of fine-looking gardens with neatly tended flowerbeds of every colour imaginable. He stopped near some Buddleia bushes. Their sweet smell, and gently moving, and noticed a butterfly as it fluttered overhead until it finally landed on the edge of a bouncing leaf. Its wings coming together like the closing of a book. He looked, the sheer pleasure of it. Now he was surrounded by more butterflies.

Further still, he came to someone's home that had an open neat looking wooden porch that overlooked a colourful garden - a profusion of packed lilacs, whites, deep purples and reds sparring with the breeze. He sat on a bench opposite. And saw that on their porch wall, they'd added a large decorative mirror, pretty in a way, with a little shelf below it. Two confused little birds were perched on the shelf, tapping away at the mirror with their beaks. Flapping their wings wildly. Trying to enter the place of their own reflections.

"What are they doing?" Alfi thought. "Trying to enter a world of their imaginations which they believe is better, is brighter, when in truth it doesn't really exist. And after all, all that they had needed and not wanted, was right there behind them."

He was shaken out of his thoughts by a sound over his shoulder. He looked behind, his face softened, as did hers. It was Lily.

❀ ❀ ❀

The days continued to pass, and in his free time he worked for Frenchie on the truck's engine. Indeed, the intellect required in working on the machine, the skill of his hands and the cleverness of the brain with the practical outcome it would bring, always gave Alfi a quiet satisfaction. It was a form of meditation, the singlemindedness of tuning in. He thought back and laughed at how sometimes, it was looked down upon by those who had no skill or intelligence for it, why even Socrates was a stonemason.

Perhaps too, it was a further reward, or that Frenchie had realised that they were probably going to get through Green Bird, that both he and Lester were given the more pleasant errand of taking the truck to Miss Chan's to deliver laundry. And all the while they were now just one week away from Green Bird.

❀ ❀ ❀

It was evening, later than it had ever been, as Thay mindfully picked up a large gold brocade and placed it over his favourite cushion resting on the floor. He admired the objects around his room; the figurines, paintings and photographs. Such things had been his constant companions over the years, as a golden light shone from a myriad of wavering candles. He settled down on the cushion and crossed his legs, as his eyes circled the room once more, finally settling on the portrait of Alexandria. He thought of all the changes a person can bring about if they put their mind to it, and how all things must draw to an end, there was a sad inevitability to it. "Is vanity all it is?" he thought. "And where would the next journey take him?" He became weak. Life and the final treachery of it.

It was strange, that then, just then, in those quiet moments, he wanted to reach out with a trembling hand to touch someone, but there was no one there. Goodbyes, their sentimentality then, seemed hurtful - the burden of grief that they would bring. Tis better, hard it may seem, to leave them. Leave it all be. Let it rest now, and slip back to nothingness. And so, he sat comfortably. Lowering his head as his hands intwined themselves unconsciously. His eyelids quivered, just a little, before beginning to shut - gently now, taking out the light, as if the descending curtains to a play.

# CHAPTER TWENTY-ONE

## Bad Faith

Calliope held her gaze as Alfi and Lily sat in front of her. Around them, like always in this quiet place, was a concert of calls and playful shrieks from the birds hidden somewhere inside the shadowy trees. Lobsang appeared - it was obvious he'd been running. Out of breath with both hands he momentarily touched his chest. 'Mr Alfi,' he called, there was tiredness in his voice. 'Come quick! Come quickly please!'

'What is it?' asked Alfi.

But he couldn't speak.

He led them hurriedly along the red corridor. The richly decorated walls, the familiar gold lighting - all as quiet as they'd always been. The door was half open as the three of them hesitated before passing through it into the middle of the room, where Thay sat meditating. Alfi crept forward not wanting to disturb the master.

Lobsang took another breath and whispered. 'He's gone.'

'What do you mean?' stuttered Alfi.

'He's gone. He's left his body. It was no longer good anymore. So he had to leave it. He knew it was the time but he couldn't tell anyone.' Lobsang's head dropped in two quick successions; his hand to his forehead, which did little to hide a tear.

Timidly, Lily stepped forward and knelt in front of the master. She lingered, taking in his quiet face. So utterly at peace, she thought, as he seemed always to be. The softly closed eyelids, the unfurrowed forehead, his lips, gently resting upon each other, but there was no breeze between them. Then his words called out telepathically to her as if they'd come from a dream, "*Do your best,*" he said, "*and leave the rest to fate.*" She looked back at the two others where Lobsang nodded, then reached out to press her thumb to Thay's tender wrist. Moving some more, her head lowered, her eyes filled, and she faced back to Alfi.

The master's two hands took Alfi back to Brother Iblan and the Brother's words from all that time ago. He looked to the wall, and to a round mandala pictured in its simple frame, painted in every colour imaginable, muted beautifully. It was a depiction of a stupa from above, its thirteen shelves, steps leading to the heavens and into enlightenment from which there is no return. Then to the master's hands again.

"One day," Brother Iblan had said. "I've dreamt you will see this simple mudra in a significant way." And so, Alfi's soft eyes were drawn to the one hand cupped inside the other. The palms facing upwards from the centre of the master's lap, and the monk's words called out to him. "Gone Home."

❀ ❀ ❀

In a fresh winter's morning, a gilded sun rose over the sea of still white figures. All the Mindgarten were there, they stood outside the Great Hall, filled the main square, along all the paths and the flowerbeds, on every walkway, in every space. A string of children held hands together, whilst some of them, the smaller ones, turned away to be comforted inside their mother's aprons; and all within this dreadful silence, broken only by a lonesome bell.

Facing them, and sitting on top of the grand steps, was Thay. His back had been kept upright, secured respectfully to a sandalwood plinth. For days his body had remained as warm as it had always been. They say, being a venerated one, a Rinpoche, that the mind can reside within the body even long after the heart beat had gone. But now Lobsang had told Alfi, now was the time.

Powdery, tightly packed branches of more sandalwood, saturated with the bright orange splashes of ghee, were stacked beneath Thay's crossed legs below his gown. Lobsang walked heavily, and without saying a word, handed a small cloth of white muslin to Alfi whose heart began to beat like a soft drum.

For the end of a life with no progeny was more significant than any other. It was a conclusion. The finish of a linage of ancestors that Thay had spoken about, that had taken thousands of years to fashion itself, and now all coming to an end. Their voices would no longer be heard.

Alfi placed the muslin into Thay's mouth, pressing each last fold tenderly into the corners of the master's lips - as a hollowness consumed him. "How could we be brought to this?" he thought, as Lobsang approached again, this time offering a candle, shielding its flame that was bent sideways in a circling wind.

Alfi lit the cloth, and watched as Thay's mouth began to take light. The head would take the longest. He stepped back, as the lips that had articulated all those careful thoughts into words and deeds, began to burn - soon to disappear to nothing. The flame became longer and jutted inwards and into the mouth quickly, like a serpent not wanting to be seen, as Alfi's eyes met Lily's in the crowd.

And all across the Mindgarten, over the gardens and the lawns, the wild leaning fields, the white shining buildings, the hills and the towering mountains that encircled them, all was quiet.

❀ ❀ ❀

It was customary to wait fourteen days after a body had expired. Whilst this was a time when some believed the soul would begin its celestial journey, for many in the Mindgarten, it was a time simply to rest, to avoid pleasures, nor even, like in Buddhism or Hinduism, to take salt, and absorb the loss of another sentient being - to become accustomed to change. In the lingering, contemplative two weeks that followed, Alfi began to feel a veracious and irresistible expectation put before him. His relationship with Thay - and in performing the ritual of his death - had of course, not gone unnoticed and there seemed to be an anticipation from the Mindgarten that he might somehow step into the breach. He wondered, did they look to him for guidance and hope? Did he have the ability to lead, and the practical wisdom to nurture people to decide things for themselves - and to compel them *always* to be compassionate to others, something that the Mindgarten did so effortlessly. Indeed, when he reflected on it for long enough, he *could lead,* with pure virtue as its foundation, the sweetest and happiest power of all.

Each night, he'd remove the small glass prism from its hidden place inside his room and in the calm meditative hours that followed, he was becoming aware of faint voices, indescribable feelings that ebbed and flowed towards him. With each gentle rhythm of his breath, it presented a further gateway, in which he could delve more deeply - so much so - that eventually he could sit quite comfortably behind his own thoughts for hours and watch the coming and going of things. The playing or teasing within the functioning of the mind, with all its preconceived ideas, notions and prejudices. The mind's aversion to being bored, not recognising the true power of it and the ideas that nothingness could bring. In some ways it was quite entertaining, and in this stillness Thay's words flew about him; *'the unexamined life is not worth living Mr Alfi.'*

Questions puzzled him. Was he living a perception of himself reflected by the expectation of others or was he truly free? Was it impossible to be free within a community, or even outside of one and alone, where you would be led by your own conditioning and biases? What was the *real essence* of Alfi?

He dreamt that night - and what was it that dreamt? That what if the mind, or at least how we thought of it, did not exist at all? Where inside, if we looked, we would find nothing. If we were solely the body, just the physical, and there was no more to it than that? If we were simply being led by a function of the brain, a biological machine, where all our interactions with the world were only through the processing of neurons, chemical reactions and electric pulses based on patterns, genetics and previous experiences; and that such things originated all our actions and thoughts, even love. Then if this be true, there was to be no spirituality and we were fooling ourselves. Individuality, as we knew it, could not exist, instead we were reduced to the highest form of artificial, of organic intelligence, where all we have rooted for, our dreams and how we made sense of ourselves were illusionary. It was a proposition that if correct, horrified Alfi and left him utterly alone, cast out with this knowledge, and outside of the race. There seemed no discourse to approve or disprove it. But he did not believe it to be true. And so, in the quiet comfort of his room he wondered, should he resolve *not* to identify his 'Self' by what he was, but instead by the freedom of choice to become who he ought to be?

Then a darker contemplation consumed him, and a tear began to collect itself into a corner of an eye; heavying, globulus, and falling with all its loneliness onto his cheek. Had he, over all these years, been defeated by a version of himself and made some dreadful, irreversible mistake? He had become anonymous, denying his own freedom, to be part of the herd. Had the sum of his life so far; his values, the preconceptions that his mind and others had given him, their conditioning; had they all been Mauvaise Foi; *bad faith?* Had he been lied to by himself and been too afraid to take risks? And was it now too late? For like everyone, his greatest treasure was time, what he gave to it, how much he sold of it, it was finite with no day, week or year to be repeated. Had he failed to examine himself as Thay had advised, and flittered it away?

Then, in the quiet spaces within the prism, he reminded himself with delectable feelings more than words, to look outwards, to dance with the world and be moved by it. To take experiences unselfishly, compassionately and make decisions unburdened by the conventions inside him. But how could he do this? How could he escape himself to such a freedom and walk outside of his own mind? *What was* the nature, the limit of human experience - and could it be transcended?

# CHAPTER TWENTY-TWO

## The Nine Muse Gompa

Lester steered the truck awkwardly as it weaved and bounced its way along the sun-bleached track. Despite the state of the road, he enjoyed the route. The view of the white mountains both left and right, against the sapphire sky and along the high ridge was spectacular, as they made yet another laundry visit to Miss Chan's. Lester was his usual enthusiastic self as he clutched the wheel with an elbow outside the blowy window. He turned to Alfi as the mountain winds blew about them ruffling their hair. 'It's another fine day my friend! A beautiful day,' and Alfi felt the immediate joy of his company. Miss Chan's shop building came, at last, into view, as Lester swerved boisterously to a sliding stop, emblematic of his mood.

Belan was already at the top of his ladder as they entered carrying a pair of heavy sacks, a place Belen always seemed to be. He was rifling through some fabric as Miss Chan called up holding her pencil and writing pad. 'Medium!' she yelled, and then began scribbling.

'Yes, medium Angel,' Belan reported back, rustling through more plastic wrappers.

Lester lent into Alfi's ear. 'Is he alright up there? At his age?'

'He just needs to be careful,' Alfi said staring up.

'Hallo Alfi, Lester!' Miss Chan called out happily.

Belan called down too. 'Oh Mr Alfi, Lester! How good it is to see you both! It's such a pleasure to see such pleasant, fine gentlemen, gives one a fine fluttering in the solar plexus.'

'Thank you Belan,' said Alfi.

'Never mind the *solar plexus!*' his wife snapped.

'How was the ride over?' asked Belan. 'The road still a bit on the slip?'

'Still not that easy,' Lester replied.

'Always a tricky one. That pass,' Belen observed. 'I can remember an attempt on it on my bicycle once in the seventies. The buffeting winds and vibration cruelly exposing a weakness in my wheel nuts.'

'Sorry to hear that,' said Lester.

Miss Chan shook her head disappointedly mumbling the words, 'Wheel nuts,' as Alfi and Lester disappeared into the laundry room.

She looked down, scribbling on her writing pad, when suddenly the nib of her pencil stopped. There was the sound, a sound of several car engines outside. She paced to the window as Belan called down. 'Next Angel?' A question that was ignored as she peered through the dusty glass.

Several black jeeps were pulling in, one by one, and parking haphazardly. Their doors opened, as a group of bullish looking men emerged, stretching themselves - it was obvious they'd been on a long journey. The jeep in front caused her eyes to grow wider. She became quite agitated. Alfi and Lester reappeared from the laundry room.

'Yup! Just another three bags,' called Lester.

'Oh,' said Miss Chan with little expression, still staring through the window.

'What?' asked Alfi.

In spite of the years, she recognized the pose, the little stagger as he stepped forward from the jeep in front, with that stick, and that slightest of limps. He hadn't changed that much at all. He lent on his cane dependably, and was convening with the others. 'Oh no,' she said. 'I knew this...I thought this could happen.'

'What?' asked Alfi.

'We've problem...outside,' she said.

'Oh?' asked Alfi.

'Problem? What problem?' voiced Lester.

'Outside,' she repeated. 'Now Thay has gone and outside. Outside. I can see...it is his brother. His real brother! Thay's brother is here.'

'His brother?' asked Lester. 'Thay had a brother?'

Belan called down again from higher altitude. 'We only have *large* Angel.'

'Be quiet Belan!' she whispered, pressing a finger to her lips.

Alfi joined her at the window. He stood back. He couldn't quite believe it. 'It's Teshi!'

'What? How you know Thay's brother?' asked Miss Chan.

'Teshi? Teshi who? Who's Teshi?' said Lester.

'That's Mr Teshi,' continued Alfi. 'We met. I met him in Madrakani. Is Mr Teshi...is Mr Teshi *really* Thay's younger brother?'

'Who's Teshi?' Lester repeated.

'Yes, he's Thay's younger brother,' she replied as Belan attempted to call from above. 'Wait a minute, Belan!' she blurted, and turned to Alfi. 'This is trouble.'

'I still can't believe it. That he's Thay's brother!' said Alfi.

'You have to believe it. And now that Thay, his brother has expired, I think he has come to take the land, to take the Mindgarten,' said Miss Chan.

'Take the Mindgarten?' voiced Lester.

'It's the law,' she continued flatly. 'I should have thought about this sooner. The Nepalese law. There's no other benefactor. No children. So the younger brother will inherit, take everything. Why else do you think he's here?' She looked more closely through the window and turned to them quickly. 'Quick! Hide! There're others with him. He is walking here. He's coming...'

Alfi and Lester shot a glance to each other and dashed into the laundry room. They all waited, where the whole shop, apart from the sound of an old ticking wall clock, went into a kind of silent limbo. Eventually the silence was broken as the door slowly opened. Mr Teshi stepped in, his walking stick tapping heavily on the wooden floor. Alongside, was his ever-vacant looking assistant, Stodge.

Leaning on his good leg, Mr Teshi looked at Miss Chan pleasantly. 'Oh Miss Chan!' he announced, trying to sound homely. 'Look at you. Look at you! After all these years. You look the same. You haven't changed at all!'

'It's been a good many years,' she replied promptly. 'Good years.'

'Yes. It has.'

'So, why you have you come here?'

'Oh Miss Chan. That's not very friendly. Not friendly, not a welcome at all, is it? I've come a long way.' He limped in a step further, surveying the shop and stopped to take a breath. 'My brother has finally and sadly, passed away. You must know. Such terrible news,' his head shook. 'And I have come to show my respects. My condolences. Such a sad demise. And the place, the Mindgarten. Is it good?'

'Everyone's been very happy there,' Miss Chan said dismissively. 'And still are. So why? Why have you really come here?'

'I told you, just to show my condolences and...'

'And?'

'Oh Miss Chan, I *do* wish you would give me a better welcome. I really do. Sometimes, I wonder, why it is that all the world seems always against me? But the Mindgarten, you're right. Since my brother's expired. We have to consider the consequences, the Mindgarten and its future. And what will become of it? The land, the buildings, everything, all the responsibility has been sadly passed on to me. It's such a burden really, for me to take on.'

'Then why don't you just go? Just leave it,' she said curtly. 'You don't need the burden of it. It can run itself. Go back to Madrakani. The people here, they can run it here, alone themselves. They can look after it.'

'Oh, I wish it could be that simple,' he replied emphatically. 'I really do. But it's not simple at all. I feel, I must take it on - what else can one do? But redevelop it. Make a go of it somehow, as a...tribute to my brother.'

'Redevelop?'

'Oh, it can't possibly survive as it is.' He studied her more carefully. 'There is a lot of people in Mindgarten? How many?'

'I would not tell you.'

'Oh Miss Chan. That's not nice. It's not nice at all. It's why I've had to bring so many jeeps, friends of mine. You know, I must tell you, there might be quite a lot of commotion over there tonight. I just wish life could be easier...a lot easier. I do. But I have to take what's mine and quickly, it's always from my experience, the best way. To be decisive, and not string things out. And, as a friend, if I were you Miss Chan, in case it gets troublesome, I'd stay away from the Mindgarten tonight.'

Miss Chan was about to speak, when suddenly her dog Brandy dashed out wagging his tail. At first, he skipped to Mr Teshi, his paws dancing noisily and sliding on the wooden floor, then he made a half jump to Stodge, and after thinking better of it, trotted with a bounce towards the laundry room. Leaping to the door, he flicked open its handle with a paw, it swung open to reveal two figures moving quickly away from behind it.

Stodge's head twitched. He asked innocently. 'Is someone in there Mr Teshi?'

'Who is it? Who's in there?' said Mr Teshi. 'Come out!' Stodge, drew out a pistol and pouted his lips. 'Come out! Whoever you are,' continued Teshi and then surprisingly added. 'Please.' A moment of thought passed. There was a creak on the floorboards behind the door as the two decided - ever-so-slowly - to tread out. Alfi with his hands in the air, like someone in the movies, was followed by a rather shaky looking Lester. Teshi took a while to take it all in. 'Oh no. Not again,' he announced.

Lester glanced to his wristwatch and did his best to lighten the mood. 'Well, what a shame,' he said checking the time. 'Is that the time? The time already? We have to move on. Sorry about that. Time flies, doesn't it? Particularly as you get older.'

'Yes, it sure does,' nodded Stodge, much to Teshi's annoyance.

Lester continued. 'We just get to meet, and now we have to say goodbye. Laundry's a busy business. Sorry about that.'

'Not so fast,' said Teshi.

'We're just doing some washing,' Lester persisted. 'We gotta go. We're on a fast cycle. Spin dry. We're just innocent, simple, launderette people.'

Ignoring this remark, Teshi clenched his lips into a half smile. 'If it isn't that Mr Alfi again! We looked all over for you - all over Kathmandu. There was no sign, and now *here* you are. All the way up here! The only place we *didn't* look. You have a habit of being in the wrong place at the wrong time Mr Alfi. It's so unfortunate. So, you have been staying in the Mindgarten *all* this time?'

Alfi began to answer. 'Well...'

Abruptly, almost as if this was his prompt, an unobserved Belan slipped a footing from above. He swung outwards like a geriatric gibbon by an outstretched arm and a leg - it was at more of an acute angle than his advanced groin could bear. He groaned as his leg came back to some degree of equilibrium which was accompanied by an apologetic 'I do beg your pardon sir,' uncomfortably high on the octaves. It caught Teshi and Stodge off-guard as Alfi and Lester seized the moment.

They ran back into the laundry room and rushed for an open window. Lester was out first, jumping through and landing on the dust outside in a rolling ball, but he was up again and galloping towards the truck - arms pumping, chin in the air - like an athlete chasing gold. Next out was Alfi, running behind and grasping the ignition keys in both hands as if they were a cherished talisman. Teshi and Stodge bolted into the room after them, Stodge thought fast, and made a lunge for the same aperture but was forgetful of his large buttock size - the way many such people sadly are in public these days - and was held up by thick, ornamental Tibetan window sills. Half inside and half outside the building, he writhed over the sills as if trying to learn the breaststroke without the use of any water. 'I think,' he whimpered, breathing heavily and trying to grab anything with his hands. 'I think I'm stuck sir.'

Teshi gripped and tugged at Stodge's thick belt. It was harder than he thought. There was an almighty crash as he finally yanked him back into the room, both of them falling into a shambolic heap. 'Sorry sir,' Stodge called out, getting up quickly and apologetically lifting Mr Teshi and patting him down. There was a clatter as Stodge broke for the door and back into the shop, with a fast-limping Mr Teshi trailing behind by ten yards with his stick - looking like someone who'd lost their horse. They staggered passed Miss Chan and out of the building where Belan was descending the ladder, surprisingly quickly for a man of his age, counting the runners as he went and proclaiming, 'By Jove!'

Alfi felt the ignition and pressed in the key. 'Come on, come on!' he said.

'They're coming!' yelled Lester.

'I know that!' Alfi twisted the key again, finally he heard the roar as the engine got going. He thrust the gear stick forward, stamped the peddle to the floor, and they were sent into an accelerated turn, right in front of the jeeps and sending up an eruption of dust over their dazed, confused standing drivers.

'Chase them! Chase them!' Teshi called, clambering outside and pointing with his stick. There was the clanking of doors as they scrambled into action.

Alfi and Lester accelerated at full pelt. Down a long dust track that rose steeply again, up towards the hills, but they were no match for Teshi's men who were soon pressing behind them, probing at their tail lights. Lester shouted amongst wind and noise. 'What are we going to do now? They're bound to get us! They've got jeeps and we've got this! And I wanna know how? How you know this Teshi guy and how we're in this mess?'

'You might had noticed we're in a car chase?' shouted Alfi, twisting the wheel as they jerked up the hill. 'We've got no time for that! I'll explain later. Now...the Nine Muse Gompa.'

'The what?'

Alfi drove as madly as he could up another steep rising ridge, he glanced to the mirror but the jeeps kept coming. He took another sweeping turn that sent them leftwards, leaning sideways and around the other side of a hill and to the very top - the jeeps still raging in a convoy behind them. Along the peak they entered a series of tighter curves, one after the other; a road he knew well. The truck skewed left and right, he was clutching the wheel desperately at full speed to stay on track - the narrow cliff they were traversing giving them glimpses; plummeting falls down both sides of the mountain below. The jeeps, now nervous with the terrain, were beginning to fall back.

'It's just a little further,' cried Alfi shifting a gear as the engine groaned - beginning to sound like it was giving up. 'I think!' He steered into a shuddering turn to the right, then to the left. The truck lost its grip on the stones and dust, and rocked the two of them sideways. Glancing to the mirror again, at last, their followers were dropping further back - and almost out of view. Accelerating forward, his mouth tensed, where he took another final yank on the wheel, this time that was so severe, that they were up on two wheels, their hearts missing a beat. And bang! The truck pounded down again, and at a right angle they were off - hurtling forwards and downwards, now careering uncontrollably down a steep concealed track. Alfi steered through scrub and around trees as they sped on; the windscreen whipped by branches, the bushes scraping violently at their doors. Finally, they heard the jeeps disappear above them on the hill - only to become a succession of faint whistles into the distance - they were gone.

The ground levelled as Alfi stomped the brake with full force. It threw the two of them forwards and back again where truck finally stopped. Alfi gasped, turned off the engine and pressed backwards in his seat. There was silence until he breathed. 'The Nine Muse Gompa.' And through the windscreen, littered with tattered leaves and broken branches, was a simple, weather-beaten dome of bricks and mortar.

Lester stuttered, still exhausted by the chase. 'So what...? What are we going to do now? And when are you going to tell me what this is all about Alfi?'

'It's a long story.' Alfi tapped the steering wheel. 'Look, briefly Mr Teshi did some gold smuggling.'

'Gold smuggling?'

'From Tibet.'

'Tibet?'

'And Teshi, he turns out to be Thay's brother. Small world, isn't it? And, as he said back there, I was in the wrong place at the wrong time. I met him when I was in jail. These things happen. And these men have got guns.'

'Jail? You were in *jail!*'

'It was nothing much.'

'Nothing much! What the hell is going on Alfi? Who the hell are you? What have you been doing before you came up here? Gold smuggling. Tibet. Guns. Jail...?'

'And now I think we've got to move quickly!' retorted Alfi. 'We've got to get back to the Mindgarten to warn everyone.'

'Go back? Oh no. Are you kidding me? Back to the Mindgarten? As soon as we get there...Get back. Guess who's going to be waiting for us? Men with guns Alfi. That's who.' Lester rubbed his forehead and looked miserably through the leaves on the tatty windscreen. 'Things were going so well,' he said. 'And I was beginning to like the Mindgarten. We were nearly through Green Bird too - and there was Number Fifteen.'

'We've got to sneak back.' Alfi interrupted.

'Sneak?'

'An element of surprise.'

'It's not possible.'

Alfi looked over his shoulder and into the back of the van where, stacked up neatly, was a collection of about to be laundered, colourful women's saris.

Lester followed his gaze. 'Surprise?'

# CHAPTER TWENTY-THREE

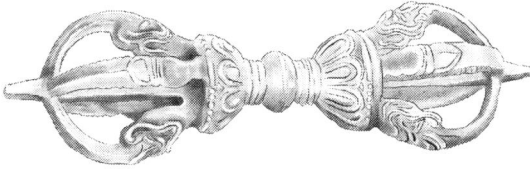

*Virtue and Power*

Men rarely look agreeable in women's clothing. They often look quite horrific, and this evening, even within the sweet allure of sunset, there proved to be no exception. Perhaps it is something to do with the lack of curvaceous hips or the high female symmetry, Lester could not quite fathom it as he faced forward, their truck slowing down to just walking pace. He was wearing a deep red silk number and Alfi was in peach, a colour that rarely looks good, even on a peach.

'I still can't believe I am...we are...doing this?' Lester complained. There was no reaction from Alfi so he continued. 'This is a stupid idea Alfi. A stupid idea. They're going to spot us immediately. Crazy.'

'Stop it,' calmed Alfi. 'And your veil's dropping. You'll need to keep it up over the face. And it would have helped if you'd shaved this morning.'

'Shaved?' Pardon me. But at seven o-clock this morning I didn't think I'd be dressed up as a woman and sneaking back into the Mindgarten. I would have packed eyeliner.'

'There's no need for that. You just need to make a bit more of an effort, that's all.'

They drove a little further, nearing the entrance to the Mindgarten. Alfi steered forward and parked tightly underneath the shadows of some trees. They got out, closed the doors as gently as they could and crept towards the entrance, with Lester tripping a little over his veil as he went. He whispered. 'It looks all quiet. It looks like this Teshi guy hasn't got here yet? So, what should we do?'

'Here, you take the keys. At least if you need to get out fast - you have the van. We need to both spread out separately and tell as many people as possible. At least so they can prepare.'

'What about you?' asked Lester.

'I have my motorbike remember? We don't want to cause a panic. If we just tell as many people as possible. At least they can start protecting themselves somehow...some might want to leave, others may just bolt down their doors for the night, barricade themselves in. Let's just get around the Mindgarten and tell people. When Teshi arrives with those men and those guns...well, we just want them to be safe.'

'Lily?' Lester asked.

Alfi checked his watch. 'Yes,' he replied pensively. 'I know where she'll be. Good luck Lester, and if all fails, we'll meet back at the Nine Muse Gompa. Got it?'

'The Nine Muse Gompa.' Lester repeated. 'Ok. Got it.'

The two separated and began walking in different directions into the night. Lester slightly tripping again as he went.

❀ ❀ ❀

Beneath her fountain, Caliope was as quiet and serene as she'd always been. Alfi caught sight of Lily's silhouette, alone and staring into the water, her hands loosely on her lap. Trotting lightly, he went up the old stone steps and into the garden. He spoke softly. 'Lily. It's me.'

She turned. 'Who?' Startled to see his sari. Then with surprise. 'What? What are you doing?'

He sat next to her. 'Look, it's a long story.'

'You're dressed as a woman!'

'Full marks for the observation. Now listen,' he said hurriedly. 'We've, got to leave tonight.'

'What, what do you mean?' she asked, staring at him up and down.

'It's Thay's brother,' he said.

'Who's Thay's brother? And why are you dressed as a woman?'

'We thought, me and Lester, that it was the safest way to get back in. To get back here. Look, Thay has a brother who's returned, who's coming to claim the land...tonight. His name is Teshi. It's going to be dangerous Lily. He's coming with men. They've got guns and they are going to take the Mindgarten back, by force.'

'What? What are you saying? I don't understand?'

'Look, I haven't got time to explain,'

'But you're dressed as a woman.'

'These people are dangerous Lily. There're dangerous people coming here tonight, believe me! Now Thay has passed away, his brother now owns the Mindgarten. We've got to warn others, as many people as we can. Then, I think, we should get out. Tonight.'

'You can't expect me to leave? Just like that. For this...story? And I still don't understand why you are dressed as a woman!'

'We've got to leave.'

'So someone is coming to take the Mindgarten?'

'Yes! He'll want everybody out.'

'And you expect me to go? Just like that. Where would I be going?'

'We can figure that out later.'

She looked at him earnestly. 'I've done enough of running Alfi. All my life.'

'But Lily, we've got to go. Don't you realise? We don't own this place.'

'Haven't you done enough of running around too? Moving away?' she had lowered the tempo of the conversation.

'But.'

'Don't you ever just want to *stay* somewhere? Make a home?'

'We can't stay,' Alf pleaded. 'The Mindgarten...it looks to be over.' And there was the shuddering of jeeps in the distance. 'We're too late,' he said, tilting his head to listen. 'I think they're coming.'

❀ ❀ ❀

The line of ten jeeps came in a rambling convoy that rolled to a halt outside the Great Hall. Their doors swung open, and as if without a care in the world, the men clambered out and surveyed their impressive new surroundings. Some held rifles, dropped loosely over their arms, almost as if they were an afterthought. With his stick Mr Teshi limped out in front and was handed a megaphone from a rather doubtful looking Stodge. Teshi fiddled with it for a while, twisting a little white dial one way then the other, and then stood more upright to take a breath. For this was his moment.

'This is the new owner of the Mindgarten,' he pronounced. His nasally tone reverberating around the buildings. 'My name is Mr Teshi,' the megaphone began to crackle so he adjusted it again, giving Stodge a disappointed look. 'So I've come here to take my land. I'm the brother of dear, beloved, Thay. And I hope you've enjoyed your stay here, but now is the time, sadly, to leave. We need everyone out please. This place. This Mindgarten, will no longer exist. It will no longer be your home. We want you to please gather your belongings and be out of the buildings as quickly as you can. Within one hour.

And please. Please, don't let me down. We'd like your departure in an orderly fashion.'

Alfi listened, half surprised as to how polite the dooming message was.

Teshi continued. 'We don't want any trouble. You will be assisted, and encouraged to leave, by my colleagues.'

'We've got to go,' said Alfi.

'But where?' Lily whispered.

❀ ❀ ❀

Illuminated under a cloudy moon in the darkness, the motorbike leant on its side-stand behind Alfi's building. The only sound, was of rhythmic cicadas calling out invisibly to each other from the barks of the trees. 'Come,' Alfi said tenderly to Lily as they tiptoed forward. He took hold of the handle bars, straightened the machine and placed himself on, and then helped Lily. She sat on the saddle behind him where they said nothing. Her head pointed downwards; they both enveloped in their own particular sadness to be leaving. Glancing to the track ahead, Alfi gave the bike a light kick and the engine quietly and reliably, rumbled into a low action. They moved off slowly, leaving only the chirping insects behind.

It occurred to Alfi that the only way to leave the Mindgarten was through a wide nut-coloured track, that would eventually make its way through the very centre of the Mindgarten - and in front of the Great Hall. He would have to pass Teshi and his men. He edged forward at an almost silent speed under the shadows of a line of trees, until sure enough, ahead in the distance, was a huddle of haphazard jeeps with Teshi standing amongst them. The two waited and watched from the motorbike, still wondering quite what to do.

Meanwhile even then, and earlier on the megaphone, Mr Teshi was beginning to feel a discomfort with power. Perhaps the

Mindgarten was already beginning to cast a spell on him. You could hear it delicately within his voice. His demands seemed rather to be requests, too polite, where he lacked the lion's roar for commanding.

Countless thoughts can arrive in a single moment, and so Teshi might had considered, why people worked for him at all? Was it, that they had a fear of doing something for themselves? Was their servitude just simple employment, and nothing more to it than that? With none, or very little, admiration for their leader and therefore not genuine at all? For the truth was, that *his* power had no virtue behind it. It was based on fear. And so, the worst power of all, and was useless apart from the actions it yielded. It could not make him, or others, happy. And if he brooded on this for long enough, it would make him feel rather pathetic and alone.

Whether their allegiance was through any semblance of charisma from his part or otherwise, what lay unarticulated for Mr Teshi, was that he truly wanted no one to follow him. Like his deceased brother, he would've preferred it, if they had followed themselves. To become a master of oneself from within, rather than exert any control over others. Indeed, had he too lacked the power to control his own Self, and take power over his senses? What *was* he really looking for - after all these years? From where had all his messages come, these messages that had driven, that had deceived him.

Indeed, these suppositions might had emanated from the symbol of the Vajra, the "thunderbolt" often seen in the Mindgarten. There was one outside the Great Hall and just above him. With its elaborate silver shaft and spherical spoked heads at both ends; and whilst it was seen as a symbol of power, a weapon of the gods in Hinduism, as well as used in Buddhism to cut through ignorance, in the Mindgarten it manifested as the simple indestructability of wisdom and truth.

It was within these feelings, more than words, that Stodge eventually approached with his dopey eyes. 'What now?' he asked with

Mr Teshi still held in his dream. 'What now?' he asked again, as they both turned to see the motorbike coming.

Alfi twisted the throttle, their heads jolted back and they were away - Lily clutching onto him tightly. The jeep drivers just stood, mesmerised with the bike racing towards them - the sheer audacity of it. But it was the revelation amongst the noise, most of all of Alfi's features in the darkness, in the wind and the dust, as his veil had slipped and was flapping on his shoulders, and the fact that he was wearing a sari, that left Mr Teshi holding his megaphone swinging by the fingertips - he was beginning to look utterly exhausted.

Just yards before them Alfi wrenched at the handle bars. He leaned and skidded, his knee touching the ground, and in a violent turn he threw up a wave of orange dust. Teshi's mouth dropped - before he yelled out. 'Follow him! Follow him!' And already one of his drivers was leaping behind his wheel - his jeep speeding off in a grinding half-circle on the turf. The chase was on.

Alfi and Lily shot like an arrow into the half-darkness. Swerving in and out between buildings and around gardens, along rows of houses in a stream of white light from their lit porches. They accelerated passed the long dark ponds, carrying on, until at last, they were beginning to reach more open ground. He looked back but somehow the jeep was still coming, even teasing at him, zigzagging in the distance. They drove further until eventually there was farmland - now they were at the very western edge of the Mindgarten. Beyond them was an undulating landscape, mostly of glowing mustard fields in the moonlight, one after another, and just up from these a road swept invitingly into a dark forest. Their heads dropped, they leaned forward and went for it. Taking the bike through one curvaceous turn then another, winding around the fields and into the forest, past fast-flowing black trees in a blaze of noise with Lily doing her best to hold on. Yet the jeep's flashing lights kept coming. Further still, and a brow of a hill was covered in a silvery mist and marking the last of the trees. He pulled back the throttle to its maximum. For a second the front wheel left the ground, and they were away, speeding through the mist and over the hill and out of the forest again, with Lily looking back - her hair wild in the wind - the jeep falling out of view. A mile passed, along a flat wilderness, until in the distance was a shining black river that divided a bleak landscape. Relentlessly, the jeep's flashing lights started coming again over the horizon behind them as the river ahead gushed and rolled, its icy white surf now bright under the full moon. Two logs had fallen on Alfi's side of the river and had wedged themselves together, pointing up over the water. He thought quickly. 'Hold on!'

'What?' she yelled, but before he could answer they were at full speed, the bike slipping along the wet timber and they were away! Lifted up and tearing through the cold air, their loose wheels still spinning in the wind. They landed with a blow the other side. Alfi shoved the bike quickly, left and right, to stay upright. It straightened and they drove madly into the wilderness.

The jeep came on hungrily. The driver gripping the wheel, his knuckles tight as he saw the sight. He rose up on two tyres over the logs, only to come down heavily again and flat into the water; his engine guzzling to a halt.

❀ ❀ ❀

The flames from the little fire crackled under a round moon that shone over the Nine Muse Gompa. Alfi mindfully shifted some twigs amongst the glowing embers and turned to Lily. 'Maybe Lester got caught?' he said. 'Or maybe he's sleeping in the van somewhere? But I did tell him the Nine Muse Gompa.'

'Poor Lester,' Lily sleepily replied. 'And the Mindgarten, I'm tired Alfi. Just tired.'

She leant into his chest where he could feel the weight of her head against him, the weight of her dependence. A cool breeze crept. It circled their backs which gave him the impulse. Telling him, gently, to do so. He put his arm around her as she nudged closer in her acceptance, and they gazed into the flames.

✿ ✿ ✿

A cockerel gave out a last solitary cry as the morning light rose up over the injured buildings of the Mindgarten. A door was left swinging open, it clattered noisily against a wooden frame in a confused wind, whilst pretty white fences that once had encircled neat flowerbeds and gardens were down, humbled and broken.

Alfi and Lily chose to walk and dismounted the bike. Someone's belongings were strewn across a side of the road, some children's toys - colourful orange and blue plastic with little grey wheels - were in a tumbled mess outside one of the buildings. Beyond them was a string of white, now empty houses, leading up to a silent Great Hall. The hall's silence, held the two of them quiet together, until eventually walking further they saw an only figure. It was an elderly Nepalese man, Alfi knew him to be a gardener. The man was sat, huddled into his knees and looking cold on a porch floor. He looked up recognising the two of them sympathetically.

'Are you ok?' Alfi asked. 'What happened?'

Lily bent down and took his hand, his grey translucent eyes coupling with hers. 'There was 'big action,' he said in his simple English. 'They come, and many people from Mindgarten run away. Others stay in home, but then they all go later. The police - they come. Many police. And I think they take them. Those that were left.'

'Police?' uttered Alfi. 'Up here? How would they know about this place and to come up here? And where did they take them?'

'Some of the people are in the jail...outside Tabiki.'

'Tabiki. Jail?' repeated Alfi.

'The others run away.'

❀ ❀ ❀

On the side of the big old barn near Tabiki, were the freshly painted, big botched unfussy letters, *District Jail*. Alfi pulled up just below it, they got off the bike, he looked sideways to Lily and then stepped up and pressed against the large wooden doors. It let in a flood of light, where they stood astonished by the sight - as over a hundred pairs of eyes stared back at them, followed by the optimistic calls of 'Alfi!'

They were surprised too by the sheer size of the place - where the whole barn had been hastily adapted into a large make-shift jail. A small number of guards, bored and solemn looking, paced around the inside walls wearing wide-brimmed cowboy hats that sent shadows down their expressionless faces. The guards glanced up as Lily and Afi entered, but didn't say a word, still disinterested. Around them, most Mindgarten residents were sitting on the floor; groups of families, or huddles of friends - some were standing or leaning against the wooden walls.

'Alfi!' There was another lively voice. He turned to see Lester sitting. Next to him was a handsome looking woman with long auburn hair that hung down in loose ringlets over her slender shoulders. She was dressed in white, a white tunic, and had the disposition of someone calm, humble and quietly sophisticated. His arm was wrapped protectively around her but on seeing Alfi he got up with the broadest of smiles. 'So, you got here my friend!'

'What, what happened? And why didn't you take the van?' Alfi asked, as Lily turned to see a jumble of other prisoners at the back of the room. Intriguingly, they were separated from everyone else by a row of trellises propped up with heavy sacks.

'Well, I went around,' Lester said. 'Starting to warn people. As you told me. You know, and then, after a big commotion broke loose, people were running all over the place. And I met...' he hesitated and glanced back to the woman. 'I met Number Fifteen.' She stood, indeed there was a natural gracefulness about her, and gave a smile that came both from her eyes and her lips. Without saying a word, she came over and slotted her arm neatly inside his. 'This is Elderberry,' he announced, admiring her fingers resting on his arm. 'It's a nice touch.'

Alfi then caught sight of another familiar face, the Guru, who was sat cross-legged on the floor. He was meditating and making quite a show of it. His hands rested on his lap, head tilted downwards and eyes closed, seemingly without a care in the world as if he was in some far-off hermitage somewhere. Frenchie stood over him, his eyes just then flickered towards Alfi, there was even a glint of admiration about them.

They were interrupted by another creaking at the doors. Another flash of light, as they fanned open - accompanied with the slow, solid sound of two heavy pairs of cowboy boots. The figures, one short, the other tall, both wearing Stetsons and silhouetted dramatically from the light outside. Alfi gaped at the sight. The Sheriff surveyed the room meanwhile, satisfied and somewhat enjoying the potent silence he'd created with Ronson standing by too - although a bit jittery looking. The peak of the Sheriff's Stetson eventually stopped in Alfi's direction as his chubby, rose coloured face morphed into a smile - as if seeing a well-loved son. 'Well,' he said with measured assuredness. 'If it isn't my old friend. Mr Alfi!'

'Well? It's...It's nice to see you, Sheriff. Strange to see you. But... but what are you doing here?'

'I told you,' the Sheriff said with obvious brightness in his voice. 'I was keeping an eye on things in Madrakani for a while. And now, I'm following my friends up here. Up, over to this place.' He nodded towards the huddle of other prisoners behind the trellises where Mr

Teshi stepped forward from amongst his men, holding up his stick and with a flick, even attempting a wave with it. Stodge was there too and looked back innocently like a puppy dog hoping to be taken out of a shop window. He raised a thumb, then held his hand up, as he couldn't quite think of anything else to do.

'It's nice to see you again Mr Alfi,' interrupted Ronson.

'You too Ronson.'

'And this time,' the Sheriff continued in an authoritative drawl. 'This time, it looks like my friend here, Mr Teshi, has gone a little bit too far,' he called out volubly so they could hear. 'Hey Mr Teshi? Maybe, we've got ourselves another *inability to assimilate?*' He sniffed and turned to Alfi. 'And it looks like, things might be changing for *you too* Mr Alfi.'

'Me? Changing? What do you mean?'

'Sprouts!' There was a clang at the door as Lobsang rushed in clutching a scroll of paper with both hands. He glanced to the Sheriff and to Alfi nervously. 'Here it is!' he said, holding out the old paper. 'Here it is! Feck you! This gravy's rancid.' He placed a hand over his mouth before adding. 'Sorry...I've...I've got it sir!'

'Ah Lobsang,' said the Sheriff calmly. 'You have it.'

'I have indeed!' replied Lobsang and watched with a kind of childish delight as the Sheriff unfurled it.

The Sheriff began to read. Turning to Lobsang, he asked him. 'And it's got the stamp? This is the stamp? And you. You were the witness?'

'Yes. Yes, I was,' he said earnestly.

Ronson fumbled for his note pad, pulled a pen from a pocket and began to write. 'Stamp. Witness...'

'Well, there it is!' the Sheriff concluded rolling up the paper. 'You foreigners, you sure are a fine, mystical thing. You sure are! Congratulations then, Mr Alfi. It looks like you've got yourself the Mindgarten.'

'What?'

Ronson scribbled in his pad and mumbled. 'The Mindgarten. Mr Alfi gets the Mindgarten.'

'It's all here,' continued the Sheriff holding up the scroll with a grin. 'In this statement, this *Will* written by the then lawful owner, the venerable Brother Thay. He has bequeathed the whole Mindgarten to you.'

'Me? The whole Mindgarten?' puzzled Alfi.

'How do I spell *bequeathed*?' asked Ronson.

'Yes you,' repeated the Sheriff seriously.

Lester butted in. 'I don't understand? He *owns* the Mindgarten? Alfi?'

'But. But. How?' asked Alfi.

'You'd better believe it,' added the Sheriff. 'It's all written here. Now what? Now what do you want to do?'

'What do I want to do?' repeated Alfi, still incredulous. 'Well. For a start. I want to get these people out of here. Get them home.'

A cheer erupted. It filled the entire barn, and amongst the noise the Sheriff pointed to Mr Teshi's and his men. 'And these?' he said triumphantly. 'How we proceed matters is largely up to you!'

# CHAPTER TWENTY-FOUR

## Condemed to Freedom

The sound of honest work echoed through the Mindgarten. Children carried broken wood, men measured and sawed timber with pencils between their lips, there was the tapping of nails, as groups of people swept, fixed and loaded things. Word had got round too, and most of the Mindgarten residents who'd run away that night had now returned.

Alfi wandered and surveyed it all. And in those first few days he'd noticed too, how something had changed for Mr Teshi. Had he been ordained with some kind of magic from the Mindgarten? He now looked kindlily towards Alfi as he, together with his men, worked contently; sweeping, fixing and carrying things - even under the brooding eyes of Frenchie and the Guru.

Had humility finally found Mr Teshi? Could he reason well by it? To understand how the previous loss of his own curiosity had reduced him so? Nothing of the world's beauty could reveal itself to him before, as his eyes had become dead. Now at last, could he sense his own fallibility? Indeed, he had begun to perceive the complexities of the world and looked to others outside of himself with interest.

And in the time that would follow, this realisation would save him, where he would no longer see himself as the victor or victim, or the judge of all things. Perhaps, at last, he could begin to grow.

As the days followed, Alfi witnessed too, how Lester had acquired happiness with all its failings. He was phlegmatic to know it was enough and couldn't last, but had the ability to retrace his steps to it where it would be replenished through love. He reflected on Elderberry, who was to be Lester's constant, and he hers. There would be no need for pleasure seeking for their happiness, at least for now, as it would come from the natural state. And with love perhaps, to create the blossom of a new family? Why forsake this for anything else? It reflected on Alfi - had this been his mistake? A procession of desires would no doubt be waiting for Lester, but he had the intelligence to choose. Lester smiled at the world, and through cause and effect, it would mostly smile back at him.

Green Bird had come to an end, and Alfi thought of the new names they were given, together with how the actions of each new day, however small, would etch, little by little upon their futures. How life seemed so pleasing then, particularly for the young, where it danced in their direction.

Lester, with all his friendliness had finally become 'Bluebell' much to his delight. A flower they said, that was a symbol of kindliness and affability. Its appearance presented the optimism of spring.

❈ ❈ ❈

Time passed, and within his nightly ritual, Alfi would carefully unwrap the small glass pyramid and sit with it. He'd notice how it would capture light from the darkness, a flickering star from far off somewhere, a passing beam of brightness. And in the hours that followed, he'd sit and watch the workings of his own mind. It was as if he was becoming separated from it, and rising above all notions of what it was to exist. Could he step outside of himself? Would this not be an oblivion, as Thay had spoken about? Should he return from it?

He wondered did he have a soul. And if so, would it survive death in the Vedic sense to be reincarnated into something anew - something that when Thay was alive, he did not agree about. Or was the idea Abrahamic, where he would enter into a proverb of paradise, an eternity, but in what form would it take? Would he remain or lose himself to the spirit? Or would he be obliterated on death - and cease to exist at all? The last of these three, that night, seemed to be the least terrifying of all. Would the glass prism finally teach him something?

And it was this night, of all nights, that it advised him about none, yet all of these things. Words and feelings came anonymously from the blackness that would both enrapture and terrify him. He looked longer, more deeply, to see if it were true. For after all this time, it had come to this - and was something of a disappointment. Mostly, that his journey had still not come to an end, or would it ever will?

He thought of himself. What construct is a man? How troubled he is. In action, a few, so noble, yet all brought so helplessly to dust. And in-between, with all the merriment, the hurt, that rises and falls like the chest - brought to nothing. A bit player, in a play of fools. An everyman, a no one, where the irony was that comfort would suffocate him. And so, a truth, a sad last laconic aphorism, finally revealed itself to him. That all along, he'd been asking the wrong question. There was no need. No need to find the Self after all, but instead to relinquish yourself from it, and become free. These were the words that said themselves to him that night, and in truth it must be said, maybe Alfi should not have existed.

It was past midnight as he lay in his bed, where, outside his window, slate-coloured clouds separated to reveal a bright half of a moon that sent opaque shadows across him. He stirred on the pillow.

His eyes half open in the quiet. Then he heard it coming. A wind hovering outside with all its coldness. It hushed, then rose fiercely again to shiver the building. And as it howled, along the loose stones the footsteps came. They moved slowly, assuredly as they drew closer. He rushed to the window, fumbled and opened the latch and leaned out to see, to greet him, yet no one was there. The footsteps were below him now and turned noisily amongst the stones to show him, before beginning to shift away again. And as the wind whispered down, down to the faintest of nothings, he heard the final, sad echoes of *his* footsteps. And that was the last he would ever hear of Thay. From his place - wherever was this place of reckoning - he had agreed.

❀ ❀ ❀

Alfi treaded mindfully along the corridor to Thay's old apartment. He wondered, should he go in? What now, were farewells like? There were far too many of them, they came regularly, too much, like the falling of leaves from the trees. He knew he would find Lobsang waiting there. Who would bow his head gracefully at the door, where inside he would find Lily. There, she would be sat on her stool. Delicately arranging her flowers in the light.

❀ ❀ ❀

'And what of my name?' Alfi whispered to himself. They had given him the name of *Culver*. A flower that can bloom anywhere they say, wherever it goes, and one that attracts a lot of butterflies. He smiled at the thought, as he tied the luggage to his motorbike. Holding out the small glass pyramid wrapped in its purple cloth, he tucked it carefully into a saddlebag, before staring out, onto the bleached, silvery white road that lay ahead of him. The sun was blinding.

❁ ❁ ❁

She glanced away from the flowers as she heard him coming, and caught her breath. Holding out her arm, her face tilted to the tips of her outstretched fingers; her palm to the ceiling - she waited 'til at last it came. The hand landing gently, and resting inside hers. Feeling its comfort, she gazed into his eyes. Mr Teshi looked back to her with the softest of smiles. Was this what he had been looking for? Had it saved him? Had he needed the love, and the good, to be good? Love had made him kind.

❁ ❁ ❁

Alfi sat up on the motorbike, where behind him, all the questions along his journey were strung out like garlands. The engine sounded, and he clicked it into gear. For in his search for self, free will and freedom, he would now have to face away from the crowd and leave all the madness of humanity. To be truly oneself, for now at least, Alfi would need to cease to be. This truth had revealed itself to him and Thay had confirmed it. The Mindgarten was not his, and he should not be seduced by the comfort of it.

And so, in the hard complicated months that would follow, he was consigned. With no one, nor even his own mind to dictate to him and no one else to blame, he would be limitless. And as he rode out and disappeared over the mountains, a monstrous silence consumed him. He became a lonely, vulnerable and insignificant figure, utterly alone yet without the wrath of loneliness. He felt the cold air again, as a smile gently creased his face. He was condemned to be free.

## About the Author

Steve Carver is a BBC presenter, writer, journalist and adventurer. He's lived in Nepal and travelled throughout Tibet, supported an orphanage, and created the ethical travel company, Angel Holidays. He's written comedy for British television, presented a number of series for Radio 4, as well as staged a play in central London. He's also written for the Sunday Times.

Suggested listening for the end of this book:
Northern Sky, Nick Drake

scinbox@hotmail.com
www.angelholidays.co.uk

+44 751 717 5030

facebook.com/angelholidays.co.uk